GET OUT OF TOWN

Sheriff Aaron Mackey Westerns
by TERRENCE MCCAULEY

Where the Bullets Fly

Dark Territory

Get Out of Town

The Dark Sunrise

GET OUT OF TOWN

A SHERIFF AARON MACKEY WESTERN

TERRENCE McCAULEY

PINNACLE BOOKS
Kensington Publishing Corp.
www.kensingtonbooks.com

PINNACLE BOOKS are published by

Kensington Publishing Corp.
119 West 40th Street
New York, NY 10018

This book is a work of fiction. Names, characters, businesses, organizations, places, events, and incidents either are the product of the author's imagination or are used fictitiously. Any resemblance to actual persons, living or dead, events, or locales is entirely coincidental. To the extent that the image or images on the cover of this book depict a person or persons, such person or persons are merely models, and are not intended to portray any character or characters featured in the book.

If you purchased this book without a cover, you should be aware that this book is stolen property. It was reported as "unsold and destroyed" to the publisher, and neither the author nor the publisher has received any payment for this "stripped book."

All Kensington titles, imprints, and distributed lines are available at special quantity discounts for bulk purchases for sales promotions, premiums, fund-raising, educational, or institutional use. Special book excerpts or customized printings can also be created to fit specific needs. For details, write or phone the office of the Kensington sales manager: Kensington Publishing Corp., 119 West 40th Street, New York, NY 10018, attn: Sales Department; phone 1-800-221-2647.

ISBN-13: 978-0-7860-4652-2
ISBN-10: 0-7860-4652-X

First printing: September 2020

10 9 8 7 6 5 4 3 2 1

Printed in the United States of America

Electronic edition:

ISBN-13: 978-0-7860-4653-9 (e-book)
ISBN-10: 0-7860-4653-8 (e-book)

he watched the drunken gang stumble around the fire in some kind of dance. He could see their saddlebags swollen with the cash they had stolen from the bank were being used as pillows by the men when they rested or passed out from too much drink.

Mackey knew why they had camped here. They were less than a day's ride back to Henry's hometown, which was aptly named Hancock for his family that had settled the town. But he hadn't bothered to go that far because he was not afraid of anyone coming after him.

The neighboring town of Tylerville didn't have a sheriff of its own, and none of the men who lived there would dare ride out after a dangerous criminal like Henry Hancock and his men.

Hancock and his gang were not afraid of the men of Tylerville. They were not afraid of the law, either.

Mackey was going to show them how wrong they were.

He watched one of the men jump to his feet as he slurred through a story before gyrating like a man being hit with bullets before he dramatically fell to the ground to the laughter of his audience. Mackey figured he was reenacting the death of Ben Harper or Van Deutcher, the two bank guards who had been killed during the robbery.

The men whooped and cheered, and one of them fired off another pistol shot in the air.

Mackey went back to Adair and pulled his Winchester from the saddle scabbard. He dropped to the ground when he reached the canyon rim. He had an ideal angle of fire down into the camp, and none of the five men were near any cover.

All five were still wearing their pistols, but their rifles were leaning against the canyon wall. Their horses had been hobbled nearby, but there was no grass in the canyon for the animals to eat and no water for them to drink. They had that restless look that hungry, untended mounts got after a day or so. At least the drunkards had removed their saddles.

Mackey watched the Hancock gang continue to laugh and goad each other on as they passed around the jug. The campfire cast sinister shadows on their faces.

Mackey brought his Winchester to his shoulder and drew a bead on the men to gauge the distance to his targets. Given the angle, he might have to aim a bit higher than normal, but the group was well within range of the Winchester. Besides, Henry Hancock had long boasted that neither he nor any of his men would ever be taken alive by a lawman, so announcing himself ahead of time would be foolish. Mackey would give them a chance to surrender after the odds had been knocked down to four-to-one or better.

Four of the men encouraged a fifth to begin acting out another pantomime of one of their crimes. The man swayed as he got to his feet and staggered to the other side of the fire. And although the lawman couldn't swear to it, he thought the performer might be Henry Hancock himself.

Mackey brought the rifle stock snug against his shoulder and took aim. He did not have to lever a round into the chamber. One was already there. When going alone against men like Hancock, Mackey found it best to be ready to fire at a second's notice.

The echoes rising up from the canyon floor made

it impossible for him to separate one voice from the other, much less understand what they were saying. But what they said no longer mattered.

Only their crimes mattered now.

He was about to fire without warning, but as he took aim at the man, decided that would be murder. It would make him no different than the men he was hunting.

Besides, he would probably have to kill them anyway.

Without taking his aim off the dancing man, Mackey called out, "United States Marshal!" The words echoed throughout the small canyon. "I have a warrant for your arrest. Throw up your hands!"

But most of the men were laughing too loud to hear him.

One of the men seated by the fire had heard him, and drew his pistol and shot in Mackey's direction. The bullet glanced harmlessly off the canyon wall.

Mackey continued to track the dancing man and fired. The round struck the man in the back, spinning him completely around before he fell to a knee. The laughter from his drunken audience had drowned out the sound of the rifle shot. They thought the man's spin was just part of his act. Mackey fired again, striking Hancock in the left side of the back. The bullet went through his chest and struck a man holding the whiskey jug in the face. Both men laid bleeding on the canyon floor.

The three remaining drunk men scrambled for their rifles as Mackey levered a fresh round into the chamber. He fired at the man who was closest to the weapons. The round caught him in the small of the back and slammed him to the ground.

The two remaining men stumbled off to the left and the right of the fire before realizing there was no cover available.

Mackey decided that now that the numbers had been thinned down, he should give the survivors a chance to surrender. "I'm Aaron Mackey, United States Marshal. Put down your weapons and throw up your hands. You boys don't have to die."

The men responded by firing their pistols in different directions where they thought the voice might be coming from. But given the echoes of the canyon, it was impossible for them to peg Mackey's position. The bullets ricocheted off the canyon walls and never came near him.

At least I gave them a chance.

Mackey took aim at the man on the right, who had stopped firing his pistol to reload. The marshal put him down with one round to his chest.

The last robber on the left was in a crouch, yelling to his fallen friend. Mackey had a clear shot at him, but could not take it. It was too easy. He had to give him one final chance.

"You don't have to die," he called out over the neighing and ruckus of the screaming horses. "Just drop your gun and walk out of there with your hands up."

The man yelled something as he aimed his pistol in Mackey's general direction.

Mackey killed him before he had the chance to fire.

Mackey remained where he was for a few minutes and listened. When he was satisfied, he stood up and looked down into the canyon. A few minutes ago, they had been five drunks around a roaring fire, pulling on a jug while reliving past glory.

Now they were five corpses on a cold canyon floor. Five murdering thieves just as dead as all of the men they had killed over the years. It seemed a shame that, after all the blood they had spilled, he could only kill them once.

One of them was Henry Hancock. That's what mattered most. To Mr. Rice and to Judge Forester. The judge would not be happy with so much death, but he would have to accept it.

Henry Hancock and his gang had been brought to justice, and that was all that counted.

Mackey began feeding cartridges from his belt into the Winchester as he walked back to Adair. The mare hadn't moved an inch. He hadn't expected her to.

He levered the last round into the chamber and tucked the rifle into the saddle scabbard. He knew he would need his weapons fully loaded for the next stop in this part of the territory.

He climbed into the saddle and patted Adair on the neck. "Come on, girl. Let's take Hancock back home. It'll be the first time in his miserable life he was ever worth anything."

Adair moved forward, guiding herself and her rider through the darkness toward the fire in the canyon below.

Chapter 2

It was just past dawn when Mackey rode into the town of Hancock with five horses in tow.

The lead horse Mackey was trailing had Henry Hancock's body draped over the saddle. The lawman had bound the corpse's feet and hands with a rope under the horse's belly to make sure his body did not fall off on the way to town. Getting him on the horse had been difficult enough. He had no intention of doing it again.

Mackey was glad to see the boardwalks of Hancock were deserted so early in the morning. The fewer people who saw him ride into town, the better. Word of his bringing their dead relative back home would spread soon enough. They would not be hanging bunting and striking up a brass band in his honor.

Mackey steered Adair to the right and rode down a side street, pulling the five horses along with him. He found an undertaker's office around the side of a larger building. The swinging sign read:

D. Dugan
Undertaker *and* Mortician

Mackey had no idea if this was the only undertaker in town, but it would be the one getting his business that morning.

He tied Adair to one hitching rail and the string of horses to the other. It was best to keep them separate from each other, as the Arabian did not abide the presence of other animals. Or humans, now that he thought of it.

After tying off the horses, Mackey adjusted his black duster and shifted the angle of his black, flat-brimmed Plainsman on his head before knocking on the undertaker's front door.

The door opened almost immediately. Inside stood a round, pleasant-looking man in a crisp white shirt and black tie. His gray hair was perfectly combed, and he squinted out at the world from behind a pair of round spectacles.

He looked up at Mackey, then at the silver star on his chest, then at the horses tied to his hitching rail. "Yes, Sheriff? How might I be of service?"

"It's not Sheriff or Deputy. It's Aaron Mackey, United States Marshal for the Montana Territory."

"Mackey?" the undertaker repeated. "The *territory*? Why, I thought you were the law down in Dover Station."

"I was and still am," Mackey told him. "Just got named as marshal of the territory a couple of months ago. Guess word hasn't gotten around as fast as it should have."

"No, I suppose not." The undertaker flattened down his hair, though it didn't need flattening. "I'm Mort Duggan." He extended his hand, which the lawman shook. "My real name is David, but everyone here calls me Mort, which is short for mortician."

"What does an undertaker do that a mortician can't?"

Duggan seemed stumped for an answer. "Provide a greater range of services, I suppose. Proper embalming of the departed. A fitting setting for mourning and of course, a fine Christian burial."

"That's fine by me." Mackey dug a paper out from the inside pocket of his duster and opened it. "I've got a prisoner who needs a burial. The government will pay for it if need be. You'll see to it that the family is notified, too. I'll pay extra for that if I have to. I just need you to make out a receipt on the back here and sign it." Mackey saw fit to add, "With your right name."

Duggan wiped his hands on his pants. Sweat had already appeared on his forehead despite the cool air of the morning. "I must say this is most irregular, Marshal. Usually, this kind of business is done in conjunction with the town sheriff. You see—"

"That can't happen in this case because the dead man and the sheriff are related." Mackey unfolded the piece of paper and held it up the mortician to see. "This is a federal warrant signed by a judge in Helena for one Henry Hancock. Wanted dead or alive for murder, armed robbery, cattle rustling, horse thievery, and just about every sin mentioned in both testaments of the Bible."

Duggan frowned. "As a resident of Hancock, sir, I'm familiar with Henry's reputation."

"Good." Mackey refolded the paper and inclined his head back toward the five horses at the hitching post. "Because Henry Hancock's remains are draped over the saddle of the Appaloosa back there. I need you to take possession of the body and notify the family, and I need you to do it right now."

Duggan's small eyes grew wider before he rushed past Mackey to examine the body for himself. His hands passed over the two bullet wounds in Hancock's back before he bent to take a better look at the dead man's face.

Duggan stood up and leaned against the horse for support. "Good God, sir. That really is Henry Hancock."

"That's what I said." He held out the back of the warrant to him. "Now, if you could write up that receipt, I'll be on my way."

"But how could this happen?" Duggan asked. "He and his gang were the terror of the territory. None of them had received so much as a scratch in all these years."

"They received a hell of a lot more than that last night," Mackey said. "I only had paper on Hancock, so I left the others where they died. I won't need receipts on them, but I will for Hancock, so let's get moving."

Duggan squinted at him. "You mean you killed all of them?"

Mackey didn't like the undertaker's tone. "Did I stutter?"

"And you left them out there? For the birds and critters to gnaw on their mortal remains?"

"You can hitch up a wagon and go out and get them if you want," Mackey said, "but on your own time and only after I get my receipt."

Duggan took another look at the face of the dead

man slung over the saddle. "Henry. It's really you, isn't it? I never would've imagined." He looked up at Mackey. "Good God, Marshal. Do you have any idea what you've done by bringing him here? You've brought a dead Hancock boy to the town of Hancock. His family owns this town and everyone in it."

Mackey knew exactly why he had brought him back to his hometown, but that was none of the ditch-digger's business. "I'm the one who shot him, so I know what I did." He beckoned to the doorway of the undertaker's office. "Now, I've asked nicely for that receipt a couple of times now, but I'm beginning to lose patience. I haven't had my supper, and I'm anxious to get something to eat before news of this spreads. I'll probably be dropping off a few more of his relatives before the day is done, and I'd like to do it on a full stomach."

Duggan trudged back up the stairs to his shop like a man in a trance. "A black day. The blackest, indeed. Hell has broken loose in Hancock now."

Mackey followed the undertaker inside. "It was like that long before I showed up. All I did was poke the devil in the eye."

Duggan looked up at him as he lowered himself into the chair behind his desk. "I'll probably be working on you before sundown."

Mackey set the warrant on the desk so Duggan could write the receipt. "Not likely."

Mackey rode Adair over to the livery, trailing the five horses behind him on a line.

The liveryman was a black man named Arthur, who was enthusiastic at the prospect of acquiring five quality mounts he could resell at great profit. But he quickly soured on the idea when he recognized the saddles and the horses as belonging to Harry Hancock and his gang.

"Well, I'll be," Arthur said as he took a closer look at the horse that had carried Hancock's corpse to town. "This animal's still got blood on her."

"Hancock's blood," Mackey said as he leaned against the livery entrance, keeping an eye on the street. "No extra charge for it, either. You could probably charge people a nickel apiece just to look at it. What do you say?"

"I don't know, mister. The Hancock family won't look too kindly on me purchasing a death horse, especially when that horse belonged to their kin and his friends. They're likely to takc these animals off me after I pay you good money for them."

Mackey noticed the boardwalks of Hancock were starting to fill up with people. They were mostly shopkeepers opening for business. He could tell they were too calm for the news about Henry Hancock to have reached them yet. Once it did, they would be abuzz with activity, flitting around from one store to another like bees in a flower garden.

That's when the trouble would start.

Trouble he knew he would not avoid. Trouble he had wanted to start by bringing Henry Hancock's body to town.

"You hear what I said, mister," Arthur repeated.

"The Hancock family will just take these animals away from me if I buy them from you."

Mackey had heard him. "I'll arrest them if they do."

"You wouldn't even know about it," Arthur said. "Hell, I'll likely be dead and strung up from that rafter up there before I had a chance to yelp, much less get word to you about it."

"They won't hurt you." Mackey kept watching the street. "They come for anyone, it'll be for me."

"You don't know the Hancocks, sir," Arthur said. "I thank you for the offer, but the answer is no. You might as well take these horses to a ranch someplace. They'd likely give you a better price for them than I ever could, anyway."

But selling the horses to Arthur wasn't about profit, just like bringing Henry's body to town wasn't about burial. It was about more than that.

It was about making sure the Hancock clan knew their place. That's what Mr. Rice had wanted. That's what Mackey had wanted, too.

"What if I agreed to stay in town until tomorrow? Agree to protect you until all of this blows over? You can keep the horses and pay me tomorrow if I'm still alive. That way, if they take them from you, you're not out any money. You can even charge me for stabling Adair if you want."

"You think this will just blow over?" Arthur looked up from one of the horses he had been examining. "Hell, mister, you just killed a Hancock. The breath of God himself couldn't blow this over."

"Why don't you let me worry about that?" He

looked back at the liveryman. "Keep them overnight and see how it goes. What do you say?"

Arthur looked at the marshal and swallowed hard. "I'd say my business is horses, mister, and not men. But you look just as bad as those crazy Hancock bastards. Maybe even worse."

Mackey turned so he could look back at the street. A bell above a storefront door tinkled as someone got their first customer of the day. The sky was high and blue. The harsh light of morning made the entire town look clean and new. It had the promise of being a nice day, but he knew it wouldn't stay that way for long.

"Write up that receipt for the horses and we'll consider it a done deal," Mackey said. "You can give me the money tomorrow before I leave town."

Arthur petted one of the dead men's horses, then began writing out a receipt on the back of the warrant, next to Duggan's list of mortuary services. "If we're both still alive."

"We will." Mackey took Adair's reins and climbed into the saddle. "Now, how about telling me where the telegraph office is?"

The telegraph office was close enough to walk to, but Mackey had been a cavalryman and never walked when he could ride. He took great pleasure in riding up the middle of the town's Main Street to the telegraph office.

He enjoyed the looks and whispers he drew from the few people making their way along the boardwalk that chilly Montana morning.

At just a shade over six feet tall in his stocking feet and clad all in black astride a black horse, the clean-shaven Mackey knew he did not fit in easily. But the black outfit made the silver handle of the Peacemaker holstered to the left of his buckle stand out and the silver star on his chest gleam. Visibility was the point. A United States Marshal should not fit in with everyone else. Especially since he had come to town to make a point.

Adair seemed to enjoy the attention, too. He could swear the horse held her head a little higher and stepped a little livelier as she drew looks from the citizens of Hancock.

For a cattle and mining town, Mackey had expected to see more activity in Hancock, even this early in the morning. The Great Northwestern Railway had not stretched this far north yet and, according to its owner, Mr. Rice, was not likely to do so any time soon.

Not until some concessions were made by the Hancock family. Concessions Mackey had come to town to get on Mr. Rice's behalf.

Although the railroad had not yet laid track as far north as Hancock, it had extended its telegraph lines northward as something of a concession to the town's promise of a brighter future.

When he reached the telegraph office, Mackey climbed down from the saddle and tied Adair to the rail out front. He rubbed the horse's muzzle as he walked inside.

The door was open and the office was empty. He rang a small bell on the counter, and a clerk scrambled out from a back room. The little man looked like he had just woken up and was still tucking his shirt into his pants. "Yes, sir. How may I help you?"

"I need a pad and paper to write out a telegram."

"I'll be happy to write it out for you, sir," the clerk said. "After all, that's what they pay me to do."

Mackey looked at him until he got the point and handed the telegraph book and a pencil to him.

The clerk crossed his arms as he watched Mackey write out the message. "I hope you know we charge by the word. Don't go getting too long-winded or it'll wind up costing you a pretty penny."

Mackey kept writing despite the clerk's prattle. "I strike you as the long-winded type, boy?"

The clerk uncrossed his arms. "No, sir. No, you don't."

The marshal finished writing and shoved the book across the counter to the clerk. "You make out my handwriting?"

The clerk read the telegraph aloud to himself:

"Judge Forester, Helena—STOP—Hancock dead—STOP—Receipts to follow by post upon return to Dover Station—STOP – Signed A. Mackey—STOP."

The clerk looked up at him. "Hancock dead? Which Hancock?"

Mackey placed enough money on the counter to more than cover the cost of the telegram. "Just send it. Now. I'll wait."

The clerk took the money and the notebook and sat down at the telegraph to begin tapping out the message to Judge Adam Forester in Helena, Montana. Mackey knew the judge would be furious with him about killing Henry Hancock instead of bringing him in alive. He had looked forward to the spectacle of a jury trial to show the rule of law had ridden west with him to Montana. He'd be annoyed, but smart enough to avoid raising a fuss about it. Forester was a presidential appointee, just like Mackey, but with one difference. There were plenty of lawyers who could be judges, even in Montana, but not many who could serve as United States Marshal. None who could have done the job well, anyway. And no one who had Aaron Mackey's pedigree. After all, he was the Hero of Adobe Flat. The Savior of Dover Station.

Judge Forester was a good man, but he was just another attorney in a territorial capital filled with men eager to take his place, especially with statehood around the corner. Aaron Mackey, on the other hand, was a local hero.

Not that such notoriety would do him much good in the town of Hancock over the next twenty-four hours.

The clerk looked up at Mackey after the telegram was sent. "It's all done, Mr. Mackey."

"Marshal, not mister."

The clerk seemed to notice the star on his chest for the first time. "Of course, sir. My apologies."

He knew the clerk would start spreading the contents of the telegraph the moment he had the opportunity. Everyone in town would probably know its contents before Judge Forester had a chance to read it.

That was fine by Mackey. He could not stop it even if he had wanted to. If anything, he was counting on the gossip to speed things along.

It was time for him to set the next part of Mr. Rice's grand plan in motion. "Tell me where I can find the sheriff."

Chapter 3

The sheriff's office was as plain as Mackey had expected it to be. The jail consisted of an old, beat-up desk, a couple of busted wooden chairs, and two cells in the back of the room that looked like they had been put there as an afterthought. Large windows that seemed to only be cleaned when it rained looked out over Main Street and whatever happened to be going on out on the thoroughfare.

As he waited for the deputy on duty to fetch the sheriff, Mackey noticed the foot and horse traffic along Main Street had picked up considerably since he had ridden into town. He figured part of that was normal, given that people in Hancock had businesses to attend to and things to buy. But he could tell by the way people darted from one business to the next that there was an undercurrent running through town. An undercurrent that likely involved him and the death of Henry Hancock.

When Sheriff Warren Hancock came to the jail, he came alone. He didn't offer Mackey a greeting, and the marshal had not expected one, either, especially after killing a relative, even if that relative was Henry Hancock.

The sheriff shut the door and plodded over to his desk. He looked like a man who had known how to handle himself once but had allowed himself to go to seed. Too many years of easy living in the town controlled by his family had made him soft. Mackey judged the sheriff to be about thirty or so, but his swollen belly had already begun to spill over his gun belt.

Sheriff Hancock dropped his bulk into a swivel chair that protested the burden with a series of cracks and squeaks. "I just can't believe it." The sheriff's skin turned red and splotchy in some places. He looked like he might cry. "I just can't believe old Henry's gone." He looked up at Mackey. "And you're the one who killed him. Why? He never went anywhere near Dover Station."

"I'm the marshal for the territory now, Sheriff." Mackey took out the warrant and laid it on the desk. "I had paper on him, so everything that happened is legal."

The sheriff looked at the warrant without really seeing it. "That doesn't make it right. You didn't have to kill him like that. He's got a mama still above ground, you know? And a daddy, too."

"I gave him the chance to surrender peacefully," Mackey told him. "He refused. That warrant reads dead or alive. Straight up or over the saddle makes no difference to me."

The sheriff scowled at Mackey. "And you walking into my office and telling me that is your way of rubbing it in my face, is that it?"

That was part of it, but Mackey said, "I'm here because you're the closest thing this town's got to a lawman, and I'm a federal marshal depositing a dead fugitive in your jurisdiction."

Hancock bolted out of his chair, but stayed on his side of the desk. "That dead fugitive you claim you're depositing is my kin, Mackey. My own first cousin, damn you. My aunt's boy."

"Henry stopped being a boy when he started robbing banks and killing people, Sheriff." Mackey pointed down at the warrant on the sheriff's desk. "I can read off the list of charges for you if you want."

"Charges he had a right to answer in a fair and open court," Warren said with more grit than Mackey thought he had. "Charges to be brought before a judge, not gunned down in cold blood while he was sleeping."

"He wasn't sleeping," Mackey said. "He was up drinking with his gang around a campfire, celebrating after robbing a bank in Tylerville. I called out to them from the darkness and gave them the chance to give up. They went for their guns instead. If it's any consolation, none of them made it out alive."

Warren slowly wiped his soft, pale hands on his pants. "You mean you killed all of them? Where are the rest of them?"

"Hank's the only one I brought back." Mackey took the warrant from the desk and put it back in his pocket. "I brought him back because I had paper on him. I left the rest where they died."

"Why doesn't that surprise me?" He pointed at Mackey. "I've heard plenty about you, and I'm not talking about all of that glory stuff about you being a hero or a savior, neither. I've heard you're a stone-cold killer and don't care about snuffing out a man's life as if it was nothing more than a candle. And for what?" he sneered. "Dover Station? Another dot on a map of the territory, no different than any other town out here. What makes Dover Station so special, anyhow?"

Mackey was glad to tell him. "A railroad station for one. A brand-new town for another. Banks, cattle, mining. Just about everything the town of Hancock wants to be, but never will." He took a step closer to the sheriff. "At least not until you and your people start realizing who your friends are and who they're not."

Warren Hancock's eyes grew small and nasty. "Is that what Henry's death was? A message from the railroad to me and my people to stay in line?" Mackey saw Warren's hand drop to the gun on his hip. "Is that —"

Mackey nailed him with a left cross to the jaw that sent him tumbling back into his chair.

Before the sheriff could recover, Mackey took the man's pistol from its holster, opened the cylinder, and let the bullets drop out onto the jail floor before tossing the empty weapon across the room.

Warren was just beginning to come around when Mackey snatched the fat man by the collar and hauled him up out of the chair, pinning him against the wall. "Henry and his bunch got killed because they refused to surrender when I gave them the chance. They got killed because they didn't think anyone would come for them for the men they killed in Tylerville. That's not going to happen anymore. Anyone who breaks the law in this territory answers to me and my deputies. Anyone in this territory who's got paper on them gets brought before a judge, no matter who they are or what their last name is. You'd best make damned sure your family understands that before any more of them try to go up against me in Dover Station or anywhere else."

Mackey released the fat man with a shove that dropped him back into his chair before Mackey backed away toward the door.

Warren recovered in time to say, "You can talk as fancy as you want in here, Mackey, but smacking me around don't mean a damned thing. You're in Hancock country now, boy. Best you remember that. Mad Nellie's going to be none too happy over what you've done. Nothing sticks together like the Hancock family."

While still facing the sheriff, Mackey opened the jail door and glanced outside. A few of the horses hitched to posts across Main Street were making manure. Great clumps of it had piled up on the thoroughfare.

Mackey grinned back at the sheriff. "Lots of things stick together, Warren. Some more useful than others. Tell your people to watch their step around me. Here in Hancock or anywhere else."

He didn't bother to close the door behind him.

Chapter 4

Mackey decided he had done enough to make sure the Hancock family knew he was in town, so it was finally time for Adair to be tended to. He rode her back to the livery and arranged for Arthur to take good care of her.

"Anyone come around asking about those horses I left with you?" Mackey asked.

"Not yet," Arthur admitted, "but it's just past breakfast time for some folks. Might not be anyone come calling until noon, if not later. And when they do, that'll be bad news for you."

"That's what everyone keeps telling me." Mackey realized he had ignored the grumbling in his stomach for too long. "Any places in town still open for breakfast?"

Arthur looked at him warily. "Plenty of places, but only one where you're less likely to get yourself shot by a friend of the Hancock family."

Mackey appreciated the liveryman's concern for his well-being. And for the agreement of protection they had made. "Sounds like the kind of place I need."

* * *

As he walked to the Hancock Dining Café and Rooms, Mackey had to remind himself that he was in a strange town without Billy or Sandborne or even Lagrange to watch his back. He was not complaining. He knew his message to the Hancock clan would stick better if he was alone. Claiming he was not afraid of them was one thing. Showing the family he had no fear of them was different.

But times were certainly changing, and Mackey found himself with no choice but to change with them. He had spent most of the past five years since his discharge from the army enforcing the law in Dover Station. Between the ranchers, the miners, the loggers, and the townsfolk, he and Billy Sunday had been kept busy keeping a lid on the busy town.

But that lid had been blown clean off once Mr. Frazer Rice and his railroad had decided to pour a lot of money into expanding Dover Station from a mere stopover to a main stop on the Great Northwestern Railway. And while Mr. Rice had left Silas Van Dorn in town to oversee his investments, Van Dorn had ceded most of his authority to James Grant. Mackey knew Grant as a man of dubious background and reputation, but there was nothing dubious about the power he had amassed in town. Not only did he oversee the daily operations of the Dover Station Company, but he had managed to get himself elected mayor. Mr. Rice objected, of course, but even powerful men have a limited reach, especially from over two thousand miles away. Besides, his shareholders saw

Grant as a miracle worker who had hewn a profitable business out of the Montana wilderness.

But Mr. Rice had plenty of power in Washington, which he had used to get Mackey named as the United States Marshal for the Montana Territory. Rice hadn't done it simply because he was civic-minded, but because the move benefited him personally. It gave him another ally with broad powers across the territory and a powerful friend who could help him corral James Grant's influence.

With statehood just around the corner, Mackey had no idea how long the post would last. He imagined being properly admitted into the union would change everything, including how he did his job. But for today, he had the full weight of the federal government behind him. On paper, the territorial governor and Judge Forester outranked him, but in reality, all three men were equally beholden to Frazer Rice for their positions.

Mackey decided he'd be glad when he could put all of this political intrigue behind him. He had enjoyed being sheriff of a small, bustling town in the middle of the territory. It was never an easy job nor a safe one, but it was manageable. Now, with a town police force headed up by Walter Underhill and controlled by Grant, he had to look both ways before he put a foot on the boardwalk out of concern about offending someone's authority. Add the friction between Grant, Van Dorn, and Rice into the mix and it became even more of a mess. Mackey enjoyed the power and privilege of a federal badge pinned to his chest, but not all of the intrigue that went along with it.

Mackey found the café just off Main Street exactly

where Arthur had told him it would be. The white tablecloths were a good sign that the place had decent food. The aromas of fresh coffee and bacon were even better signs and made his stomach grumble a bit louder.

A Chinese man who carried himself like the manager eyed Mackey carefully as he walked toward the new customer. The man had a full head of hair gone almost gray and sported a pair of black holders on each arm to keep his shirtsleeves rolled up.

"Can I help you?"

"I'd like some breakfast if you're still serving."

The manager seemed to have to think about it, even though Mackey saw a waiter bring out a couple of plates of bacon and eggs to a table. "Yes, we are. Follow me, please."

Given the place was empty except for the one occupied table, he didn't know why he needed to follow the manager anywhere, but he did. He understood what the man was up to when he stopped at the table in farthest corner of the dining room. "I thought you might enjoy your privacy back here, Marshal."

"Sounds like you've heard of me." Mackey pulled off his duster and laid it on the back of the chair before taking the seat facing the door. "That didn't take long, did it?"

"Hancock is a small town," the manager said as he handed him a menu. "And if you'll take some friendly advice, it's a town you'll leave as soon as you're able."

"Let me guess. You're a Hancock, too." He looked the Chinese man over. "You don't look like a Hancock."

"Me?" The Chinese man bristled. "I hate the bastards. Just don't want to see a good man gunned down on account of vermin like Henry Hancock. His family run this town, Marshal, and if I know you're here, they probably know it, too. Most likely, they've got people riding down from their ranch right now to see their brother's body with their own eyes. They'll see to it that you're on the next table to him, too, if you're not careful."

"That's what everyone keeps telling me." He checked the clock above the front door. It wasn't even nine in the morning yet, but a world of trouble was already headed straight for him. But he had asked for it, so he had no complaints. "Guess that's why you didn't sit me at the table by the window."

"It's a nice window," the manager said, "and I would not like to see it damaged. Or to see you shot without having a chance to at least defend yourself."

Mackey extended his hand to him. "Name's Aaron."

The manager shook his hand. "And mine is Norman Fong. My father was Chinese and my mother was Mexican, in case you're wondering."

He wasn't. "I'm was wondering more about the kind of breakfast you folks serve here than about who your father was."

"Eggs fresh this morning, as much bacon as will fit on your plate, and the best coffee in town limits."

"Sold." Mackey handed him back the menu. "Let's start with the coffee and make the eggs fried. If a bit of the bacon fat winds up mixed in, all the better."

Without bothering to write it down, Norman began to head for the kitchen before Mackey stopped him. "You said some of the Hancock family was on their way into town. Any of them I should watch out for in particular?"

Norman looked at the table at the opposite end of the room. The two burly men Mackey pegged for miners were too busy quietly tucking into their breakfast to pay attention to anyone else. Still, Norman kept his voice low when he said, "All of them are dangerous in their own way. They're as nasty as they are plentiful. I wouldn't go so far as to call them feral, but they're not far from it. Their women are every bit as dangerous as the men. Mad Nellie's the one to watch for. She will cut your throat sooner than her menfolk, and do a better job of it, too."

Mackey had heard about her. "Sounds lovely."

"And there are a lot of them, too," Norman went on. "I've been here over two years and I still don't know who all of them are. And that doesn't even count the cousins. They've got different names, so you don't always know who you're talking to."

Norman stole another glance at the door, then nodded at the Peacemaker handle poking out above the table. "Might be a good idea to keep that handy, Aaron. Trouble's liable to come at you in any direction and in any form."

It sounded like good advice to Mackey. "Any back door to this place?"

"No," Norman said. "Just the front. And watching that will be plenty."

Mackey had been a lawman for too long to not be suspicious. "Why are you being so helpful to me?"

"Because if there's one thing the Hancock family like less than blacks or Mexicans," Norman said, "it's the Chinese. And a half-blood like me doesn't rate too highly in their book."

Mackey let the waiter go put his order in with the kitchen before drawing the Colt and placing it on the table.

Norman returned with a mug of coffee. "Just be careful. We serve it plenty hot around here."

Both men looked up when the front door of the café flew open and a tall, rangy man of about twenty stormed into the dining room.

Mackey figured he was a good inch or two taller than himself and wider, too. Not fat like the sheriff but lean the way years of ranch work tended to shape a man. Despite the long face and droopy eyes, he still bore a certain facial resemblance to Sheriff Warren Hancock and Henry Hancock that told him he must be a relative.

Mackey had been expecting some kind of confrontation by one of the family. In fact, he had been counting on it. He had just hoped it would happen after his breakfast.

Norman approached the man with nothing more than a scowl. "Just who the hell do you think you are, busting in here like this?"

The man pulled a pistol and aimed it at Norman's head. "I'm Al Brenner, you half-breed son of a bitch, and I'm here for the man who killed my kin. Someone said they saw him walk in here. Now, you either point him out or you'll be shaking hands with my poor uncle Henry in a minute."

From his seat at the back table, Mackey said, "There was nothing poor about Henry Hancock. And since you're looking for the man who killed your uncle, I'm the one. Might as well leave everyone else out of it."

Brenner lowered his gun as he looked over at Mackey.

The two miners having breakfast threw some greenbacks on the table as they abandoned their meals and ran outside. They had to force their way through the crowd that had gathered at the café entrance to watch what was happening.

Mackey didn't blame the miners for running. They weren't wearing guns, and this wasn't their fight. He just hoped Norman didn't try to be a hero. That pencil he was holding wouldn't do much against Al Brenner's pistol.

"Best head inside, Norman." Mackey had laid his hand flat on the table beside his Peacemaker. "Give me and Mr. Brenner here some privacy."

Norman looked at the mob of people who had pressed their dirty faces against his clean window. "Yeah, privacy."

He went into the kitchen as Al Brenner turned to face Mackey. His pistol remained at his side. "You the bastard that murdered Henry?"

Mackey drank his coffee with his left hand. "I'm the federal marshal who attempted to bring him in on a warrant a judge swore out for his arrest about a year ago. Henry and his bunch made the decision to start shooting instead of coming along peaceful. They got what they had coming to them."

Brenner's right arm trembled, but he kept his pistol low. "I'd call that murder."

"Only a fool would call five-on-one odds murder. I'd call it survival." Mackey patted his pocket without taking his eyes off Brenner. "And the warrant I've got right here says it's legal. I had a right to bring him in, and that's exactly what I did."

"You brought his *body* into town," Brenner yelled, "not my uncle. I'll bet you were too yellow to even give him a chance to surrender."

"Men like your uncle don't surrender." Mackey shrugged to goad the boy into doing something stupid. Another dead Hancock boy might be enough to drive his point home. "Straight up or over the saddle makes no difference to me, Brenner, so long as the body matches the name to satisfy the warrant."

"To satisfy the warrant?" Al Brenner's droopy eyes narrowed. "You can talk about ending a man's life like it was some kind of chore on a list someplace. What kind of man are you?"

"I'm a lawman." Mackey kept an eye on Brenner's right shoulder. He knew if the cowboy began to raise his gun, the first sign of movement would come from there. "In fact, I'm a federal law man, to put a finer point on it, and a hungry one at that. Now, either do what you came in here to do or get the hell out of here before my food comes out. Killing people once I start eating upsets my stomach, and I've got no intention of missing another meal on account of another Hancock man."

The big cowboy's shoulders shifted as he began to raise his pistol, but Mackey had grabbed his Peacemaker and leveled it before Brenner had raised the pistol above his gun belt.

The young man froze.

Mackey remained perfectly still as he kept the gun aimed at Brenner's chest. "Drop it. Right now."

He didn't take his eyes off Brenner when a woman dressed in rags stormed through the crowd that had gathered in the café doorway and yanked Brenner's gun arm down.

The woman was round and half his size, if that. "Just what the hell do you think you're doing?"

"Avenging Uncle Henry," Brenner said.

"How did you plan on going about doing that?" the small woman yelled up at him. "By getting yourself killed?"

He glowered over her and stared at Mackey. "Who says I'm the one who'd get killed?"

She slapped him in the face, breaking his stare. "I'm saying it, and it's a good thing I came in when I did. This ain't the way I wanted it done, Al. Now all you've done is make things worse." She grabbed him by the sleeve and shoved him toward the door. "Now get out of here before I step aside and let him do what he was fixing to do to you."

Al took a few steps back from the short, roundish woman wearing a man's work pants and shirt. "But, Aunt Nell, I—"

She held her ground and pointed for the door. "Get back home like I told you and wait for me there."

Nell scowled at the faces peering into the café at her and wagged a dirty crooked finger at them. "And I don't want none of you idiots fillin' his head with any nonsense about comin' back in here with his cousins, understand? I want that boy home where he belongs."

Mackey knew this had to be Mad Nellie Hancock, the matriarch and leader of the entire Hancock tribe. According to Mr. Rice's people, Nellie ran the entire family, including all the cousins and in-laws. Though she was a Hancock only by marriage, she had spent the better part of the last twenty years defending the corrupt legacy of the family she had joined as if it was her own birthright rather than that of her children. The file Mr. Rice had sent him offered little information on her children's names or which Hancock was their father, not that it mattered. Mackey pegged the woman to be only thirty, which meant her children were probably too young to be a problem just yet, though the file also said the family had a reputation for spawning early.

Now that her nephew was gone, Mad Nellie turned her attention to the marshal. "Mind pointing that thing elsewhere?" She held up her hands, showing she was unarmed. "I'm not packing, Marshal." She winked. "You can pat me down if you want."

"No thanks." He slowly laid the Peacemaker back on the table, but did not dare holster it. Only a fool would put away their weapon when facing Mad Nellie.

She offered a yellow-toothed grin as she began to slowly amble over to his table. Mackey watched every move. She might not be armed, but from what he had heard of her, she was even more dangerous with her bare hands. She dressed like a man because she had been doing men's work out on her family's ranch since her husband was hanged for armed robbery and murder in Helena more than ten years before.

Mad Nellie gestured to the chair where Mackey had put his duster. "Mind if I have a seat?"

He nodded toward a chair at another table. "Over there is close enough for both of us."

She pulled out a chair from the table next to Mackey

and sat down. She pointed at him with a filthy hand that hadn't been washed in days, maybe longer. "I know all about you, Aaron Mackey. What's more, I know who sent you and why they done it, too."

"I know you, too, Nell." Mackey kept his hand close to his pistol, but not on it. "Who you're working for and why."

"Of course you do," she said. "Everyone who calls themselves anyone in this part of the territory knows about me and mine. Hell, I hear they know about the Hancock clan clear down to Texas. Maybe even Mexico."

"I'm not talking about that," Mackey said. "I'm talking about places a lot closer than that. I'm talking about Dover Station, and you know it."

"Dover Station." Nell's dull blue eyes grew even duller. "To hear people talk, the place was nearer to heaven on earth than the fly speck of a town it is."

"It's got a railroad station," Mackey said, "which is more than can be said about Hancock." He kept his gun hand still as he leaned forward. "Which is why you and your family have thrown your lot in with James Grant, isn't it? He promised you he'd run the railroad up here to Hancock if you and your family agreed to work for him, didn't he?"

He could tell by her reaction that she had not expected him to know so much. She tried to cover her surprise, but did a poor job of it. "Where'd you go and get a damned fool notion like that?"

Since Mr. Rice owned the telegraph office, it was not hard for him to read telegrams that had been sent between Nell and James Grant. But there was no point in telling her that. "Who cares where I heard it? The only question is whether or not it's true."

The flesh under her jaw wagged as she jerked her chin up at him. "And what if it is?"

"Then the bad times for the Hancock family are only beginning."

Mad Nell sat back in her chair and drummed her filthy fingers on Norman's white tablecloth. He watched her closely in case she decided to take a swing at him or lunge for his throat. "I could be forgiven for taking that as a threat, Marshal."

"You a God-fearing woman, Nell?"

She stopped drumming her fingers. "Indeed, I am."

"Then take what I said as prophecy. Stick with Grant and things go from bad to worse for the Hancock clan."

She began drumming her fingers again. "We Hancocks ain't used to being threatened, Marshal. We're better at striking out first and thinking about it later."

"Same as me," Mackey said. "Because if you agree to do James Grant's dirty work for him, you and your family better have plenty of shovels ready. You're going to need them."

She nodded to herself as she kept drumming a pointless tune on the tabletop. "I guess you bringin' Henry into town like you done would be your way of makin' a point?"

Mackey was glad she wasn't as dense as he feared. "Just enforcing a warrant is all. His name's on the paper, just like a lot of other names."

Nellie kept nodding. "Maybe bringin' him here like that was your way of tryin' to rile us up into doing somethin' stupid. Like makin' you grab that pistol you've got right there on the table and laying me out."

"That's a lot of maybes, Nell. But everything I've told you about working for Grant is a fact."

Her chins waggled as she shook the head that was as round as the rest of her. "I'm not stupid enough to go up against a man like you. Henry was, and like you said, got what was comin' to him. Had been comin' to him for a long time, I'd imagine, just like my Joshua had it comin' to him ten years ago. Left me with five children to raise on a ranch that ain't worth a damn and a farm where only crabgrass grows."

"Sounds to me like you're trying to justify something."

She stopped drumming her fingers. "Not to the likes of you, Mackey. See, I might not place much stock in that hero nonsense they peddle about you, but I believe it's near enough to the truth to call for what you might call discretion on my part."

She pointed a grimy finger at the star pinned to the lapel of his duster on the back of the chair. "See, I know how you got that fancy piece of jewelry. And I know who got it for you, too."

"Sure, you do. The story was in all the papers, from what I understand," Mackey said. "I'd suppose word even reached as far as a jerkwater town like Hancock."

Still, Mad Nellie wouldn't be baited. "I never had the time to waste learnin' how to read and never missed it, either. I get my information in other ways. By word of mouth. And that's why I know you may have gotten that fancy star from the president back in Washington, but the man who got it for you is Mr. Frazer Rice himself."

Mackey was quickly beginning to realize that Mad Nellie wasn't so crazy after all. "Mr. Rice made the recommendation, but it was the president's decision."

"Men like Rice tell presidents what decisions to make," Nellie said. "Men like Rice make towns like Dover Station. Can break 'em, too, all with the stroke of a pen."

She leaned closer to Mackey, but Mackey didn't budge. "Towns like Hancock. See, I know why, out of all them warrants you must have in that pocket of yours, that you went after poor old Henry first. On account of Rice sendin' you here to do it. To deliver a message to me in the form of the corpse of one of my relations."

Mackey saw no reason to admit it so quickly. "You've got a nasty way of looking at the world, Nell. But maybe you're on to something where Mr. Rice is involved."

"I'll just bet I am."

"And I'll bet you've heard about Rice and Grant not always seeing things the same way. I'll bet you've also heard that Mr. Rice doesn't like some of Grant's plans for the town. Plans that include some Hancock men to help him run more saloons, whorehouses, and maybe an opium den or two when he opens that new sawmill of his in a couple of months."

She smiled, "Can't say I know anything about any of that, Marshal. But let's just say James Grant was planning on doing all of those things. You think it's smart to go up against him the way you're doin' it? By making an enemy of him and the Hancock clan at the same time? I've heard tell that you're a smart man, Marshal. Goin' against us ain't the way of a smart man."

"Neither is going against Mr. Rice," Mackey countered. "Or me."

She sat forward and pointed a grimy finger at him. "Except there's a difference between what you're doin' and what I'm doin'. I'm protectin' me and mine the same as any other woman in her right mind would do." Nellie sat back. "I'm admittin' that I know that you're tryin' to goad me and mine into choosin' between a man who ain't never done anythin' for my family and one who has no reason to lie to us."

"Grant's got no reason to do anything for you, either," Mackey said. "Not after you give him what he wants."

"Except what I'm offerin' ain't a onetime deal," she told him. "Not even close. It's more permanent than that."

This was what Mackey had come to Hancock to find out. Lagrange had learned the Hancock family was working with Grant, but he hadn't been able to discover how deep their dealings went. "How permanent?"

But Nellie was not as mad as she seemed. "No way, lawman. You'll find out when the time comes. I know why you brought Henry's body here. You came lookin' for a fight and figured we'd be dumb enough to give you one. Then you'd have every right to come back here with a whole passel of deputies to arrest us for tryin' to kill you. Bet you'd manage to kill a few of us in the bargain."

She smiled. "It'd be a good plan, too, if you was

dealin' with a Hancock man. They've been known to charge at whatever's in their path like a wild boar and to hell with the consequences. Well, I ain't that stupid, see, but that don't mean I'm weak. I might not be a Hancock by birth, but I've become one by sweat and the blood that runs through my children's veins. I'm the only one in the whole family that's got any sense, and I'm not fool enough to let you wipe us out legally just to make some old man in New York City happy."

Mackey had heard enough. "You keep telling me you're not stupid. How about showing me how smart you really are?"

"Smart enough to know there are a hell of a lot more of us than there are of you," Nellie said. "And just because I'm smart enough to keep you from goadin' me and mine into a fight doesn't mean we won't cut you down the first chance we get."

"You'll try," Mackey said, "on James Grant's orders, of course."

"Grant plays his game and we play ours," Nellie said. "And you're missin' my point, lawman. I've got no more allegiance to Grant than I do to Rice. But since Rice ain't offerin' anything after years of our beggin', I've decided to back a different horse."

Mackey slowly shook his head. "Mr. Rice knows you want a rail spur up here, but he's never lied to you about building it. There's no money in it. Not for him and not for you. None of Grant's lies to the contrary are going to make a damned bit of difference."

Nellie's face softened to the point where he knew she understood that. "So what's your fancy man putting on the table to allow me and mine to enjoy some of Dover Station's prosperity?"

"You back out of your agreement with Grant," Mackey said, "you get to live. All of you. It'll prove you're serious about law and order, and Mr. Rice will be impressed. After a while, maybe he'll consider some options. Maybe buying out your ranches well above any fair price you ask or maybe some other arrangement when the time is right."

"And what if we keep on working with James Grant?"

"Then Mr. Rice will be disappointed." He made sure Nellie was looking at him when he said, "And so will you."

Mad Nellie pushed the chair back as she stood to leave. "Then you might as well head on back to Dover Station and wire your boss and tell him his offer ain't good enough. Tell him the Hancock clan ain't scared of him, you, or anyone else who crosses us. Tell him we've chosen our side and the only way to change our mind is to build that spur from Dover to Hancock. Rice does that, we won't need Grant anymore. Until he does, we don't need Rice for anything." She turned and walked toward the door. "If he gives you another message for me, be sure to ride back up here and let me know. But it'd better have gold, Marshal, and lots of it."

Mackey saw his chance to goad her into a public fight in town slipping away, so he gave it one last try. "The next message will involve lead, Nellie. And more of it than you'll be able to count."

She laughed as she pushed her way through the crowd that still gathered at the café entrance. A good number of the crowd thinned out behind her, and Mackey wondered if they were all relatives. He had no idea how large the family was. No one did, except that there were a lot of them. More than most men would try to take on by himself.

But Aaron Mackey was not most men.

He saw Norman appear at the kitchen door, holding the plate containing his breakfast. He beckoned him to come forward.

"I said I'd be damned if I allowed my breakfast to be ruined by a Hancock." The plate of food was so large he gladly holstered his Peacemaker to make room for it on the table. "And that's one promise I aim to keep right now."

Chapter 5

Back in Dover Station, Deputy U.S. Marshal Billy Sunday leaned against the porch post in front of the old jailhouse while he built a cigarette with dark, nimble fingers. He was glad the wind was not strong enough to blow his tobacco leaves all over Front Street.

The wind in that part of town had changed considerably since they had finished the ornate Municipal Building across the thoroughfare a few months back. Billy mourned the loss of the quaint blacksmith shop and hotel they had torn down to make room for the red brick and iron monstrosity that now lorded over the town like a castle.

The new building even had a clock in it that chimed like a church bell every hour on the hour all day and all night as if to remind all within earshot that another hour of life had just passed by. Billy thought it was a quaint enough sound when he was on the other end of town or riding on the hillside, but being right across from the damned thing when it rang wasn't so quaint, especially when he was trying to sleep.

But neither he nor Mackey had given Mayor James Grant the satisfaction of complaining about it.

Grant's first order of business upon his election to mayor had been to abolish the office of the town's sheriff department and replace it with a larger police department made up of gunmen loyal to him. Grant had been smart enough to hire their old friend Walter Underhill as chief of police. After all, their town was on the rise, and terms like "sheriff" did not quite fit with the Dover Station Company's plans to make the town the jewel of the territory.

Grant's second official act as mayor was to lead his new police force to the old jailhouse and demand Mackey and Billy's stars and the key to the jailhouse. He planned to destroy the squat old building and expand the livery to include horse stables for his new police force.

Grant did not know that Mr. Rice had pulled strings with his friends in Washington to get Mackey named United States Marshal of the Montana Territory and that the jailhouse was now federal property.

The black man smiled at the memory of the look on Grant's face as he sealed his cigarette around the tobacco.

He stood because he didn't feel much like sitting on the wooden bench, and the rocking chair beside it had always been Aaron's. Plenty of other people had taken a seat in the rocking chair, though, after Aaron got famous following the whole Darabont business a year or so ago. Nearly everyone who came to town or was just passing through wanted to see the jailhouse from where the Savior of Dover Station defended justice. They all wanted to sit in the great man's rocking chair and pepper Billy with questions he usually ignored.

Does the sheriff's Peacemaker really have pearl handles? Has he really killed all those men the papers say he did? Is he really seven feet tall?

Billy never ceased to be amazed at how so many facts could be jumbled in the retelling or just flat-out made up. His friend hated his newfound notoriety, which men like James Grant had turned into a tourist attraction, but Billy managed to find a way to enjoy it. It was nice to see people genuinely happy to see them, which was rare for a lawman.

After answering a few questions, Billy usually directed them over to the Dover Station General Store and Mercantile, where Aaron's father, Brendan "Pappy" Mackey, would gladly tell them all about his part in the Battle of Dover Station and how his son had come to be known as the Hero of Adobe Flat when he was in the cavalry.

Billy imagined Pappy's store was the birthplace of a lot of the embellishments in what had become known as the Battle of Dover Station and other stories associated with Mackey.

Billy Sunday had been with Aaron at both engagements and at a few dozen more that had been too bloody for anyone to want to hear about. People tended to only like the stories they wanted to hear. The kind where the heroes and the villains were plain to see, like lines of troops on a battlefield. They didn't like it if the tales blurred lines between good and bad. They shied away from stories of the real world where the hero didn't always get the girl and the villain didn't always die on the last page of the story.

They didn't like stories where the hero wasn't always the hero.

In that regard, Billy Sunday had never thought of Aaron Mackey or of himself as heroes. He thought of Aaron as a good man who did right whenever he could. That was enough for Billy Sunday to consider him a friend.

Billy had struck a lucifer match off the post and lit his cigarette when he spotted Mayor James Grant and Chief Walter Underhill come down the stone steps of the Municipal Building and head his way.

He cursed to himself as he waved the match dead and tossed it into the thoroughfare. A pleasant Montana morning ruined just like that.

Mayor Grant was a tallish man in his mid-forties whose sandy blond hair and a full beard had begun to gray in all the right places for a politician. He had one of those faces where the gray made him look distinguished. He was broad shouldered and thick around the chest. Billy always thought he looked more like a laborer who had become a foreman than a man who had come to wield so much power.

He had the common man's touch, having been a rancher, a stagecoach station manager, and operator of a telegraph office for the railroad. Rumor said that he had once served as a lawman in some capacity in Nebraska, though the town and the time of his service was a matter of some debate.

Somewhere along the line, he had managed to get the ear of Silas Van Dorn, Mr. Rice's partner in the Dover Station Company, who hired Grant to manage the company's operations and transformation of Dover Station.

Billy figured his agreeable appearance was a good reason why the people of Dover Station had seen fit to elect the son of a bitch mayor.

Since his election, James Grant had beaten or killed just about everyone and everything that had stood against him since he had arrived in Dover Station.

Everyone except Aaron Mackey and Billy Sunday.

Chief Underhill hung back as Mayor Grant approached the jailhouse alone. The big Texan with the long blond hair usually looked robust and powerful, but on that morning, his skin was pale and he looked sick.

Billy knew this was going to be an interesting visit.

Grant removed his hat before speaking to Billy. A delicate gesture of an indelicate man. "Morning, Deputy Sunday. I suppose I can still call you that, given your new post with the federal government."

"The badge is different," Billy said, "but the title's the same. Easier to remember that way."

Grant forced a smile as he asked, "Is the marshal around, by chance? I'd like to talk to him about a matter of some urgency."

"Just so happens that he's away on a matter of some urgency. Federal business." Billy had no intention of telling Grant that Aaron was off tracking down Hancock and his gang. Grant might already suspect that Mackey was after his allies, but Billy would be damned before he confirmed it for him.

"Do you have any idea where he is so I might send him a wire?" Grant asked. "As I said, it's a matter of some urgency."

"I'll tell him to stop by to see you when he gets back to town," Billy said.

"When will that be?"

"Don't have any idea. Could be a day or two. Could be a week. Federal business is hard to peg down sometimes."

Grant masked his disappointment well. He glanced back at Underhill, who silently prodded him on.

Billy could tell by the glance that something good was, indeed, coming his way. "Do you think you might be able to help me?"

Billy blew out the smoke from the side of his mouth. "Depends on what it is."

Grant looked back at Underhill once more. "What do you think, Chief? Could Deputy Sunday help us?"

Underhill squinted as he slowly nodded. It was as if he was trying hard not to be sick. "I already told you he could, didn't I?"

Billy saw Mayor Grant bristle at Underhill's tone. He tried to cover it, but not quick enough for the deputy to miss it. "I'm afraid you'll find the chief in poor spirits today. We have something of a situation on our hands, one that I believe your time and experience on the Great Plains might help us understand."

Billy had no idea how his time in the cavalry could help either Grant or Underhill. But given Underhill's sickly expression, he imagined it wasn't anything good. "I'll be happy to help. Lead the way."

"You won't need my assistance." Mayor Grant quickly put his hat back on as he stepped back into the thoroughfare. "Chief Underhill here will be able to show you everything far better than I could. Besides, I'm already late for a meeting in my office." He touched Billy's arm and lowered his voice. "Thank you in advance for your discretion, Deputy. We deeply appreciate it. Please come by my office later once you've had a chance to fully grasp the situation."

Billy squinted through his cigarette smoke as he watched Mayor Grant walk across Front Street and go up the stairs into the Municipal Building.

Billy noticed Underhill still hadn't moved. The big man just stood there as if he was waiting to be helped across the street. "Should I bring my rifle for this help I'm providing?"

Underhill slowly shook his head. "Just a strong stomach."

Billy pulled the jailhouse door shut and locked it. He couldn't recall a time when the Texan had been so subdued. He slipped the key into his pocket and walked down the steps to the thoroughfare where Underhill stood. "Sounds serious."

"It's worse than serious, Billy. It's evil." He nodded to the alley across the street next to the Municipal Building. "Follow me. I'll show you."

Billy had always been able to sense trouble before and after it happened.

Whether he was out on the trail or in town, that sense of death and danger had been the advantage that had saved his life more times than he could count.

And as he followed Chief Underhill through the alley and toward three new houses that had just been built across the street behind the Municipal Building, Billy's instinct kicked up once again.

A hint of stale blood and worse reached him as they cleared the mouth of the alley.

Billy looked at the three new buildings. They had been painted a dark blue, and he could still smell the fresh-cut wood underlying the stench of death. "What happened in there, Chief?"

"Talking about it won't do it justice. You'll have to see it for yourself, and I mean that, Billy. You'll have to go in there by yourself. I went in there once." He stopped and brought a hand to his mouth. "I won't be making that same mistake again."

The wind picked up, and the stench of death grew even stronger. Underhill stopped again and turned to the side as he retched.

Billy walked past the chief, knowing the Texan wouldn't be much use to him anymore.

He saw the door of the third house on the right was open. He also saw a dark smear on the boardwalk connecting the three houses, a smear that ended in the dirt below the porch.

Billy pulled the Colt from the holster and held it at his side as he walked toward the death house. He slowly stepped up onto the boardwalk and squatted to take a closer look at the smear on the porch. He saw a bloody footprint leading off the boardwalk.

A very large boot print.

He looked back at Underhill. "That would be your boot in the blood, wouldn't it?"

The big Texan nodded the best he could as he heaved once more into the mud.

Billy slowly stood up and saw the trail of blood led back to the house with the half-open door.

This is where it happened. This was why they had asked him here.

He nudged the door inward with the barrel of his gun, and the putrid smell of death only grew worse.

Billy minded his step as he moved inside. There was no reason for him to wait. Death was no stranger to him.

Chapter 6

Billy opened up the back door of the death house and took a deep breath of fresh air. He sat down on the edge of the porch. The steps hadn't been put in yet, so his feet dangled just above the dirt.

He had to get the images of those bodies out of his mind.

He focused on the lots across the street from the death house and saw they were already plotted out with stakes in the ground. He knew this part of town was the next slated for expansion by the Dover Station Company. They were planning on diverting part of the river to flow through a dry bed at the end of Front Street for the new sawmill they would start building in a month or so when the weather got warmer. The mill was supposed to increase the town by a third and be a big boost to its lumber industry.

This entire area was supposed to be the site of the town's future. But the three dead women he had just seen reminded him of the town's deadly past. They were gone, but the living kept on planning and building and growing.

In a year or so, no one would remember the three

dead women he had just seen in the house behind the Municipal Building. And if they did, they wouldn't even care. Because Dover Station was a boomtown and boomtowns had short memories. The past was an expense they could ill afford. There was simply no money in it.

But Billy had always been a sentimentalist, and letting death go was not in his nature.

He pulled out his pouch of tobacco and his rolling paper and began building a cigarette, hoping the routine might take his mind off what he had just seen. Three dead women—Chinese from the looks of them—posed sitting against the wall in an upstairs bedroom. The oldest of them might have been thirty. The other two had been no older than twenty.

Each of them had died from a sharp blade drawn across their throats. Billy was sure of that. The other things that had been done to them were best forgotten about until Doc Ridley could take a look for himself. He had seen injuries like that before. Horrors from the parched lands of the southwest. Men found bound on scorched wagon wheels. Women found in burned-out houses. Mutilated bodies left on the side of the road for the buzzards and the coyotes to pick at. The bodies of cavalrymen stripped bare and desecrated, left to swell and bake beneath the harsh desert sun.

And the flies. The damned flies were always there. Everywhere, and now they had come to a row of tiny houses behind the Municipal Buildings on the edge of town. The flies and the same death that always brought them.

Billy didn't notice Underhill had been standing off

to the side until the chief cleared his throat. "Grant told me it was pretty bad in there."

"It's not good." Billy made sure he had rolled his cigarette nice and tight before sealing it. "But you didn't see it for yourself, did you? No, I'd wager you didn't get much past the front door."

"That's right." Underhill lifted his head. "How'd you know?"

"Saw your boot print in the . . . mess . . . just inside the house," Billy said. "Looked like you slid as you ran out."

Underhill toed at the dirt. "Didn't know a man could tell so much from a lousy boot print."

"Most people can't," Billy said. "I can."

"It was the smell that got me," Underhill explained. "I've seen a lot of things in my time, Billy, but I've never smelled anything like that."

Billy couldn't hold that against him. Most people could handle the sight of death and even a fair amount of blood. Not many could handle the amount of gore he had just seen in that house.

Underhill's lips moved as he struggled to find the words. "Grant said there's three squaws in there, all cut up."

"Squaws?" Billy struck a match on the porch and lit his cigarette. "Grant doesn't know what he's talking about. They're three Chinese women. And from the general look of the place, I'd peg them as whores. That's not to say they deserved to die that way, but I'd imagine the nature of their profession might help you figure out who did it."

"Chinese women?" Underhill repeated as if trying the idea on for size. "You sure?"

"I'm sure they're not squaws, and I don't know why Grant would say otherwise. I know he's been cooped up in an office for the past couple of years, but squaws and Celestial women don't look much alike."

Underhill still frowned like he didn't like the idea. "But that doesn't make any sense. We don't have many Chinamen in town."

Billy didn't know what to tell him. "Well, however many you had yesterday, you've got three fewer of them running around today." He thought of something. "You sure Grant told you they were Indian women?"

"Squaws was his exact term," Underhill said. "He was all set and ready to tell that to Doc Ridley and that old drunk Harrington down at the *Record* before I stopped him."

Billy flicked his ash off the porch. "Why'd you stop him from getting Doc Ridley?"

"On account of Ridley being the biggest gossip in town, second only to Mackey's father," Underhill said. "And I didn't want this in the paper until we knew more about what happened here and why. Maybe it would've been different if I'd been able to go in there and take a look at them for myself, but, well, I couldn't, and that's all there is to it."

That was more to it than Billy thought there would be. He had never known Underhill to stand up to Grant in the past. He was surprised he had done so now, but he was glad he had. "Seems Grant was in a hell of a hurry to put a period on this, wasn't he?"

"Seems so," Underhill said. "Why do you think that is?"

Billy smoked his cigarette. "He's your boss, not mine. You tell me."

"I won't be able to tell you anything," Underhill admitted. "I'm not a tracker, Billy. You are. You track men and you track down facts. You're used to finding things you're looking for. I'm not like that, and neither are any of the men working with me. They're tough boys, but . . ."

"They're gunmen," Billy said. "Gunmen aren't lawmen, Walter, not even after you pin a badge on their chest."

"And right now, we need a lawman for this kind of work." The wind shifted again, and Underhill had to step to the side to avoid another blast from the death house. "I want your help on this, Billy. Hell, I'm not ashamed to admit I need it. Grant wanted these murders public, and I don't know why. Once he brings other people into this, the truth will get stomped out, and I don't want that. You said you thought those ladies were whores. Well, someone saw fit to kill them. And with Grant rushing to make it public, I figure there's got to be a reason why. Maybe it's the same reason why they got killed in the first place."

Billy took his first deep drag on his cigarette while he thought over everything that Underhill had just said.

The notion that James Grant had been in the death house first bothered Billy. Grant's decision to involve him and Aaron bothered him even more. Grant never did anything by accident.

Billy asked Underhill, "Who told you about these dead ladies?"

"Grant did," the chief admitted. "Said he passed by

Chapter 7

After checking into the Hancock Hotel, Mackey waited until nightfall before taking the back stairs to the alley and walking across the street to the livery, where he bunked down in the hay for a good night's rest.

Arthur clearly could not understand the marshal's logic. "You mean you were able to check into the hotel, even after you brought a dead Hancock back to town?"

"I was," Mackey told him. "They were even nice enough to give me the big room with the balcony out front."

"And you paid for it already?"

"One night in advance," Mackey said. "They insisted. Gave me the nicest room in the place to make up for the policy."

"So, you've got the nicest room in town and you're sleeping on some old hay in the livery. Why?"

"Safer that way," Mackey said. "Nice sheets and a fluffy pillow don't do you much good if you're dead."

Now, the marshal's reasoning was beginning to

"The Land Office is right down the hall from mine. I should be able to find out easy enough once old Bill Donohue finally gets around to coming to work. Why?"

Billy slapped the dust from the seat of his pants. "Because that title just might tell us who killed these women and why."

perfectly content to lie atop its rider until it caught its wind. Mackey had seen many a man get trapped beneath their horse and knew every second under the two-thousand-pound animal was pure agony, assuming he was still alive. The last rider had thrown down a rope to the others trying to pull horse and man free from each other.

In another place and time, Mackey might have felt sorry for the Hancock men. But he could not forget they had gotten themselves into this predicament by trying to kill him.

It was tough to work up much sympathy for them after that.

He had no intention of staying hidden by the watering hole for the rest of the day.

It was time to do something.

As Mackey rode toward them, he saw they had managed to drag the fallen horse off their relative, who was as dead as his horse. The one horse they had left stood hobbled close by and was more interested in the grass at its feet than the troubles of the humans.

Mackey brought Adair to a stop about forty yards away from the men. The butt of the Winchester was flat against his leg. "Looks like you boys are in a bad way. Kind of takes all the fun out of running down a man."

The men flinched as they looked up to see the man they had been trying to kill looming over them on horseback.

The biggest man in the group reached for his

sidearm, but one of his friends stopped him. "Don't be a damned fool, Al. He could've started slamming into us from way over there if he wanted."

Mackey looked the would-be gunman over. "Al. You're the same hothead from the café, aren't you?"

"I am." Al struggled against his kin to get to his pistol. "And I'm the same one who'll put you in your grave."

Mackey lowered the Winchester until it was aimed at the center of Al's chest. "Let him try."

The man, who looked like the oldest of the bunch, wrapped his arms around Al and glared up at Mackey. "Don't you think you've killed enough of us for one day?"

"You counting just here or back at the hotel?" Mackey asked. "I'm afraid I'm losing count."

"I don't know about that business back at the hotel," the man said. "I only know what's happening here." He looked around at the rest of his men. "Unbuckle your gun belts, boys, and toss them over there. Let's not give this bastard any excuses to kill more of us."

Mackey watched the man unbuckle his belt and swing it away from him. The others did the same, except Al. The older man took his pistol from the holster and tossed it on the pile with the others.

"You're the first Hancock I've met who talks sense." Mackey shifted the Winchester so it aimed at the sky. "What's your name?"

"Carl Winslow," the man told him, "but I'm a Hancock just the same. My daddy changed it when he tried going respectable a few years ago. Made the rest of us change it, too, but Hancock's my right name."

"A man can change his name, but not who he is. Mad Nellie send you out here after me?"

Carl nodded. "We call her Nellie, if it's just the same to you."

"And I'd call you stranded afoot in the middle of nowhere with two dead men, a cripple, and a halfwit like Al here to make things worse."

Al moved toward the pistols, but Carl and two other Hancock men were able to hold him back.

Carl let the other two handle Al as he walked toward Mackey. "You ride all the way back up here to gloat, mister, or help?"

"What makes you think I didn't come up here to finish what I started?" Mackey asked.

"Because you would've done that from farther away if you had blood on your mind. You didn't tie down your rig for a silent ride just to gun us down in broad daylight."

Mackey liked the way the man thought. "Guess that means I'm not the cold-blooded killer Nellie says I am."

"You're a killer, Mackey, and one who deserves to be put down for what he's done," Carl said. "To Henry and maybe some other folks, too. But none of us are in a position to do much about that now, so there's no use in discussing it at present. Just about the only thing that matters is what you plan on doing to us right here and now."

Mackey knew these men had tried to kill him once and would probably try again. But they were unarmed, on foot, and stranded in a valley in the middle of nowhere. Only one of them still had a horse. He probably had every right to kill them where they stood, but that would be wrong. The war might not be over, but this particular battle was done.

He looked down at the man who had been crushed by his horse. "He looks pretty bad."

"Damned near every bone in his chest is crushed or busted," Carl said. "I don't have the heart to put him down, and neither do any of the others. Not even Al, here. If we had our horses, we might be able to figure out a way to get him back to the ranch, but he won't survive on foot."

"Won't survive it on horseback," Mackey said. "Or by you dragging him somehow. You boys know that."

Carl looked at the other Hancock men. None of them looked at him. "Yeah. We do."

Mackey knew the injured man had been intent on killing him only a few moments before, but the sight of another human being writhing in agony made him set that aside. "How about we come to an agreement?"

Carl glowered up at him. "What kind of an agreement, seeing as how you're the son of a bitch who did this to him."

"While he was trying to kill me," Mackey reminded him. "Along with the rest of you. But I'm in a charitable mood, so here's what we're going to do. Carl, you're going to get on that horse and gather up the mounts who rode off. They're pretty tired after your big chase, so they didn't go far. Probably just past those foothills over there. You shouldn't have any trouble finding them."

Carl thought it over. "And what about the rest of us?"

"Al here will lead them in walking back the way you came. Once you gather the horses, you'll bring them to the others and keep riding back to your ranch and stay there." He looked at Al when he said, "I've already stopped you boys once, and it cost three of you your lives. Come at me again, and none of you ride out alive. Understand?"

The Hancock men grumbled, but it was Carl who spoke first. "What about our guns?" He gestured at the dying man on the ground. "And poor Dan here?"

"You can pick them up when you come back to collect Dan's body later on." He gestured back to the watering hole. "I'll hide them over there so no one comes along and takes them. And if you go peacefully, I promise I won't throw them in the water."

Carl drew in a ragged breath. It was clear he hated the idea of giving up and going away. He did not like anything about any of this. And he also did not have a choice. "You promise you'll help Dan pass as painless as possible, Marshal? You give me your word?"

"I give you my word on everything I've told you today." Mackey had Adair take one step closer to him. "Every single thing."

A heavy wind picked up and blew down the length of the wide valley. Mackey dipped his brim below the wind to keep his hat from blowing away.

"Just wait a second," Al protested as Carl and the other remaining Hancock men began to walk away. "We can't just leave Dan here! Not with the likes of him!"

But the other men urged the younger man to join them as Carl swung up into the saddle. The others were cowhands and older than Al. They had spent more of their lives grateful for the pleasure of sunrises and even more so for the sight of the setting sun.

They knew a good day's work when they saw it and knew what a man could expect from himself. They had lost and their men were dead. Best to get home and get ready for tomorrow.

Carl kept his horse back until his men were out of earshot.

Mackey watched them go. "You'd best get on, too, Carl. You don't want to be part of what happens next."

"That's just it," Carl said. "I didn't want to be part of any of this. I don't even know how it all started."

He looked down at Dan, who had quieted some in the past few moments. "But none of that really matters anymore because, after today, you and me have our own score to settle, Marshal. I don't know what happened between you and Nellie and I don't care, either. You killed three of my family today, Marshal Mackey, and law or no law, I won't let any man get away with being able to claim that. Not before he answers to me. I'm grateful for you letting me and mine live, but I also know gunning us down would've been murder, and you ain't no murderer. But the next time I see you, you're a dead man."

Mackey could not blame Carl for being angry. He also had no reason to doubt every word that Carl said was true. He imagined the man would kill him the next time he saw him. And just like he might have felt sympathy for him in other circumstances, he may have saved himself the aggravation of anticipation and simply shot Carl right out of the saddle. He'd be well within his rights to do so, both as a man and as a lawman.

But he knew that would also be playing into Mad

Nellie's hands again, and he wouldn't allow himself to make that mistake.

"I'll scabbard my rifle if you'd prefer to go at it with pistols right here and now."

Carl seemed to think about it for a moment. "I'd like to, but I've got men afoot who need horses and good men who'll need burying before tomorrow. Can't do that if I lose."

Mackey was glad the man had made a wise decision. "You ever been to Dover Station?"

Carl gripped the reins tighter. "I could ride there blindfolded in the dead of night."

"Good, because if I ever see you there, it won't be by accident, and you won't have a chance." He jerked his chin toward the men on foot. "Get to riding, Carl. Right now."

He watched Carl wheel the big bay around before putting the heels to her flanks, bringing her to a full gallop. The horse had rested some since they had been forced to stop, but it still looked winded from the charge and the excitement. If Carl wasn't a good horseman, he'd wind up afoot like his relatives.

Mackey waited until the men had walked a good five hundred yards or so away before he nudged Adair closer toward the fallen man. He was proud of the way the warhorse didn't shy away from the scent of blood or the moaning of the broken man.

Dan's ragged breath came in shallow gasps as he struggled to breathe. To live.

Mackey lowered the Winchester to the dying man's head and fired once. The shot killed him instantly.

He heard Al's shrieks of "No!" echo throughout the

valley, followed by the sounds of struggle from the men who tried to keep him from running after Mackey.

The man who had caused that misery in the first place.

Mackey had no idea what relation the dead man might be to Carl or Al. He could have been a brother or a distant cousin.

None of that mattered now. Not to Mackey. Not to the man he had just killed. Blood didn't mean much to the dead. Only the living.

He tucked his Winchester into the scabbard under his left leg, touched the brim of his hat to the soul of the dead man, and began the long ride back to Dover Station. He changed his mind and decided to leave the pistols where they were, piled like a nest of snakes in the tall grass.

Al's cries of mourning were carried on the wind that followed Mackey through the valley.

Chapter 8

In the front parlor of The Campbell Arms, Billy told Robert Lagrange about the three women he had found butchered in the house at the edge of town.

When he finished telling him the entire story from the beginning, Lagrange looked at him over the rim of his coffee cup. "Strange." He sipped his coffee. "Yes, quite strange indeed."

Billy waited for more, but Lagrange was still mulling over the situation in his mind.

He remembered he had not liked the Pinkerton man back when they had first met on Mr. Rice's private car all of those months ago. Mr. Rice had assigned Lagrange to remain in Dover Station and keep an eye on James Grant's influence over Silas Van Dorn and the Dover Station Company.

Robert Lagrange's gray suit and shined shoes were city attire, and his matching bowler hat had no place in a Montana frontier town. His brown moustaches and chin whiskers were as perfectly groomed and waxed as his wavy hair was styled. Even after living among the people of Dover Station for so many months, Mr. Lagrange had remained quite the dandy who bore the confidence of a man better suited for a boardroom than horseback.

But Billy had seen how Lagrange could handle himself when the bullets flew and knew this city man was much tougher than he looked. Billy normally didn't like city men, but he had grown to like Lagrange.

With Aaron chasing down Henry Hancock, the Pinkerton man was the only man in town he could trust to help him with the house of dead women. Because if there was anyone who distrusted James Grant as much as Aaron and Billy, it was Robert Lagrange.

The detective set his coffee cup back in the saucer. "Underhill's reluctance to go public is as encouraging as Grant's rush to involve the public is troubling. Do you think the chief is finally turning on the mayor?"

"I'm not sure he was ever really with him," Billy admitted. "He would've been a fool not to take the chief's job when Grant gave it to him. Maybe he's looked the other way a couple of times, but he showed good sense in keeping these murders quiet."

"At least until we've had a good look at the bodies." He looked back at the clock at the other end of the parlor. "And I'd say we'll want to get moving as soon as possible. Decay will settle in fast now that the warmer weather is upon us."

"Decay won't make much of a difference," Billy said. "They were killed some time last night and found after sunrise this morning."

Lagrange filed both of their coffee cups. "According to our fair mayor."

Billy frowned. "Seems like everything we know so far is based on what that bastard tells us."

"It's like that with most things in Dover Station." Lagrange tapped a finger against his coffee mug as he thought things through. "Grant has become far more dangerous now than he was when I first came to town. His growing alliance with the Hancock family proves that." He tapped his saucer with a fingernail. "I wonder if the deaths of these women have anything to do with the Hancock clan moving into town."

Billy had not thought of that before, but did not think there was much to it now. "The Hancocks have been known to run saloons and joy houses, but I've never known them to bother with the Celestials and the troubles they bring."

"You mean gambling and opium," Lagrange concluded. "Yes, I can see why. The Chinese are a stubborn lot when it comes to the administration of vices. Best to take a cut of their action and let them do as they will. They'll wind up doing that anyway, so fighting it is pointless. But I find the presence of three Chinese women in that part of town to be a fascinating development. Why there? Why not in the heart of town? Why not in a saloon? Certainly, they could have carved out a niche for themselves in one of the other establishments."

Billy fought down the bile that rose in his throat. "Don't use that term."

"Carve?" Lagrange repeated. "Why?"

"You'll see for yourself when you come see the bodies," was all Billy would say. "Best if you make your own conclusions."

Lagrange smiled as he sipped his coffee. "Now I'm positively intrigued."

The detective brightened when Mrs. Katherine Campbell approached the table. Billy noticed there wasn't anything lustful in the way he looked at her. It was just the effect she tended to have on people.

"What's all this talk about intrigue?" she asked. "I hope it doesn't have anything to do with my place. Intrigue is hard on the furniture."

She bent and kissed Billy on the cheek. "Morning, Deputy."

"Morning, Katie."

Billy knew he was one of the last people in town to still call her that. Mrs. Katherine Campbell was not only the owner of The Campbell Arms, but Aaron Mackey's lady friend. She had been born into a fine Boston family and had an accent to match, a nicer accent to Billy's ear than Lagrange's. He knew she was older than Aaron by a few years and might even be closer to forty, but it wasn't easy to tell. She had developed fine lines around her eyes and mouth from smiling so much since she'd come to Dover Station to find Aaron, her true love.

Billy knew the two of them had been through a lot together, and he kept hoping Aaron would ask her to marry him one day. But Aaron Mackey was a stubborn man and wasn't easily rushed. If he wanted to ask her, he'd ask her and in his own time. Not a second before.

She rearranged the silverware on the table to make it more orderly. "Have either of you heard any news from our traveling marshal?"

"Not yet," Billy said, "but I expect him along today or tomorrow at the latest. Hancock's not that far."

"I'm not worried about the distance," Katherine said. "I'm worried about what he'll find once he's there. Henry Hancock has crafted himself quite a dangerous reputation."

"So has Aaron Mackey." Lagrange laughed. "I'm sure the marshal can handle himself, Mrs. Campbell. I've seen him do it plenty of times, and I haven't known him for that long."

"Well I've known him longer than that," she said, "and as the marshal himself is fond of saying, it only takes one bullet to change everything." She looked at Billy. "You said he might be back today?"

Billy hated hearing the concern in her voice. He was sure Aaron was fine, but she was right. All it took was a single bullet to change everything forever. He had seen a lot of forevers changed that way. "It's possible, but don't hold me to it. But if he's not back by tomorrow, I'll send a wire to Hancock before I go riding up there. Can't speak to the accuracy of the response as the town most likely hates him, but I'll send it just the same."

"I'd appreciate that." She rested a hand on his shoulder. "I don't know why he just didn't let you go with him in the first place."

"Said he wanted to handle it himself." Billy shrugged. "He can be stubborn."

"Don't I know it. Can I get you gentlemen another pot of coffee?"

"No thanks," Lagrange said. "Deputy Sunday and I have some work to attend to, don't we?"

"Oh?" Katherine asked. "That intriguing kind of work you were taking about when I interrupted."

Billy liked the fancy man, but often wondered if his elegant ways might get them all in trouble someday. He wasn't worried about Katherine saying something, but about one of the guests roaming through The Campbell Arms overhearing something. "It might be nothing. Just something I've asked Robert here to help me with."

"Does it involve Aaron and that damned Hancock clan?"

"Nothing at all," Billy assured her.

Though, now that she had mentioned it, he wondered if it could.

If Lagrange was bothered by the prospect of gore when he followed Billy into the house, he did a good job of hiding it. The Pinkerton Detective Agency had a well-earned reputation of training its men in all of the most modern investigative techniques. It wasn't just book learning, either. They saw real bodies in real life.

"That sickness I saw in the front yard," Lagrange said. "Do we know where that came from?"

"Underhill."

The detective smiled at the deputy marshal. "Really?"

"Said the smell got to him. Didn't get past the front door on account of it."

"I never would've guessed that." Lagrange pointed to Billy's lantern. "Light that up and let us see what we can see."

Billy had borrowed a lantern from The Campbell Arms and lit it as they moved deeper into the house.

It was well on into the afternoon and some areas of the house were darker than others. He lit the lantern and handed it to Lagrange.

The detective raised the lantern high as he examined the first floor. "I see there's a large amount of blood on the walls and on the floor by the front door," he observed, "but very little on the steps themselves."

Billy hadn't noticed that the first time he had been in the house that morning. "What does that mean?"

"I won't know until I see everything," Lagrange explained. "I was taught that if I concoct a theory now, I'll fit what I find to match it. That's no good for anyone, especially the victims."

Billy followed the Pinkerton man upstairs.

"More smears on the walls and floor up here," Lagrange said when he reached the second floor.

He stopped when he saw the three dead women who had been placed between the bed and the wall. Billy thought the shadows cast by the lantern on the bodies made the macabre scene look even more horrible than it already was.

"They're certainly Chinese and most certainly dead," Lagrange observed as he moved closer to the corpses. "Now I can also see why Grant would want to make this public."

Billy had not expected him to say that. "Why?"

Lagrange set the lantern on the table beside the bed. "Because this kind of butchery qualifies as a massacre, and any reporter worth his salt, even one working for a local rag like the *Record*, ever got hold of this, it would cause a great panic."

Billy still didn't understand his reason. "Why would a mayor want a panic in his own town?"

"Panics can be tricky," Lagrange said, "but beneficial to a leader if handled properly. Given that Grant holds sway over the business and political interests in this town, he could arrange it so he benefited nicely from his people's fear."

Billy looked from the detective to the three dead women. "You think he planned this?"

"Not at this point," Lagrange admitted, "but I wouldn't put it past him to try to capitalize on the deaths of these poor women in a way that benefits him. The greater the crisis, the greater the glory to the man who captures the villain and brings him to justice. Imagine how heroic the police chief of London would look if he were able to capture the fiend behind those murders in Whitechapel."

Billy still had not gotten down the knack of reading, but he had heard people talk about the murders in London and how the city was terrified. If something like that could happen in the biggest city in the world, Billy could only imagine what it would do to a place like Dover Station.

He was beginning to see Lagrange's point. "And Grant could benefit from that kind of trouble."

"Most certainly," Lagrange said. "Create the panic so that he could stem it and look like the hero. With statehood right around the corner, what better way for him to look like a man who can get things done than to stomp out the villain he created? Probably pin it on some poor drunk. Although the town's image would suffer in the short term, Grant could personally profit greatly in the long run."

Billy knew Grant was capable of a lot, but he didn't want to think the man was capable of killing three women for the sake of headlines. Lagrange's theory explained why Grant had been so eager to involve Doc Ridley and the *Record*. "Think we prove it?"

"Probably not," Lagrange said as he held the lantern aloft and examined the three corpses that had been positioned beside the bed. "You didn't arrange the bodies in the seating position, did you?"

"I haven't touched anything," Billy said. "All I did was check under the bed to see if the knife was there. It wasn't. Checked the rest of the house and the yard out back. Didn't find anything there, either, so whoever did this must have taken the knife with them."

"For good reason," Lagrange said. "A blade that can cut so deep so easily is hard to come by." He inched the bed aside with his leg as he moved in to get a closer look at the three corpses. He held the lantern close as he examined the neck wound of the young woman on the left before moving on to wounds of the other two beside her.

"The flimsy nightgowns, cheap rouge, and powder on their faces tell me they were whores. Am I right?"

"I've got Underhill looking into that," Billy said, "but it looks that way. Decent layout for one. Three rooms upstairs and the front parlor downstairs for entertaining guests. I'd say the oldest one there at the end might've been the madam."

"I'd say she was around thirty." Lagrange ran the lantern over the bodies. "They were seated on the floor like a child's dolls. They certainly didn't fall this way. They were posed like this."

That was another question Billy needed answered. "Why?"

"It's all part of his ruse," Lagrange declared as he continued to examine the corpses.

Billy didn't understand. "What the hell are you talking about?"

"The bloodstains show the women died where they fell," the detective explained. "One downstairs who opened the door and two in this room. Probably made a last stand against the killer or something. He brought the unfortunate girl from downstairs and carried her up here with the others. We know that he carried her because of the lack of blood on the stair treads themselves. He placed all three of them in a seated position and went about desecrating the corpses afterward. We know they were already dead by the lack of blood from the head and other stab wounds."

Lagrange stood up and looked at Billy. "Chief Underhill was right to bring you in first, Billy. Your experience on the frontier helped you see through the other horrors the killer left to distract us from what really happened here."

Billy still wasn't sure what Lagrange was talking about. "Which is?"

"A man with a sharp blade cut the throats of three whores," Lagrange explained. "All the rest of it is just a distraction. The placement of them, the other horrors he committed. None of them matter. All that matters is the deaths."

Lagrange thought of something as he moved the lantern to look over them again. "It shows whoever did this was cunning enough to lay a trap for us."

Billy realized he must have seen the confused look on his face, for Lagrange explained, "I mean look at all the lengths he went to in order to make this seem worse than it already was. And then to leave the door open like that for Grant to find? It doesn't make any sense."

Billy finally understood what Lagrange was getting at. And he was able to make a conclusion of his own. One that changed everything. "It only makes sense when you realize who benefits from all of this. Grant."

He looked at Lagrange. "Underhill told me how he found out about this. Grant came and got him."

Lagrange pushed his bowler farther back on his head and began to scratch. "Given that it's James Grant we're talking about, I'd say there's an excellent chance he's involved in this somehow, and, as usual, we have no evidence whatsoever to arrest him, much less bring him before a judge."

Lagrange pulled his hat properly on his head. "I'm getting tired of being outfoxed by this bastard, Billy."

"You and me both." But Billy wasn't as discouraged as Lagrange. "You know why I asked you here, don't you?"

"To give you a fresh set of eyes on what happened here?"

"That was part of it," Billy allowed, "but the real reason is that I needed an official witness to what happened here. Someone who knew what they were talking about and could write it up real and proper without Grant or Underhill knowing about it. Someone who could make sure Mr. Rice knew what had happened before Grant put his own angle on it."

"Then there isn't a moment to lose." Lagrange

picked up the lantern and began leading them back downstairs. "I'll get back to my room and start working on a report to Mr. Rice immediately while the details of the scene are still fresh in my mind. Would you like to read it over before I send it?"

Billy knew Lagrange wasn't aware that he couldn't read or write. There was no reason why he should find out, either. "We saw it together. I know what it'll say. Just send it to him when you're done."

"Good, then I'd best be at it." Lagrange opened the door and began to head back to The Campbell Arms. "Do you mind if I run ahead?"

"Go on," Billy said. "In the meantime, I'll talk to Underhill about who built these houses and owns these lots. I might have something for you to add to that report pretty soon."

As Lagrange rushed back to The Campbell Arms, Billy shut the door to the death house and began walking toward the Municipal Building. He hoped Underhill had found the ownership records for the lots and the houses. He hoped he had found some answers that would help him pin these murders on Grant once and for all.

He had wanted to bring down Grant as much as Mackey, but he hated that it might take the deaths of three women to do it. But if that's what it took to break his hold on the town, then that's what they'd use.

As he walked along the boardwalk, he noticed a new signpost had been stuck in the ground. "Lower River Street" had been written in black paint on the wooden sign. He guessed that's what they would call the place once the sawmill was finished. About a year before, this had been nothing but unused land that ran along the road out to the JT Ranch. Now it was about to have a new business and a new name on it. He only hoped that, with all that progress, no one forgot the three dead women in the house behind him. He hoped James Grant never did.

That's when Billy heard a board creak behind him just before a thick arm wrapped around his throat and yanked him up off his feet.

Billy's right hand blindly shot back and grabbed hold of his attacker's right arm as the man tried to jam a knife into his side.

The attacker grunted as his left arm squeezed tighter around Billy's neck and he tried to bring the knife closer. But Billy's arm was locked in position, and the knife wasn't going anywhere.

Billy tried to pry his attacker's left arm from around his neck, but the arm was too thick and the man was too strong. Though his legs were off the ground, Billy kicked in the air, hoping to at least throw the man off balance.

It only caused him to squeeze tighter in an effort to keep Billy from gaining a foothold. Billy turned his head and sank his teeth deep into the man's fist.

The attacker screamed as his grip on Billy's neck finally loosened enough for his legs to hit the ground.

Billy dug his heels into the dirt and began pushing the man backward. His grip on the right arm didn't falter as they stumbled back until they slammed into a porch post.

The building shuddered as Billy slammed the man's

arm into the post once, then twice, followed by a third time.

The man managed to keep hold of the knife, but lost his grip on Billy's neck. The attacker let go, only to slam an elbow into the back of Billy's head.

The blow broke Billy's grip on the knife hand, and he managed to jump backward, narrowly avoiding the sweeping arc of the blade.

Billy lost his footing and fell backward but finally got a good look at his attacker. He was a massive bald man with a patch over his eye, and he wore a heavy black cloak with a fur collar. His hands were wrapped in rags and wielded a knife with a long, curved blade.

A buffalo knife; ideal for hunters who used it to skin the large beasts.

Billy went for the Colt on his hip, but the man leapt at him before he could pull it. The deputy only had time to bring his knees up to his chest and flip the larger man over his head and into the street.

Both men got back to their feet at the same time. The skinner charged, his knife ready to swing down in another deadly arc.

Billy drew his pistol and fired into the center of the man bearing down on him. He knew all three shots had struck the man, but it didn't stop him from barreling into the deputy. The force of the impact knocked the Colt from Billy's hand as the big man tackled him to the ground.

His pistol gone, Billy struggled to find the man's right arm amidst the flurry of fabric. He needed to get control of that buffalo knife before he found it sticking out of his belly.

He could feel the man's strength beginning to

weaken from to the three shots Billy had pumped into him. But he was still a dense, powerful man with more than enough strength to cut him to ribbons.

Billy found the skinner's right arm just as he tried to drive the knife into the left side of Billy's stomach. The coarse heavy coat made Billy lose his grip on the man's arm, only to catch it again at the wrist.

The more Billy fought, the more he could feel the man's strength begin to ebb. He knew he didn't have enough time to wait until the man bled out, and the man apparently didn't have enough time to wait, either.

The skinner brought his left arm up and moved to a crouch to put all of his weight down on Billy's neck. It had been a clumsy move that mostly caught Billy's chin and slid down to his upper chest.

In a sudden burst of energy, Billy brought up his left knee between his attacker's legs and caught him in the groin. The attacker yelped as Billy kicked a second time. He was about to hit him a third time when the man fell off him to the left.

Billy rolled on top of him as he pulled his own bowie knife from the back of his gun belt with his right hand. He kept the man's knife hand pinned to the ground with his left.

The attacker flailed at him with his free hand, but Billy's blade at the attacker's throat made him stop.

Both men were breathing heavily from the struggle. "Let go," Billy panted, "of the knife."

The man's grip weakened enough for Billy to grab hold of the skinner's knife and throw it aside.

Now fully in control, Billy kept the man pinned to the ground. Although the life was beginning to slip from his good eye, Billy didn't dare release his hold to check his wounds. The wheezing in his chest said it wouldn't be long now.

"Who are you?" Billy put more pressure on the bowie knife he held at the man's throat. "Why did you kill those women?"

The bald man sneered. "Whores ain't women and women ain't whores." He coughed up a small amount of blood, which rolled down the sides of his mouth. "And that's all you'll get from me."

Billy grabbed the man's collar and shook him. "Why did you kill them?"

"Why?" Another cough brought more blood. "Why not?"

Billy snatched the man's cloak and pulled his head off the ground. "There's always a reason, damn you. Why? Who paid you?"

The man's head lolled back as the vacancy of death appeared in his eyes. His entire body went limp. Billy shook him again, hoping he may have just gone into shock, but the attacker's body moved like an old rag doll.

He placed his bowie knife under the man's nose. The polished blade did not fog. His attacker was dead.

Billy stood up and looked around for anyone else who might be able to serve as a witness to what had happened. But as the new buildings in that part of town were still mostly vacant, he found himself alone.

He sheathed his bowie knife and found the pistol that had been knocked away. He couldn't believe the big man had died so quickly and expected him to spring back to his feet any second. But the unknown man in the buffalo coat was dead on an unnamed street beneath the dying light of afternoon. The only color on the man was the blood from the three holes in his chest. One for each of the women he had killed.

Billy opened his pistol, removed the spent rounds, and replaced them with live rounds from his belt before sliding the Colt back into the holster on his hip. He figured his attacker had been alone, but he also hadn't figured on being attacked in the first place, so it paid to keep his gun loaded.

He found the man's knife under a half-built boardwalk. The blade was dirty, but clean of blood. He was grateful there was no blood on it, particularly his. He tucked the knife in his belt to show Underhill later.

Realizing there was no use in leaving the corpse in the middle of the street, he grabbed the skinner by his heavy coat and dragged him back toward the death house. His corpse lying with the women he had killed seemed as close to justice as they were likely to get. He'd keep there while he got the answers he needed to make sense of this mess.

Answers only Underhill could provide now.

Chapter 9

When he entered the grandeur of the Municipal Building, Billy slapped the dust from his clothes and looked for a place to wipe his feet.

Even though he had watched the ornate monstrosity being built from the ground up, being inside the place always gave him an uneasy feeling. Maybe it was because it was bigger than any building he had ever been in before. All of that iron and plaster and stone and glass stacked so high made him nervous. And the echo of his own footsteps on the polished marble floor set him ill at ease.

He preferred the squat, solid old jailhouse across the thoroughfare, which was more like the cavalry buildings and barracks he had grown accustomed to living in before coming to Dover Station.

The town's courtroom and jail were on the main floor of the Municipal Building between the two wings of the marble staircases that wrapped around the lobby like arms in an embrace. Billy walked up the left arm of the staircase to the second floor, where the office of the commissioner of police was located. It was directly down the hall from doors with gilded lettering that read THE OFFICE OF THE MAYOR and THE OFFICE OF THE TOWN ASSESSOR.

Billy thought the whole building was a lot of ornate nonsense for a town that had barely even had a mayor two years before. There hadn't been a need for all of this formality then, and there wasn't any need for it now as far as Billy was concerned.

But Billy knew his opinion was not considered. James Grant's opinion was the only one that mattered in Dover Station these days. He had insisted on constructing a grand Municipal Building designed to put Dover Station, Montana, on the map. It was all part of Grant's grand plan as Silas Van Dorn's manager of the Dover Station Company to rebuild the town in the Great Northern Railroad's image of what a proper railroad town should be.

Grant had succeeded in earning himself a reputation as a visionary who got things done. Even Billy and Aaron had to admit Grant had fulfilled every promise he had made to the people of Dover Station since coming to town two years before. His buildings had been constructed ahead of schedule and under budget, not that Mr. Van Dorn seemed to concern himself with budgets or anything else regarding Dover Station. He seemed content to spend his days in his darkened library while James Grant interpreted his wishes.

No, it was the public accomplishments of James Grant that concerned them. It was the things Aaron and Billy knew he was hiding that bothered them.

Billy had already suspected Grant of murdering a rebel-rouser in the town's Tent City the year before.

Billy had seen him leaving the man's shack, but he hadn't seen him actually kill the man.

And now there were three dead Chinese women that he had reported earlier that day. To Billy's mind, James Grant's ability as an administrator was only rivaled by his knack for being around murder victims.

Neither Billy nor Aaron could prove Grant had been involved in any of the murders, but they suspected it. At the very least Grant was a complicated man. At the most, he was responsible for at least four murders within town limits, not to mention all the people who had died as a result of the unrest his people had stirred up the previous year.

That's why Billy didn't trust James Grant. Men like Silas Van Dorn and Frazer Rice never hid their wealth or ambition. Everyone knew they had built empires and had most likely hurt plenty of people along the way.

But men like James Grant remained in the shadows, wielding the influence of other, more powerful men to achieve their dreams. Grant was content to run Mr. Van Dorn's operation for him in exchange for controlling the business and political aspects of the town. He had kept his position with the Dover Station Company while serving as mayor part of the time.

But Billy knew James Grant worked only for himself one hundred percent of the time. And maybe having him attacked outside the murder house served his needs somehow.

Billy opened the door to the police commissioner's office and was quickly reminded how big the office really was. There was an ornate, hand-carved wooden railing that separated the entrance from the rest of the office, but Billy had been here before and knew where it opened. He made his way inside and found Walter Underhill alone, behind a wooden desk that was even more ornate than the handrail outside. He was reading over some kind of ledger in his lap with his back to the door. A dangerous position for a lawman.

"You sure have come a long way from Texas," Billy said as he leaned against the doorway. His struggle with the skinner had left him almost too tired to stand, but not quite.

Underhill looked up from the ledger on his lap as if he had just been wakened from a sleep. "What? Oh, this barn? It's too much space, even for all of my men."

Billy inclined his head back toward the lobby. "I didn't see any of your constables out there."

"Day shift is out on patrol," Underhill said. "I'd rather have them out there doing nothing where they're visible than sitting in here doing nothing except sleeping."

Billy looked up at the high ceilings. "At least you've got this nice big place all to yourself."

"You should've had your office in here too, Billy. You and Aaron." He pushed himself out of his chair and walked to the window. He nodded toward the large windows that looked over the old, misshapen jailhouse across Front Street. "I asked Mayor Grant if I could put you and Aaron in here so we could get rid of that eyesore outside. God knows we've got the room, and that old jail is nothing more than a sad relic of the past. It just doesn't fit in with the kind of town Dover Station is today."

Billy shrugged. Leaning against the doorframe felt good. He was so tired from fighting for his life, he was afraid he might fall asleep if he sat in one of those big, comfortable chairs by Underhill's desk. "That building has been through a lot and is still standing. Just like Dover Station."

"It doesn't matter," Underhill said. "Grant wouldn't listen to me about bringing your U.S. Marshal's office in here anyway. I guess he's still stinging about you two showing him up on his inauguration day by announcing you boys had joined up with the federals."

Underhill finally took a good look at Billy and saw the condition he was in. "Christ, you look like you're about to fall over." He rushed to the deputy and offered to help him to a chair. Billy sat down on his own power before he had to accept the help.

Underhill said, "Your clothes are dusty and you've got blood all over you. What the hell happened?" He seemed to remember something and looked through the open door into the lobby before saying, "I hope it doesn't have anything to do with that house we were at this morning."

"Didn't happen at the house, but right outside of it. And it had everything to do with it."

Underhill closed his office door and went to his desk. "Now we can speak freely. You've got no idea how far voices can echo in this place. Never know who might be listening."

"Or waiting to jump you with a knife, like happened to me just now."

"Where?" Underhill asked as he opened his bottom drawer and set two glasses on the desk. "Out on Front Street?"

"Over on River Avenue across from the house," Billy told him. "A guy wearing a buffalo coat grabbed me from behind and tried to slit my throat with a buffalo knife, so I think he was probably a skinner or worked in the buffalo trade."

Underhill slowly took the bottle of whiskey out from his drawer as he set it on the table as an afterthought. "Did the guy get away?"

"Shot him three times in the chest," Billy said. "The fight kind of went out of him after that, but not soon enough. He was a big bastard. Never saw him before."

"I'm just glad you made it through. Where is he now? Did anyone else see what happened?"

Billy decided not to tell him he had brought in Lagrange to take a look at the women. He could never forget that Underhill ultimately worked for James Grant. "No. When it was over, I dragged him inside the house and left him there until we figure out what to do with him later."

"Good thinking," Underhill said as he began pouring the whiskey. "We'll head over and tend to him later after you've got some of this medicine into you." Almost as an afterthought, he added, "And you're sure you've never seen this man before?"

Billy normally was not one for spirits, but seeing as how he almost just became one himself, he decided this was an occasion. "I'd remember a big bald pale guy with an eye patch if I had seen him before. I've never seen him before, but given how many people come in and out of town these days, that's not surprising."

Underhill toasted him before downing his shot. Billy left his glass untouched.

Something was off about the way the chief was listening to him. Kind of like he was hearing a story he already knew the ending to.

Underhill set the glass back on the desk and quickly refilled it. "And he used a skinning knife, you said?"

"A damned sharp one, too." Billy leaned forward, pulled it out of his belt, and tossed it on the desk.

Underhill cursed as he pushed himself back from the desk. "Damn it, Billy, be careful. That could be the murder weapon."

"No doubt about it to me," he said. "It's a fine blade. Sharp as hell. Strong, too. Would have to be to cut through a buffalo hide. Could cut through a Chinese lady's neck easy enough. Kind of makes me wonder what a guy like that is doing in that part of town"

"I know that tone." Underhill set down his glass of whiskey. "What are you getting at?"

"Just been wondering why he'd be lurking around River Street when the place doesn't even have a name yet."

"The women," Underhill said. "He was probably a customer. Maybe he showed up without money, they told him no, and he went to work on them with the blade. You know how skinners are. Even the best of them is half crazy."

"Plenty of whores in town," Billy said. "Plenty of other women to try to kill, too, if he wanted. Why'd he want to kill those Chinese ladies, Walter?"

Underhill leaned forward. "Some men have preferences. Maybe he liked Chinese ladies."

Billy leaned forward, too. "Then why come to Dover Station, where there aren't any Chinese ladies? I can think of five towns in the territory that have them."

"Guess he was brought here on other business, saw them, and took his opportunity," Underhill explained. "It's an explanation that works as good as any other."

"Maybe why he'd be in Tent City or drinking in one of the new buckets of blood in town," Billy said, "but not why he'd be in a deserted area stalking three women."

Billy pushed the whiskey glass aside. "Now would be a good time for you to tell me about who owns those lots and who built those buildings."

"That sounds an awful lot like a threat."

"Sounds like good sense to me," Billy said. "We're supposed to care about who killed those ladies. Or have we started to care about something else since this morning?"

"Here." Underhill pushed the ledger across his desk to Billy. "Read it for yourself."

Billy felt a cold sweat break out across his upper lip. Underhill didn't know he couldn't read, and now was not the time to tell him. "How about you save me the trouble and just tell me?"

Underhill stabbed a finger at a line in the ledger. "I know the lots and the three houses built on it all belong to the same person, but I don't know who it is."

Billy looked at the strange letters he was pointing

to in the ledger. "What do you mean you don't know? It's right there, isn't it?"

"I don't know their names, because they're written in Chinese."

Billy slumped in his seat. *Damn.*

That would make sense. The dead women in the house were Chinese. Whoever owned the lots and the houses that were built on them were probably Chinese, too. Maybe even one of the dead women themselves had come to Dover Station, bought the land, and built the homes. Three whorehouses on the edge of town. A small empire, no different than the one built by Mr. Rice and Mr. Van Dorn, except a lot more honest about what it was.

Just like Mr. Rice and Mr. Van Dorn, Billy thought. The idea stuck with him for some reason. Their names turning over in his mind. The women were building an empire just like Mr. Rice and Mr. Van Dorn.

He spoke without realizing it. "The lots."

Underhill snapped out whatever fog he had been lost in. "What?"

"The lots," Billy repeated. "Tell me who owns the other lots around the ones the Chinese lady owns."

"We don't know if it's a lady, Billy. The writing's in Chinese."

Billy practically threw the ledger at him. "I don't care if it's written in nonsense. I want you to look in that book and tell me who owns the rest of the lots in that area. I saw them staked out when I was out back this morning."

Underhill set the ledger aside without opening it. "I don't need to look it up. I already know who owns it. The Dover Station Company does. They're looking to put a mill across the road on those lots. Construction's set to begin next week. The houses for the workers are already done."

Billy felt things were coming together, but he was too close to it to see it fully, just like the old jailhouse was too close to the Municipal Building to realize how big it really was. A man needed distance for that, and he was too close to this. "Who the hell would build a sawmill by a dry riverbed?"

"It's not going to be dry for long," Underhill told him. "Not when they divert two streams into it. The engineers are starting work on it today. The water's just flowing into nowhere now. They're changing the course of two streams just enough to make it run by the new sawmill they're building. It won't be a mighty river or anything, but it'll give them enough water to generate the steam to run the mill. And it'll come out in the same place where the two streams come out now anyway. No one gets hurt."

Billy looked at him. "People have already gotten hurt, damn it. Three women dead and I've got a feeling I know why, too."

"I'm glad to hear you say that." Underhill got up and took his hat from the peg on the wall. "So will Mr. Grant, too. I think we should get over to see him and tell him about this right away."

Billy wasn't so quick to get up. And it wasn't on account of being tired, either. He had already recovered from that. This was about something else. "We're not going to see Grant just yet, Walter. I want you to lay eyes on the man who attacked me." Billy slowly rose from his chair. "And I want to see the look on your face when you see him."

He picked up the glass of whiskey and held it out to Underhill. "You take it. Think you're going to need it."

Chapter 10

Mackey was glad to be so close to home before dark.

Although he had only been gone a few days, he was eager to get home to Katherine and to see Billy again. Norman's coffee was good, but it didn't compare to the fine brew Billy made on the jailhouse stove. And the hay of Arthur's stall was a poor substitute for Katherine's bed. Or Katherine herself.

He had Adair pick up her pace a bit as he rode along the main road to town, past the old JT Ranch that sprawled to his left and his right. It had been a thriving ranch when John Tyler had owned the place, but had doubled in size since it had been purchased by the Dover Station Company following the Darabont raid. Now the ranch had more cattle, horses, and men than ever before and, if the articles in the *Record* could be believed, they looked to grow even bigger in the years ahead.

Mackey was one of the few original residents of the town that did not mind the Dover Station Company's success. He supported anything that benefited the only place he could truly call home.

But he despised James Grant's desire to use the town's ambition to mask his own crimes. He should have resented Silas Van Dorn for allowing it to happen but didn't. Van Dorn was a New Yorker, a Manhattanite worst of all. He was accustomed to the pleasant comforts of Washington Square, not the harsh realities of Montana living. He barely left his home, preferring to allow James Grant to run his affairs for him. Grant had abused the privilege, but Van Dorn did not seem to notice or mind if he did.

Mr. Rice wanted them both replaced, but it was difficult to find qualified men who wanted the position. Grant and Van Dorn were a profitable pair, and Mr. Rice's shareholders were reluctant to change simply because Rice didn't like them. The notion that Grant had been behind several deaths in the territory meant little to them.

Mackey had spent enough time back east to know how they thought. Montana was still just a territory and such lawlessness was to be expected, even encouraged, in such a place. If a few people died in the process, so be it. Better it happen now than when they became a state and the laws actually meant something. Even then, they'd probably shrug at Grant's deeds as long as the balance sheet was healthy. Mackey doubted even news of Grant's alliance with the Hancock family would make much of a difference in their opinion of Grant.

Mackey didn't resent the shareholders, either. They had a duty to make the company as wealthy as possible. He just wished they had more of a conscience while doing it.

Mackey rounded the main road into town that

would ultimately become Front Street. The red brick of the Municipal Building dominated the left side of the approach to town while the simplicity of Cemetery Hill stood on the right.

He saw the outlines of the crooked tombstones that poked out from the ground like rotting tree stumps and the budding shrubs that lined the perimeter of the place.

He also saw a solitary man standing at one of the graves. That was odd, because no one ever went to the cemetery so late in the day. People preferred to visit their dead early in the morning or in the afternoon, not as night was about to fall. Mackey wondered what the man was doing up there. He wondered if he might be one of the Hancock men looking to take a shot at him as he rode into town.

But the closer he looked at the man, the more he realized there was something familiar about him. His face was in shadow, but his height and the way he carried himself reminded Mackey of someone he couldn't place.

As he rode closer to the cemetery, he saw a dappled gray and a packhorse hitched to a tree stump at the side of the road. Both animals looked trail worn and in need of a week's worth of care at the livery. The rifle boot on the saddle was empty.

Mackey hitched Adair to the rail at the base of the hill, away from the other animals. She was tired after the ride and today's run-in with the Hancock family. It was best to keep her away from other animals.

He slowly walked up the hill to the cemetery. He chose to leave his Winchester behind. If the man was a simple mourner, he didn't want to disturb his time with his loved one.

If he was more than that, Mackey figured the Peacemaker would be enough to handle the problem.

He stopped when he crested the hill and got a good look at the man standing beside a grave. It was Sim Halstead's grave and, for a moment, Mackey wondered if the man might be Sim's ghost.

He was the exact same size and shape as Mackey's departed scout and friend. He was tall and thin, his head bowed in prayer, his long hands clasped atop the barrel of his rifle.

Then Mackey began to notice the differences. The tan skin and the wavy black hair. The cheekbones weren't quite right, and the angle of the nose was not quite as sharp as Sim's had been.

The mourner looked over at Mackey and appeared to recognize him, too.

"What's the matter, Uncle Aaron? Don't you recognize your own godson?"

Mackey knew that face or at least another version of it. It was not a ghost but flesh and blood. It was not Sim Halstead but his oldest son. "Jeremiah?"

Sim Halstead's oldest boy smiled at his uncle. "Glad you remembered before you shot me."

Mackey saw that the boy was as tall as him and maybe a good inch taller. He got his height from Sim and his bronze skin from the Mexican woman who had been Sim's first wife.

He shook hands with the young man and found a firm grip. He hadn't seen Jeremiah since his mother had died and his father had sent him to a missionary school. It was a better life for him than dragging him around from one fort to another in the Southwest.

"We tried to find you," Mackey said, "but no one knew where you were. We sent letters to different places, but we never knew if they found you."

"They found me." He watched the young man's eyes well up. "Found me at a good time, too. Found me at a time when I needed a home and figured I might have one here with you and Uncle Billy." He looked down at the grave. "And my father."

Tears streaked down Jeremiah's cheeks, and Mackey quickly embraced him. His good friend's oldest boy. His godson.

Jeremiah quickly grew embarrassed by his emotions and slowly pulled away. "Knowing he's gone and actually seeing it are two different things."

"I know." Mackey decided to change the subject and take some of the sting out of the moment. "Couldn't help but see your mounts are worn out. Where'd you ride in from?"

"Does it matter?" Jeremiah asked. "I'm here now, and that's the point."

Mackey decided it didn't matter. Not here at his father's graveside. And not yet, either. But he'd find out the truth in time and, when he did, he would probably be disappointed. The effects of a man's deeds tended to hang on him long after he'd done them, and Jeremiah Halstead was no different. Mackey sensed he had seen some trouble in the years since he'd left missionary school, but now was not the time to ask him.

Jeremiah crossed himself after finishing a silent

prayer and looked around. "Is Mackey's Garden around here? Father told me a lot about it in his letters."

Mackey smiled. "It's just a section of the cemetery where the town buried paupers. Since most of the people who broke the law were drifters, that's where they got planted. The town undertaker began planting the people I shot in one section on their own and took to calling it Mackey's Garden because of all the plantings that took place."

"Funny how a man can get a reputation just for doing his job."

Mackey decided to change the subject. "Sounds like you know something about that."

"I knocked around here and there after I got out of school. Didn't my father tell you?"

Mackey realized Jeremiah had not seen Sim since Sim had been discharged from the army and came to Dover Station. A lot had happened since then. "Your father stopped talking after your stepmother and brother were killed."

"He did? He never mentioned it in his letters."

"Guess his silence was his way of mourning their loss," Mackey said. "He never offered an explanation, and we never asked for one. We just accepted it for what it was, and that was it."

Mackey remembered Sim's last words, but as they were about his second family and not Jeremiah, he saw no reason to tell the young man that part. "We mostly communicated by him writing things down in a notebook he carried with him. Turned out not to be a problem. And your father always had an elegant hand."

"I enjoyed his letters," Jeremiah said as they walked

around the graveyard. "He told me all about you and Dover Station and the home he had made here. He told me Billy was well. I've missed him, too. I've missed all of you from the fort, even though I was sent away when I was ten."

"You weren't sent away," Mackey said. "Sim didn't have any way of taking care of you, and dragging you around from one hellhole to another wouldn't have been fair to you. Fort Concho? Adobe Flats? Fort Martin? I don't know how I survived those places, and I was an officer."

"The best one my dad ever served with," Jeremiah told him. "Said he liked you because he caught you when you were green and he could rid you of all those damned fool notions about soldiering they put in your head at West Point." Young Halstead held up his hands. "My father's words, not mine."

Mackey laughed. "Your daddy got his bad habits from my father when they served together in the war. But he taught me a lot and saved my life more times than I can count."

"He knew you were grateful." Jeremiah stopped talking, and an uneasy silence settled over them. "I've heard a lot of rumors about how my father died, Uncle Aaron, but I'd like to hear it from you since you were there."

"I wasn't there," Mackey admitted. "That's the problem." He didn't want to relive the Darabont matter, and he didn't think Jeremiah needed to hear it. He painted the picture in the broadest strokes possible.

"Your daddy helped us defend the town from a group of men who attacked it. He helped us track down some hostages and lost his life in the process.

But he killed the man who killed him, which was exactly the kind of end Sim would've wanted."

Jeremiah seemed to accept it. "Sounds like he died the best way he could."

Mackey tried to keep his throat from tightening. "That's about the best anyone could hope for."

They continued to walk among the crooked tombstones of the cemetery, passing through the area they called Mackey's Garden without the marshal calling attention to it. He had never liked the name and did not encourage its usage. Or the reputation that came with it.

The wind on Cemetery Hill had grown still, and the echoes of hammering and sawing and shouting from the construction crews building the town's future filtered up their way.

Mackey figured now would be as good a time as any to confirm a suspicion that had been growing since the first moment he saw Jeremiah. "When did you get out?"

"About a month ago." Young Halstead frowned. "What gave it away?"

"You avoiding the question every time I asked it." Mackey shrugged and toed the ground along the path. "Other things, I guess. Do this kind of work long enough, you tend to pick up on what people say and what they don't say."

"I suppose so." Jeremiah looked at him. "Want to know what I was in for?"

"Only if you want to tell me."

Jeremiah looked back at his father's grave. "Maybe someday I will."

Mackey hated to ask the next question, but had to ask it. "You do your full stint? I'm only asking because I'm a federal now and if you escaped, there'll be paper on you."

"I'm free and clear," Jeremiah told him. "No need to worry about anyone coming after me, either. I had nowhere else to go when I got out, so I figured I might as well come here. Don't know how long I'll stay. But given how you know about me now, I'll move on in the morning if you want."

"Haven't seen your name on any wanted posters, Jeremiah. And I don't have any warrants with your name on them, either. You're welcome to stay here for as long as you want as far as I'm concerned. Anyone who knew your father will feel the same way."

Jeremiah kicked at some weeds that had taken root along the pathway. "I appreciate that, Uncle Aaron. I really do."

"And I'd appreciate it if you'd quit calling me Uncle Aaron. Makes me feel like I ought to be in a rocking chair with a long beard pulling on a pipe. Just plain Aaron is fine with me."

"Me, too." Jeremiah grinned. "Makes me feel less like a kid. And as long as we're settling names, I go by Jerry most of the time these days."

"Jerry it is, then." Mackey couldn't understand why someone with a perfectly solid name like Jeremiah would want to be called Jerry, but it wasn't his name, and it wasn't his choice. "If I slip, you'll remind me."

"You've known me long enough to call me anything you'd like. Aaron." It sounded like he had tacked on the name at the end as if he was trying it on for size.

"You picked a good time to come here." Mackey looked around at the town he had left only a few days before. He tried to avoid looking at the gaudy behemoth that was the Municipal Building, but it was impossible to do so from this angle. It was also impossible to ignore that Dover Station was no longer the sleepy Montana town he had grown up in. Everywhere he looked, a new building was either going up or had just been completed. Iron buildings, too, not the cheap wooden structures that had dotted the town of his youth. Mr. Rice and his Dover Station Company had promised to make a permanent investment in the town, and Mackey was glad to see them making good on that promise. "The place has changed a lot, even since your old man was alive. Plenty of work to be had if you want it. Buildings going up all over the place, businesses going in them before the paint's even dry. Guess you could say we're a boomtown with no signs of slowing down."

"I was kind of hoping you'd be able to take me on as a deputy, Aaron."

Mackey stopped to look at the man. "You sure? With your background?"

"I was a lawman myself when I went to jail," Jerry told him. "Got arrested for doing the wrong thing for the right reasons. Kind of like a young captain I heard of who got drummed out of the army for keeping an Apache prisoner from getting beaten to death."

Mackey didn't know Sim had told him about that. "Your daddy wrote a lot in those letters."

"I was too young to read them at the time, but I

went through them when I got older. He lived quite a life. So have you and Billy."

"It hasn't been boring," Mackey admitted. "Especially lately. But I don't know about if I can take you on as a deputy. I'm not the law here in town anymore. A guy named Walter Underhill is the police chief now."

"Police chief? Here?" Jerry looked around at the townscape. "Guess the place will grow into needing a real police force soon."

Mackey nodded to the south, behind the Municipal Building, to where James Grant sought to expand the town even further. He had mapped out parcels along the newly named River Street, despite the fact that the river was little more than a creek at best and only during heavy rains.

"That redbrick building is the Municipal Building where the police and the mayor have their offices. Behind that is where they're going to be building a sawmill to help the town's logging trade. It'll increase the town's size by a good bit. Plenty of workers and people who feed off them, too. Should—"

Mackey stopped talking when he spotted Billy Sunday and Walter Underhill walking down River Street toward three new houses that had been built there in the past month or so.

And, judging from how Billy was walking, he was hurting.

And he had his hand near the Colt on his hip.

Mackey asked Jeremiah, "You mind if I tend to some business for a while?"

"Sure. Anything wrong? I can help."

"I'll be fine." Mackey began walking down the hill toward his horse. "Why don't you head over to a place called The Campbell Arms at the end of Front Street. Tell them who you are when you get there. I'll meet you there when I can."

"Miss Katherine Campbell," Jerry called after him. "Dad told me about her."

Mackey unhitched Adair. For a man who had not spoken for a decade, Sim was mighty chatty with a pen.

Chapter 11

Mackey climbed off Adair when he heard Billy shouting from one of the new houses on River Street. He couldn't hear what his deputy was saying, but since Billy rarely raised his voice, something must be wrong.

He drew his Peacemaker as he ran into the house with the open door. He caught the unmistakable stench of death coming from the house but went in anyway.

He found Billy aiming his Colt at Walter Underhill, screaming, "You recognized him, didn't you? Who is he?"

Mackey aimed his pistol at Underhill as well. "What the hell is going on here, Billy?"

His deputy turned as if shaken from a dream. "When did you get back?"

"A few minutes ago." He nodded toward his deputy's gun. "I've got him covered, so why don't you put that away while you tell me what's going on?"

Underhill fumed at Mackey while Billy holstered his pistol. "You mean you're pointing a gun at me without even knowing why?"

"Billy was pointing at you," Mackey told him. "That's reason enough for me. We'll work the rest out when one of you tells me what the hell is going on around here."

Billy laid out all that had happened as plainly as he could. The three dead whores upstairs. The mutilations. Grant's involvement. The dead man on the floor being the same man who had attacked him less than an hour ago.

Mackey had slowly lowered his weapon as Billy told his story, but his deputy hadn't noticed.

Billy concluded by saying, "I brought Underhill over here to take a look at the bastard who tried to kill me. I can tell he recognized him but won't admit it."

Underhill argued, "I never said I didn't know him, damn it. I just was surprised he was the one you'd killed is all. Then you pulled that hog leg and started screaming at me before I could say anything."

Mackey quietly tucked his pistol back in the holster. "Well, now's your chance, Walt. Might as well tell us who it is."

"His name is Dana King," Underhill told him. "He's an old buffalo hunter who works for Mr. Grant in this part of town."

"Imagine that," Billy sneered.

Mackey ignored him. "What kind of work did he do for the mayor?"

"Nothing for him as mayor," Underhill said. "He worked for the company. Did a little bit of everything, really. Foreman, clerk, watched the place at night sometimes when we were short a guard to make sure tools didn't get stolen by the rabble over in Tent City.

Signed for deliveries of materials when the teamsters brought them in."

"And you didn't know who I was talking about when I described him?" Billy pointed down at the corpse. "How many bald, one-eyed buffalo skinners does he have on the payroll that look like that?"

"Not too many," Underhill admitted, "but you can't blame me for wanting to be sure. You want me to think of you every time someone reports a crime that a Negro committed in town?"

Mackey was not buying it. "That's pretty thin, Walter."

"The hell it is," Underhill argued. "Sure, Dana's a rough customer, but I never thought of him as the killing kind. Scared people just by the way he looked more than anything else. Always did whatever Grant said needed doing and never raised a complaint as far as I know. Never had a problem with any of the workers. Ran a good crew. Men seemed to like him. Never had a complaint about him, either."

"Well I'd sure as hell like to make a complaint," Billy said, "because the son of a bitch tried to gut me just before I walked into your office today."

Mackey moved between his deputy and Underhill. Now that some of the steam had blown off, he figured they were past the point of gun pointing. "You got any reason to think he might've been the one who killed the women Billy says are upstairs?"

"No," Underhill said, "and I really need to get outside before I get sick. I can't take the stink of this place." He pointed at Billy as he left the house. "And if that crazy son of a bitch points his gun my way again, it'll be a whole different discussion."

Billy went to follow Underhill outside, but Mackey

grabbed his arm. "Steady. Getting into a fight with Underhill is only going to make things worse."

"Then let's go upstairs so you can see why I'm so damned prickly about it," Billy said.

Mackey followed his deputy upstairs and saw the mutilated corpses for himself. It was just as Billy had described earlier. Killings made to look worse than they already were.

"I can see why Underhill wanted one of us to look at this before anyone else," Mackey admitted. "It took a special type to do this kind of work. The kind of work a man like Dana King is used to. You said Underhill went against Grant's wishes to tell you?"

Billy looked away. "Yeah, he did."

"Then it sounds like he might be on our side in all of this, doesn't it?"

"He might be," Billy allowed, "but he's still Grant's man."

"Maybe he's changing his mind on that score," Mackey said.

"There's something else," Billy told him. "I didn't want to mention it in front of Underhill, but since you weren't around, I brought in that Pinkerton boy Lagrange to look at this. He thinks this is a setup, too, plain and simple."

Mackey knew Lagrange's involvement meant Mr. Rice was going to hear about it back in New York. That might not be a bad thing, considering Grant's involvement in all of this, but Mackey still wanted to know more before the millionaire got involved. "And this dead man downstairs came at you with a knife after Lagrange left."

"Came up from behind me as I was crossing the street. Strong bastard. Almost beat me."

Now Mackey knew what was bothering his deputy. This was less about Underhill and more about the notion that he had almost lost his life. That clarified things. "Almost doesn't count in our line of work. Either you do it or you don't. And you shot that man full of holes before he had a chance to carve some into you. I'd say that's a good day."

Billy ran a hand over his face and agreed.

"We're going to go back down there and talk to Underhill," Mackey said, "and I do mean talk. I don't want you two mixing it up again. He's got a direct line to Grant, and we don't want him starting to look at him as an ally in this."

"So you agree he's got the blood of these girls on his hands?" Billy asked. "Grant, I mean."

"Grant's got blood on his hands already. What's three more lives to him?" He beckoned his deputy to follow him downstairs. "Let's go talk to Underhill. And keep it civil."

Underhill was down the boardwalk a piece in front of the third house. Mackey could still smell the fresh-cut lumber and paint mixed in with death. The wood smelled a bit too young and probably should've been allowed to cure a bit longer before being used for housing. All three buildings would probably begin to sag in a year or two. But Dover Station was a boomtown, and safety came second to necessity.

"How are you feeling?" Mackey asked the bigger man.

"A lot better now that I'm out of there." Underhill pointed at Billy. "Even better now that he's not pointing a gun at my head. You'd better keep an eye on him, Mackey. I know he never liked me much, but he's starting to fray."

"And you ought to consider yourself lucky," Mackey said. "First time I ever saw him pull without shooting someone." But he wouldn't gain anything by making the chief feel more embarrassed than he already was. "Besides, we all know who the true enemy is here, and it's none of us."

Underhill looked at him. "You think Grant's behind all of this, don't you?"

"Looks like King did the killing, but him working for Grant makes Grant part of this whether you like it or not."

Underhill sat on the boardwalk, making the whole structure shake. "Maybe. Hell, I don't know. I think one of those Chinese ladies upstairs owned the house and these lots they're built on."

Mackey looked around at the stakes around the site. "Given that the company owns the rest of these parcels, seems like he might've wanted them out of the way. Maybe he sent King here to talk them into selling. Maybe things got out of hand and King went too far. Could explain why Grant was in a hurry to make this public, because it would give him the chance to come up with a story before one of us found out the truth?"

"That's a lot of maybes," Underhill said, "and you don't pull down a man like Grant with maybes. I know he's done a lot of wrong, Aaron, but this?" The chief shook his head. "I don't know. Grant's the type who'd buy out the whores or throw in with them. This close to the new mill, they could've been good earners for him. He's got a piece of every other house in town. Didn't see him kill anyone to get it. What makes this one so different?" Underhill shook his head. "Maybe Grant sent King here, but the killings seem more like King's doing alone."

Mackey asked Billy, "Sound reasonable to you?"

Billy shrugged. "It's never that simple where Grant's involved."

An idea sparked in Mackey's mind. He grabbed onto it quick before it disappeared altogether. "Anyone check what's in these other two houses?"

Billy and Underhill looked at each other, then shook their heads.

"I checked the records," Underhill said. "Same person owns them all. Chinese name and a Chinese signature. Could be a man or woman. You know how tough it is to tell the difference with Celestial names."

But Mackey didn't care about that. He cared about the houses.

He walked to the second house and tried the front door. It was locked. He put a shoulder into it, but it didn't budge. He took a step back and tried to kick it in. It didn't give at all.

"Something's behind it," Billy said. "That lock's not that strong. Want me to shoot it?"

"Wait." Mackey stepped off the boardwalk and looked underneath it. The death house didn't have a basement. He could look straight underneath it and see the stakes in the ground behind it.

But the two houses attached to it both had basements.

He got to his feet and tried the front door of the

third house with the same result. "Let's go around the back."

Billy and Underhill followed him around to the back of the house. He tried looking in through the windows, but they had all been painted over with black paint.

He went around the back of the third house to try the doors there, but they, too, were sealed shut and the windows were also painted over.

"This doesn't make sense," Underhill said. "Why build houses with no way into them?"

"There's a way," Billy said. "We just weren't looking for it because we were too caught up in those dead women."

The three lawmen went through the back door of the murder house and began to examine the south wall connected to the two houses next door. Underhill gagged as he joined Mackey and Billy as they knocked on the walls, hoping to find some entry behind the walls.

Underhill called to them from the front parlor. Mackey and Billy rushed in to find him next to shelves that had been built into the wall.

"Look at this," he said. "I noticed it was built deep into the wall, so I pushed on it."

He pushed on the shelves and they swung into the house next door. Whatever laid before them was pitch black.

All three men drew their pistols at the same time.

Billy struck a match off the wall and walked in first. Mackey and Underhill followed.

Billy held the match in front of him and found an

oil lamp hanging from a nail on the wall. He lit it and waved the match dead just as the lamp bathed the space in amber light.

It didn't take long for the men to realize what they were looking at.

Mackey took the lamp off the wall and held it before him as he walked into the open space, careful to avoid stepping on any of the beds and pillows that were scattered around the house.

He looked to where the front door and windows should be, but they had been walled over. That was why the door didn't budge when Mackey tried to kick it in.

Underhill said what the rest of them were thinking. "Looks like an opium den."

Billy toed a brass pipe next to one of the beds. "No doubt about it."

Mackey saw the wall between these two houses had never been built. It was a straight line of beds and pipes that spanned both buildings.

"More beds," Mackey said. "Probably where they keep the opium, too, if they have any. Doesn't look like the place has been used, yet."

"How do you know?" Underhill asked.

Billy laughed. "You think the stench next door turned your stomach? An opium den smells just as bad. Had one near Concho that smelled something awful. It's not the opium so much as how men lose control of themselves when they're smoking the stuff."

Underhill held his nose, even though all they could smell was cut wood and paint in the houses. "What do we do next?"

Mackey had already thought about that. "Nothing."

Billy looked like he wanted to say something, but held his tongue.

Underhill said it for him. "What do you mean nothing? We can't just forget about this, Aaron."

"Just for now," Mackey said. He could tell Underhill hadn't known about this, because he obviously wasn't that good at masking his feelings. And he wasn't sure Grant knew about it, but imagined he probably did.

Mackey intended on asking him, but only when the time was right. Now wasn't it.

"We're going to blow out this lamp, shut that door, and act like it never happened," Mackey told them. "Walt, when Grant talks to you about this, you tell him Billy's been stingy with the facts and has been nasty to you since he looked the place over."

"That won't be much of a stretch," Underhill said.

Mackey let the comment go. "Suggest he invite Billy up for a talk. I'll go with him and confront Grant with this personally. See what he says."

Underhill seemed to get the point. "He'll think it'll be two against one, but it'll actually be the three of us putting the question to him. As lawmen."

"That's right," Mackey said as he hung the lamp back on the nail. "As lawmen."

He blew out the lamp, and the three men stepped back into the death house, shutting the fake door behind them.

CHAPTER 12

As Underhill walked back to the Municipal Building, Mackey gathered up Adair's reins. She hadn't wandered far since he had jumped out of the saddle and rushed into the death house. The smell of blood hadn't bothered her for years.

He asked Billy, "How about you help me livery Adair before we head over to see Katie for some dinner?"

Billy fell in beside him as Mackey walked his horse to the livery where he kept Adair.

His deputy said, "Mind if I ask you a question?"

"Never have before."

"Why don't we go public with this now? Go to the *Record* and bring Doc Ridley into this like Grant wanted to, but do it our way? With the truth this time."

"Because we don't know the truth," Mackey told him. "Besides, he controls the *Record,* and there's no guarantee that Harrington would print it anyway. And if he did, they'd focus on the gore, not the cause. Sure, Doc Ridley would run his mouth, but this has moved way past rumors."

"You mean on account of the opium den."

"I mean on account of us not knowing much more now than you did this morning. All we've got is three dead Celestial whores and an opium den that hasn't been used yet. There's also his alliance with the Hancock clan. If we start telling people about this now, we might have only half the story and lose any advantage we have over Grant. I don't want to give that snake a chance to slither out of this one."

Mackey knew how Billy thought, so he added, "And if we barge into his office right now, he'll know something's wrong. He doesn't know about King being dead, and he doesn't know we've got this figured out. Let him invite us in, lower his guard, and then we hit him with it. See what happens. I'd rather corner him, then scare him out into the open."

"Guess you're usually right about things like this."

"Hell, Billy, we've never gone up against anything like this. I'm as new at this kind of thing as you are. Opium's not really a crime, though people take a dim view of it. If we can tie Grant to it and the plot to kill three prostitutes, we might have enough to bring him down once and for all."

"Don't see how anything we've found out so far can do that," Billy admitted. "We've got nothing to prove he knew about any of this. Just a lot of guessing."

Billy wasn't telling Mackey anything he didn't already know. "That's why we're heading over to the livery."

Billy looked over at the marshal. "Now you've completely lost me."

He clapped his old friend on the back. "James Grant keeps his horse in the same livery as I do. Bet he was riding when he found those women. Maybe after, too."

Billy stopped walking. "Underhill said they walked over to the house from the Municipal Building."

"And if we find something on his saddle that tells us different, then we've caught him in a lie, haven't we?"

Billy caught up with Mackey again. "I hope Lagrange has plenty of paper. Looks like we've got a lot to add to that report he's going to send to Mr. Rice."

"We'll see."

Billy said, "You think pretty good sometimes."

Adair snorted as she smelled the livery nearby. Mackey patted her neck. "Sometimes."

Ed Horan, the new owner of the Dover Station Livery and Stable, was in a flutter. "Now, you know how much esteem I hold for you, Sheriff, but answering questions about the comings and goings of my customers would just be a gross violation of confidence."

Mackey let the horseman gas on while Billy was somewhere in the livery looking for James Grant's horse and rig.

"You're not a priest or a doctor," Mackey told him. "You shovel feed into one end of a horse and muck out the stalls when it comes out the other. You tend animals, not souls, so quit acting like you're doing the Lord's work and answer my question."

Hearing the tone of Mackey's voice made Adair knock against the sides of her stall.

Horan looked nervously in that direction. "I'd appreciate it if we could keep a civil tone, Sheriff. Your mare is a handful on a good day. Your agitation only serves to darken her mood."

Mackey took a step toward the livery owner. "Then quit agitating me and answer the question. I won't ask again."

Horan backed up as far as he could until he banged into the back wall of the livery. "Mr. Grant had his horse out all day yesterday. Brought it back here this morning just after dawn."

Mackey knew getting information out of him wasn't going to be easy. The stables were brand new. The operation had been built and run by the Dover Station Company, so Horan worked for Grant. But self-preservation had a way of overcoming professional loyalties, so Mackey kept crowding the shorter man. "How did he look?"

"It was morning," Horan shrugged, "so the light wasn't very good, but I could tell he looked tired. Not just tired, but taxed in a way. I don't know if that makes any sense."

It did. It sounded like Horan was trying to put too fine a point on it. "What did you do before you were working in a livery, Horan?"

"I was an English teacher, sir." His back straightened a bit. "A rather good one, but, alas, I allowed drink to get the better of me, and here I am."

"That explains why you keep trying to put a shine on what you're telling me. Keep it plain. Did he look any different than normal? Act different?"

Horan sagged again. "No, sir. He walked the horse in and kept his distance, not that he's ever been warm to me. I was still half asleep and hadn't had my first cup of coffee yet. Come to think of it, he looked more drawn than he normally does. I didn't see if he was injured. I don't think he was limping or holding his arm or anything like that. But I do remember him making an odd request."

Finally. "Go on."

"He told me to give the horse a good bath. The bridle and the saddle, too. Said the whole rig needed a good cleaning and oiling. I didn't think much of it at the time. We haven't been here long, so I haven't had many requests to wash down horses or repair tack, but I did find it a bit odd."

"Aaron," Billy called out to him from inside the livery. "Take a look at this."

Mackey went inside the stables and heard Horan trudging close behind. "I see what you two were doing here, Sheriff. You kept me distracted while your man there went through my place of business with impunity. Very underhanded, sir. Very underhanded indeed, Sheriff."

Mackey snatched the liveryman by the collar. "I haven't been the sheriff in this town for six months. I'm the U.S. Marshal for this entire territory. I tell people what to do and they do it or face the consequences. And if you breathe one word about what we're doing here to anyone, including Grant, a hangover will be the least of your problems. Understand?"

Horan nodded quickly, and Mackey let him go with a shove. The man stood in the middle of the livery while Mackey joined Billy at a stall where a dappled gray mare was kept. "This Grant's horse?"

"The one he calls Philly," Billy told him as he stroked the nervous horse's neck. "I heard what Horan said about being told to give her a bath, but I don't think he has. Look at her mane. Right above where the saddle horn would be."

The horse's mane was a streaked blend of black and gray. But something brown had caked at the edge of the mane, close to where the reins might sit when Philly was being ridden.

Mackey gently moved the hairs away to get a better look. "Looks like dried blood to me."

"Can't imagine anything else that would cake up like that." Billy beckoned him to follow him to the vacant stall next to where Philly was kept. "She was awful fretful when I started looking her over. Shying away to as far back in the stall as she could. I know horses, so it couldn't possibly be me. But then I saw her saddle and bridle were hanging right next to her. When I moved them away from her, she calmed right down. Still shy, but not as bad as she had been. If you take a look at the rig, you'll see why."

Mackey walked over and took a look at the items Billy had laid out for him. It was a dark leather saddle with a matching bridle. He looked back at Horan, who had been too petrified to move from where Mackey had left him. "This James Grant's rig?"

The hostler shut his eyes and nodded slowly.

He looked at the parts of the stirrups and the fender where Billy was pointing. "That look like smeared blood to you?"

It did. "Would've had a fair amount of it on his pants if he did. On the inside of his thighs, anyway."

Billy squatted and made like he was wiping his hands off on his pants. "A careful man might do it that way. Make it less obvious. Now, look at the bridle."

Mackey examined them and found the same dried dark spots there, too, right where Grant would hold them.

"Looks like he didn't get all the blood off his hands," Billy pointed out.

"No," Mackey said, "looks like he didn't."

Mackey had seen enough and went back to Horan, who closed his eyes as the two lawmen approached. "As the federal marshal for the Montana Territory, I am ordering you to keep James Grant's horse and rig as is. You are not to touch them or clean them in any way. You are also not to let the horse leave the property. If you do, I'll arrest you. And if you defy me, remember there's no booze in prison, Horan."

Horan nodded quickly again. He looked to be on the verge of tears.

"And if someone comes to take the horse and gear from you," Billy added, "you're to come directly to the marshal's office and report it. Not the Municipal Building. The old jailhouse across the street from it. Understand?"

"You're putting me in a horrible position, gentlemen, between my job and the law."

Mackey pushed past him to bring Adair out of her stall. He hadn't taken the saddle off her yet, and he didn't want to keep her in the same place as James Grant's mare. Billy had the same idea as he took out the chestnut roan he'd never got around to naming and got her ready to ride.

Mackey swung up into the saddle. "Our job is the law, Horan. Don't make me prove it to you."

Chapter 13

They let their horses lope at their own pace on Front Street as they made their way up to Katie's hotel. Mackey was aching to see Katie, but he wanted to stop by and see his father first. Brendan "Pappy" Mackey rivaled Doc Ridley for being the biggest gossip in town. Every chatterbox in Dover Station made their way to the Dover Station General Store, where Pappy held court throughout the day.

"Hot damn, Aaron, we've got him," Billy said. "We've finally got that bastard Grant lined up and ready to take the fall. I knew Grant had a hand in killing those girls, and so did you."

Mackey could not recall a time when Billy had been so excited about anything. Not in all of the battles they had fought with the Apache, Comanche, and Lakota. Not against rustlers or gangs or brawlers, neither. Billy had always managed to keep an even keel to the point where Mackey wondered if his old friend was capable of feeling much of anything at all.

But the murder of the three whores had obviously sparked something in him that made it personal. He would make it a point to ask him about it when the time was right, but it was not right now. Billy was too worked up over it.

"Dried blood on a man's tack doesn't mean much. Could say he cut himself and wiped the blood on his pants. Could say he was hunting and laid the carcass across the saddle horn. Could say any number of things. There's no way we can prove he was in that house at the time the women were killed. Hell, he could say it came from when he found the front door open and went in to investigate."

"Damn it, Aaron. I've spent most of the day in that house. Look at how much blood I've got on me." He held up his hands and gestured to the rest of him. "Maybe some on the soles of my boots, but nothing anywhere else."

"I'm not defending him," Mackey said. "I'm just telling you what he's liable to say when we throw it in his face."

Billy looked like he had more to say, but again held his tongue. "Say, how'd you know where to find us anyhow?"

He decided Billy needed some good news and figured Jerry Halstead being in town would do the trick. "You'll likely find out when we get to Katie's place."

Billy looked over at his friend. "I've got enough mysteries in my life right now without you adding to them."

"Relax," Mackey grinned. "This is one mystery you're going to like."

They rode on in silence for a bit before Billy said, "With all of this other stuff going on, I forgot to ask you how it went up in Hancock."

"As expected," Mackey told him.

"See much action?"

"Enough to make the point. They'll come gunning for us at some point, but they're reckless and angry. We're not. Mad Nellie admitted she's working with Grant, though she wouldn't say how. I figure we'll find that out in the coming days."

"Seen a lot of Hancock men in town over the past week or so," Billy said, "more than when you left. How many they got up there, anyway?"

"Not as many as they had before I came to town." He steered Adair over to the right side of Front Street. "Let's see Pappy. I want to talk to him first before heading up to Katie."

Even from half a street away, they could see Pappy in front of his store, regaling a small cluster of men and women with some tall tale that held them enthralled.

Pappy had spotted his son and Billy as they approached his store and quickly dismissed the busybodies who had been crowded around him. Pappy came to the edge of the boardwalk to greet his son.

"As I live and breathe," he said with his gentle Longford brogue, "it's my son come back from dispensing justice. Did you get the bastard?"

"You must be starting to dodder, old man. You never used to ask stupid questions."

Pappy laughed. His father could never have been described as a tall man, but what he lacked in height he made up for in size. His broad shoulders, strong back, and thick forearms were more worthy of a blacksmith than the shopkeeper he was. He was going on sixty, but still often did the work of three men half his age. His hair and beard had long turned steel gray, making his stern countenance appear even more so, though his eyes belied a vibrant spirit and a wicked tongue.

Billy asked, "What's new on the grapevine, Pappy?"

"Most of the talk is about the work that'll be starting on the new sawmill at the end of River Street next week. The promise of jobs for the newcomers and services to be provided by us shopkeepers has done wonders to bolster our already high spirits."

Billy nudged his roan forward. "Any gossip on your new boss?"

Pappy's face soured. "The Dover Station Company may have bought out my business at well above a fair price and pay me to run it, but that's a far way from that lizard being my boss."

Mackey ignored the bluster. He had heard it every day since Mr. Rice had bought the store from Pappy to make sure only his products got sold and he had a sense of who was buying what merchandise. Mackey was no businessman, but he saw it as a smart move that hurt no one, least of all Pappy.

He bent low and spoke to his father. "He means it, Pappy. Anything about Grant at all?"

The old man gave it some thought. "Nothing new. Almost half of the people love him, almost half of the people hate him, but the majority really couldn't care less." He winked. "But I'd wager he'll remain on everyone's good side so long as jobs are plentiful and the drunks stay corralled in their saloons." He raised his finger to the sky as a new thought came to him. "Speaking of which, have you heard—"

Billy cleared his throat and said, "I'm kind of

hungry, Aaron. We ought to get to Katie's place for an early supper. Heard tonight's stew night."

Pappy opened his hand and flattened down his hair, though there wasn't a hair out of place. "You're right, Billy. Supposing I join you, too. God knows they don't need me here. Place practically runs itself these days."

But Mackey had heard too much to let it go. "Never knew you to be shy, Pappy. Finish what you were going to say."

The elder Mackey shook his head in disgust at himself. "Someday my big mouth will get me killed." Pappy relented. "Well, there's a drunk down at the Ruby who's been talking out of turn for the day or so about how he's here to kill you for killing his kin. He's been drunk for days, boy. He's probably passed out by now, suffering the worst hangover this side of hell."

"This one of the Hancock family?"

His father looked away. "One and the same."

Mackey had been afraid something like this might happen. He'd learned firsthand that the Hancocks weren't the inbred yokels most people thought them to be. They were a crafty bunch of criminals who came at a problem from several sides. Despite their awkward attack on him outside their town, they never just came in guns blazing. They checked a place out first, made sure they understood how it worked, put a plan together, and moved in.

They had done that with stagecoach lines they had hit, the banks they had robbed, and the cattle they had stolen. Now they were doing it here in Dover Station and using Henry Hancock's death as an excuse.

Mackey had enforced the warrant on him because he was one of the leaders of the family. He had more brains than the rest of his kin, and Mackey thought bringing him down would shut the family up.

Instead, he had given them a martyr to grieve in every saloon, general store, and kitchen in the territory. Before the month was out, Henry Hancock might even be a hero and Mackey the villain. That was why he had always discouraged names like Hero of Adobe Flats or Savior of Dover Station. Because he knew the difference between being a hero and a villain was only a matter of a few drinks at the wrong time.

Mackey looked back at Billy. "The Ruby is that new place that opened up on Lincoln last month?"

"Yeah," Billy told him, "but I'd let it go, Aaron. It's just saloon talk, nothing more."

"Good. Ought to be easy to put it down." He looked at his father. "I'm going to need you to stay close to the store tonight, Pappy. Might need you to put some of your old skills to work."

The old man's eyes brightened. "A little insurrection, is it?"

"Just stay close." Mackey didn't risk telling his father any more than that. He might be a gossip, but he was one of the only men in the world Mackey trusted with his life. And he might be doing just that before the night was over.

Mackey jigged Adair back toward the thoroughfare and toward the Ruby. "Come on, Billy. Let's introduce you to the Hancock clan."

Chapter 14

The Ruby was one of the newer saloons that had opened up in Dover Station in the past month or so. Most of them had good food and catered to a higher-end crowd Grant had hoped to attract to town. But Mackey knew that no matter how fancy Dover might get, there would always be room for a place like the Ruby.

The fancy carvings of Indians in headdress carved into the porch posts out front spoke of the owner's original intentions for the Ruby to be a respectable place. But bars, just like people, tended to find their own level, and the tonier crowd had never quite gravitated to the place as the owners had intended. So, when the owner ran out of money, he sold out to the first buyer and took the next train out of town to Helena.

Mackey couldn't decipher the song the drunks inside were singing as he swung down from Adair and handed the reins up to Billy. "I'll just be a minute."

But the deputy didn't take the reins. "There's no way I'm letting you walk in there alone."

"They're not throwing your name around in there,"

Mackey said. "They're throwing mine. That makes it personal, not federal business."

"Since when has that mattered to us?"

"Since we became federals." He smiled at his worried friend. "I won't be long. We'll be having that stew at Katie's place within the hour."

Billy reluctantly took Adair's reins.

Mackey pushed through the batwing doors and wasn't surprised to find one of Underhill's constables in the lookout chair. He sat high over the customers with a Winchester across his lap. He sat up a little straighter when he saw Mackey walk through the door, but otherwise didn't move. He simply nodded at the marshal, and Mackey nodded back. He had no idea whether or not the man should be on patrol. He didn't care, either. It was none of his business.

A trickle of murmurs slowly spread among the men at the gambling tables and those standing at the bar. It was a mixed crowd of cowboys and laborers from the Dover Station Company's buildings and even a few miners who must have come to town on their day off. A few painted doves flitted between the tables looking for potential customers.

They all came to a gradual stop and looked at the federal lawman dressed in black standing in the middle of the saloon.

"My name is Aaron Mackey." He made a point of looking at each face as he spoke. Some of them looked familiar, but most of them were part of the newer breed that had moved into town in the past year. "I've been told that someone in here has been threatening to kill me. Heard it was a member of the Hancock family." He held out his hands from his sides. "Well, here I am."

A glass shattered at the bar, and a large, broad man pushed his was forward and stood before Mackey. He had the same long face and dead eyes most of the Hancock men had.

This one looked like he might be in his twenties and any muscle on him had come from working a field. He wasn't a cowboy, and he wasn't wearing a gun, at least none that Mackey could see. The big man was obviously a farmer, not a cowpuncher. In Mackey's experience, the solitary labor of a farmer often meant they were less likely to just bluster and more likely to back up their threats when they felt driven to it.

Mackey subtly shifted his stance so his left foot pointed at the man. It was easier for him to draw and fire the Peacemaker holstered on his belly that way.

The man said, "My last name might be Brenner, but I'm a Hancock, by God and by blood." The big farmer may have been drunk earlier, but appeared to be sober now.

"You gunned down poor Hank like he was nothing more than a wild animal and we're not going to let you get away with it, you murdering bastard."

A few at the bar murmured their assent, but no one stepped forward to join him.

"I didn't murder anyone," Mackey told him. "A federal judge in Helena issued a warrant for his arrest for armed robbery, thievery, and murder. I went after him because a judge told me to, not because I wanted to or because his last name was Hancock. Everything I did was legal."

"What's legal ain't always right." Brenner pointed at the star on Mackey's lapel. "And that star don't make you God."

"But it makes me a lawman and a federal one at that. I had paper on Henry Hancock. Even announced myself and gave him and his bunch the chance to surrender. They fired at me instead. I gave him more of a choice than he gave me."

"You snuck up on him in the middle of the night and ambushed him while he was sleeping."

"Sleeping." Mackey grinned. "That's a good one. There were five of them and one of me. Henry was drunk, but awake and able to defend himself. So were the others. I gave him a choice."

Brenner's florid face grew redder. "And he's dead, and you're here."

Mackey felt something in the mood of the place change. "Looks like he chose wrong."

Mackey looked out over the crowd that was less anxious to meet his eye now that he'd had his say. "I'm not the sheriff of Dover Station anymore. I'm the United States Marshal for the Montana Territory. When I have paper on a man, it's my duty to bring him in. Straight up or over the saddle, makes no difference to me."

Brenner lowered his head and glowered at him. "Why do I think you prefer to bring 'em in dead?"

"My job is to bring them in, one way or the other. No matter what their last name is."

Brenner charged him like a bull and surprisingly fast for a man of his size.

But Mackey sidestepped the charge, tripping Brenner as he went past and giving him a good shoving in the bargain. His momentum sent him crashing through the empty tables and chairs behind him.

Mackey kicked away the debris and placed his boot on the back of Brenner's neck, pinning the big man to the barroom floor. The customers gasped when Mackey drew his Peacemaker and aimed it down at the prone man's head. The sound of the hammer being pulled back snapped through the saloon like a lightning strike.

Brenner quit squirming and went completely still.

Mackey said, "You're not in a position to do much talking now, are you?"

"No, sir," Brenner mumbled as clearly as he could with Mackey's weight pressing him on the floor.

"And seeing as how you just attacked me in a saloon full of witnesses, I'd be within my rights to arrest you. Maybe put you down like the mad-dog killer you say I am. I could do that, couldn't I, Brenner?"

"Don't," Brenner mumbled.

"Guess you're seeing things clearer from down there, aren't you, Brenner?"

Brenner nodded the best he could under Mackey's boot. "Yes, sir."

"If I let you up, I won't have any more trouble from you. Of any kind, right?"

Mackey turned when he heard the familiar hammer of Billy's Sharps rifle being pulled back. He saw his deputy aiming the rifle up at the constable in the lookout chair.

"You touch that rifle again," Billy said, "and I'll blow you right out of that seat."

The constable slowly lifted his hands. "I was just covering the marshal, damn it."

Mackey turned his attention back to Brenner under his boot. "That means no more running your mouth, no more threats, and no more accusations. I'm not even asking for an apology. I just want it over." He put enough pressure on the man's neck to make him cry out in pain. "Is it over?"

"Yeah," Brenner groaned. "But I don't speak for my family."

"Didn't expect you to." Mackey took his boot off Brenner's neck and stepped away as the big man rolled over onto his back.

He looked up at the barrel of Mackey's Peacemaker as the marshal rode the hammer down easy before holstering the weapon, then extended his hand down to Brenner. "Let me help you up."

Brenner took his hand and Mackey helped the big man to his feet.

But the marshal kept hold of his hand and squeezed. "This better be the end of it. Because the next time I put you on the floor, you won't be getting up."

He forced a smile for the benefit of the crowd and patted the big man on the back, sending him toward the bar.

Mackey glared up at the Underhill man in the lookout chair who had clasped his hands behind his neck, nowhere near the rifle on his lap.

Mackey backed up through the batwing doors while Billy covered him with the Sharps.

"Thanks," Mackey said as he took Adair's reins and swung up into the saddle.

Billy slipped his rifle into the scabbard on his saddle and climbed aboard his roan. "Figured you'd need me."

"Always have." Mackey climbed into the saddle and gave Adair a bit of a kick to move her quickly away from the Ruby. "Always will."

Chapter 15

Mackey noticed Billy draw up short when he saw Katherine on the porch of The Campbell Arms talking to Jerry Halstead.

Since they had been riding together for the better part of ten years, Mackey knew what his deputy was thinking before he said it. "What's Katherine doing talking to that breed? Where's Sandborne or Lagrange? One of them ought to be out here keeping an eye on things."

Mackey grabbed his deputy's arm before he jumped out of the saddle. "Easy, Billy. The boy's not a breed. I know him."

Billy looked at him. "How?"

"Same as you do. Look closer."

Billy slowly stepped down from the saddle and hitched his roan to the post as he walked up the stairs to the hotel's boardwalk.

Jerry Halstead turned when he saw Billy looking at him. He excused himself from his conversation with Katherine and stood to face Billy. "Guess you don't know me anymore, do you?"

Billy took a few steps toward him like a man in a trance. "I'm not sure."

"Sure you do. My father was white. My mother was Mexican. I grew up in Fort Concho with a young sergeant who made sure I could ride a horse before I could even walk. Taught me how to shoot straight even before I could spell my name."

Billy broke out of his trance and hugged the young man with more enthusiasm than Mackey had ever seen from him. The two had always been close when Jerry had been a boy. As an officer, Mackey had made sure that the duty roster always kept Sim or Billy at the post while little Jerry was around.

For Mackey, the only thing better than seeing Billy let down his guard for once was seeing the look on Katherine's face as she watched it happen.

Mrs. Katherine Campbell was tall for a woman, though not as tall as him and Billy. She was thin but strong, and her hair was light brown, which suited her fair complexion. A streak of gray had appeared in the middle of her hair, undoubtedly hastened by her experiences as a captive of Darabont. She had not made any effort to conceal the gray streak, and neither she nor Mackey ever mentioned it. If anything, he saw it as a badge of her courage during that horrible ordeal, an ordeal from which Mackey and the others had rescued her.

Katherine's high cheekbones and bright blue eyes gave her a strong, yet friendly, countenance. Peaceful, Mackey thought, though far from innocent. She came from a good Boston bloodline and could trace her heritage as far back as the *Mayflower*.

Their affair had begun in Boston, back when she had been the young wife of a much older major and Mackey was a lieutenant awaiting his promotion to captaincy. They only had the pleasure of one summer together before his reassignment to the Arizona Territory came through, but those few precious weeks had formed the foundation of a love that had lasted ever since.

It was that love that had brought her to Dover Station in an effort to rekindle their romance following the death of her husband. It was an unrequited romance, because Mackey was already married when she arrived unannounced. It was that love that haunted Mackey when Darabont had taken her, and he cursed himself for being too selfish to send her back to her family back east.

She was made for carriage rides around Boston Common and hosting parties in her family's town home on Beacon Hill. A refined woman like her had no business being in the harsh Montana wilderness, yet here she was, and he was the reason why. He had begged her to return to Boston after he had brought her back from Darabont and his men.

Yet, despite all she had endured, she refused to let him take away the life she had chosen for herself. Her life with Aaron Mackey.

She saw him looking at her, and her smile changed the way it always did when she looked at him. A softening to an expression they shared only with each other.

A smile that warmed him in a way nothing else ever had and served to drive all thoughts of dead Hancock men and a house full of dead whores from his mind.

"Evening, Marshal," Katherine said as Mackey climbed down from Adair.

He touched the brim of his hat before hitching Adair to the rail. "Evening, Mrs. Campbell." They were always more formal with each other in public, even among friends.

He clapped the young Halstead and Billy on the shoulders as he passed them on his way to the chair next to Katherine. "Today's what I'd call a happy day."

"The happiest I can remember in a long time." Katherine snuck a kiss on his cheek as he sat beside her. "I've missed you."

He was glad to hear it. "I've missed you, too, but it was only a couple of days."

"The fear made it feel longer than that this time." She grabbed his hand under the tablecloth and held it tightly. "Did you do what you had set out to do?"

When he had been sheriff of Dover Station, it was difficult for him to hide many aspects of his job from her. If he broke up a fight or killed a man, she always found out about it. But now that he was a federal lawman, his duties involved more than just Dover Station. He wanted to keep that part of his life from touching her own. "I served the warrant," was all he felt comfortable saying.

Katherine had learned that was all of the answer she was likely to get, so she accepted it. "You've already received two letters from Judge Forester in Helena this week. I opened them just as you asked me to, and they all say the same thing. That your place is in the capital, not here in Dover Station."

Normally, Billy would have handled the mail, but

since he couldn't read, Mackey had asked Katherine to take all posts and telegrams on his behalf. He told Billy everything after he had a chance to read it over.

But Mackey had been expecting Forester's annoyance. The old judge liked to think he ran the territory, not the governor. Forester didn't like to be reminded that he was a presidential appointee, too, one from the previous administration. He could be replaced with the stroke of the president's pen. So could Mackey. "My job is wherever the criminals are, and right now, most of the warrants he's issued are for people in this part of the territory. He just wants me to kiss his ring."

"He is a judge, Aaron. Don't make him order you to go to Helena. I know that would only make you angry."

Sometimes Mackey forgot how well she knew him. "I'll send him a telegram, telling him I'll make it out there as soon as I can." He looked out at the men and women walking along the boardwalks of Dover Station. "But for now, we've got troubles brewing right here in town."

Her smile faded, making Mackey all the sadder for letting that much slip. She didn't miss much. "You mean there's more trouble with James Grant, isn't there? Trouble from the Hancock family."

Mackey quickly kissed her hand before slipping it back under the table. "Sometimes, I wish you were dumb."

"No, you don't," she said, "and stop avoiding the question."

"I'm not avoiding it." He looked at Billy and Jeremiah as they sat on the hotel steps and caught up on all they had missed over the past decade or so. "I'd just like to quit talking about it for a while. Maybe focus on some happier things."

She rubbed his back, and it made him want to fall asleep. "I didn't even know Sim had a son, but I got chills the moment I saw him. He's the image of his father. Having Jerry here is almost as good as having Sim back, isn't it?"

"Jeremiah's his own man," Mackey said, "but it's nice to have a reminder of Sim around."

"He told me about what he's been up to the past few years," Katherine said. "Life hasn't been very kind to him."

"He grew up in a nasty part of the world." Mackey looked at the young man. There were times when he could've sworn he was looking at Sim and other times where he looked nothing like his father at all. "He's here now, and it's up to us to make him feel welcome. I want him to stay, but it's his choice."

"We'll make to leave a good impression on him. Guess we're becoming something of a refuge, aren't we? First, the girls from Hill House, then Joshua, and now Jerry."

"Don't forget me," he said. "You took me in, remember?"

"How could I forget?" She nuzzled into his arm and whispered. "God, how I missed you."

He glanced around the street to make sure no one was looking. Their relationship had become less scandalous since his wife, Mary, had left town the year before. And with each new arrival in Dover Station, whatever scandal there had been seemed to drift into the past. "I missed you, too."

Mackey looked up when Joshua Sandborne ran out of the hotel onto the porch. The expression on his face ruined Mackey's mood.

After Darabont's attack on the town, Mackey and the rest of his posse had found the boy wandering the burnt-out wreckage of the JT Ranch where he had worked. Despite a bad head injury, he had refused to ride back to town to the doctor. Instead, he healed on the trail and helped him defeat Darabont and his men. He had shown more courage at that time than half of the grown men in town.

Since then, Katherine had made the boy her right-hand man at the hotel. Mackey knew Joshua's dream job was to be a lawman someday, but he wanted to give the young man something of a trade before he encouraged him to pin a star on his chest.

Mackey could tell the boy had something to say but didn't want to interrupt the reunion on the porch. The marshal squeezed Katherine's hand before he got up to see what was troubling the young man.

He guided him back into the parlor of the hotel. "What's wrong?"

Sandborne handed Mackey a piece of paper. "One of Underhill's men came around the back door and told me to give this to you. Said it's from Mayor Grant himself, as if that's supposed to impress me. But he said it was important." He looked longingly out to the porch. "I didn't want to interrupt all the happiness going on out there, so—"

"Quit thinking of yourself as a bother," Mackey said

as he opened the letter. "You live here now, same as all of us. You're family."

Sandborne nodded and looked away as Mackey read the letter.

It was on official Town of Dover Station stationery, another wasteful expense incurred by James Grant's administration.

He recognized the writing as Grant's own hand,

Marshal Mackey,

I hope this letter finds you well. I see you are enjoying a pleasant evening on the porch of The Campbell Arms with friends old and new, so I hate to intrude on your evening like this. Unfortunately, there are several items we must discuss at your earliest possible convenience. Please come to my offices in the Municipal Building this evening so we may review them.

Fondest regards,
Mayor James Grant

Mackey refolded the letter. For as long as he lived, he would never get used to the idea that James Grant had been elected mayor of Dover Station. He didn't share that with young Sandborne, as his displeasure would only encourage the boy to challenge Underhill's men.

"Is it bad news?" Sandborne asked.

"It's not good." He knew Grant had probably been waiting until he returned to town to talk to him about the three dead women in the house on River Street. He had pulled Billy into it now, and as Billy was his deputy, it involved Mackey, too. Given that Grant claimed it was an urgent meeting, Mackey was sure he was ready to make some grand revelation about the murders, undoubtedly to his own benefit.

He had served the warrant on Henry Hancock to stall Grant's growing control over the town. If the drunk in the saloon had known Mackey had killed Hancock, Grant must have known it, too.

Grant thought he had the upper hand. Mackey had an idea.

He led Sandborne over to the front desk and picked up a pen. He wrote an address on the back of the letter and handed it to the young man. "I want you to deliver this note to my father. Tell him to read the letter, then look at the address I've written on the back. Then tell him this: 'The general sends his regards.'"

Sandborne looked puzzled when he repeated it, but he got it right. "What does it mean?"

"Don't worry," Mackey said. "Pappy will know what it means, and that's all that counts. After you give it to him, come back here and keep an eye on Mrs. Campbell. She's your responsibility no matter what else happens. Get Lagrange and Jerry out there to help you. Understand?"

"Yes, sir." He looked out to the porch. "Will your new friend be staying long?"

Mackey caught the hint of jealousy in his voice. He'd seen how resentment could eat away at a young man's confidence and he didn't want to see the same thing happen to Joshua. He was a good boy with all the qualities of being a fine man. Maybe even a fine lawman if he chose. But he was still young, and like most young things, needed training.

"Jerry Halstead is the son of an old friend of ours. He might be staying here for a while. He might even decide to call this place home. But you've got your place, too, and never forget that. The sky's big enough for more than one star."

The words seemed to make the young man feel better. "Thanks, Marshal. I'll deliver this right away."

Mackey watched him sprint out the front door, barely touching the steps as he went to deliver his message. He envied the boy's youth until he saw Katherine looking at him through the window on the porch.

Then he was reminded of what was at stake and what he had to do next.

He walked out onto the porch and gave Billy the bad news.

Billy frowned. "Him wanting to see us that quick isn't good for us, is it?"

"Meeting Grant is never good for anyone but Grant," Mackey said. "But he wants us to go, so we'd better be about our business. He'll only send Underhill and his boys after us if we don't, and that might force something ugly."

Jerry stood up, too. "Want me to come along?"

Mackey had thought better of it. "Best if you stay around here. Help Sandborne guard the place. If you see a dandy walking around, his name is Lagrange. He's a Pinkerton man, but don't hold that against him. We'll be back as soon as we can."

Billy and Mackey climbed down the steps and swung into the saddles of their respective mounts. He looked at Katherine, who blew him a kiss and mouthed the words, *Be careful.*

Mackey tipped his hat, then brought Adair around and rode up Front Street toward the Municipal Building.

Billy followed close behind.

Chapter 16

Mayor Grant made Mackey and Billy wait for him in his office. The room was even more ornate than Underhill's. What the commissioner's office lacked in drapery and paintings, Grant's office made up for in spades.

Deep blue fabrics with gold trim adorned the huge windows that not only looked out on the old jailhouse, but north to the newer part of the town, including Katherine's hotel and Mr. Van Dorn's house. Mackey wondered if Grant had a pair of field glasses in his desk so he could keep an eye on his boss. Not that he could see much, since Van Dorn kept his windows covered at all times.

The brass oil lamps fitted to the wall behind Grant's grand desk had already been lit, and between them hung a painting of what Dover Station would look like when it was completed.

Mackey easily located the spot on the painting where the corpses of the three Chinese whores and their killer were rotting away.

The painting did not show the three houses currently on the site. Instead, it showed a large brick building that encompassed the three lots with writing stenciled on the side: Dover Station Saw Mill Company. Beside it, and alongside a flowing body of water, was the sawmill building Mackey had heard about.

Mackey would have pointed it out to Billy, but his deputy was looking at the same thing.

"Interesting painting," Billy said.

"Sure is," Mackey said. "Considering everything."

Mayor James Grant opened the door and swept into the office with a flourish, trailed by Underhill and four policemen armed with rifles. Their brown dusters and hats marked them as Dover Station policemen before anyone bothered to look at the badges pinned over their hearts.

Underhill acknowledged Mackey and Billy with a slight nod, but that was all.

It was clear Grant was eager to use up all of the oxygen in the room. "I apologize for keeping you gentlemen waiting, but I was unavoidably detained. Between my duties with Mr. Van Dorn and as mayor, I don't know where I find the time to eat, much less sleep."

Mackey watched Grant take off his gray derby and hang it on a peg. His hair was still a rich brown, and the graying at his temples hadn't increased since his election to office. He also seemed to have lost quite a bit of weight since his election to mayor. Though he never could have been called a heavy man, his face was certainly thinner and his stomach flatter than it had been when he had become Mr. Van Dorn's right-hand man.

His style had changed, too. Mackey noticed Grant had given up his love of brocade vests for those that matched the rest of his subtle attire. He looked far more respectable and much more established.

Which told Mackey that James Grant had never been more dangerous than at this very moment.

Grant didn't offer to shake hands before taking his seat behind his desk and neither did the two lawmen.

"I know your time is precious," Grant began, "so I won't keep you any longer than I have to."

Mackey looked at Underhill. "Get your gunmen out of here."

"They men aren't gunmen," Grant said. "They're sworn officers of the law, no different than you."

"We're federal lawmen now," Mackey said.

Billy added, "They're flanking our position, and we don't like that. Either they leave or we do."

Underhill was about to order his men to leave, but Grant raised his hand to stop him. "What makes you think they would allow you to leave if I told them not to?"

"Because the last time we met like this, I knocked you on your ass. Five gunmen or even ten won't stop me if I want to do it again. Now, like Billy said, either they leave or we do. Your choice."

Grant laughed as he nodded to Underhill, who dismissed them. The four men filed out as they had come in. The last one closed the door behind him.

"I've granted your request," Grant said, "but Commissioner Underhill stays. I insist on that point."

"Fine," Mackey said. "Just tell us what you want."

Grant folded his hands on top of his desk. They were large hands. Worker's hands that showed the kind of man he had been before he found his way into Mr. Van Dorn's good graces. The kind of man he seemed to want to forget now.

"I have important information to share with you gentlemen that I pray won't leave the confines of this room."

Neither Mackey nor Billy reacted. Mackey figured it was about the dead people in the house on River Street, but he didn't encourage him. They just waited for him to keep talking.

Grant gladly obliged. "I have just learned that our patron, Mr. Silas Van Dorn, has reluctantly decided to leave Dover Station and return to his native home of Manhattan."

Mackey didn't see how that news impacted either of them. "Hope you'll be going back with him."

Grant looked at him. "Unfortunately, no. In fact, I will be needed here more than ever as I will be serving as his temporary replacement until such time as Mr. Van Dorn and his partner, Mr. Rice, send someone else to take his place. Once Mr. Van Dorn leaves, I will be serving as the acting director of the Dover Station Company and the mayor as well."

Mackey could only imagine how happy Grant must be that he now had what he had always wanted: full control of the empire he had helped build with Frazer Rice's money.

Mackey could see Grant was fishing for some kind of reaction. He refused to give him one. "What's that got to do with us? It's a town matter, not a federal one."

"The transition of power is not your concern, Marshal." Mackey could see the joy in his face as he said the words. "But Mr. Van Dorn's safety in transit across territorial lines is a federal matter."

"No, it isn't," Mackey said. "The Pinkertons can handle it for you. Robert Lagrange is already in town. He could have a contingent of his men here within the week. Ten men or more."

"Perhaps he could," Grant allowed, "but I speak on behalf of the entire town when I say they would be relieved if both of you agreed to make sure our patron arrives at his destination safely. Not all the way to New York, of course, but certainly as far as Laramie. I know it would be a great comfort to me and to the rest of us in Dover Station to know Mr. Van Dorn is in the capable hands of the Savior of Dover Station and the ever-loyal Deputy Sunday, of course."

Mackey let the request soak in for a moment. "Particularly given all of the violence that has plagued the town lately."

Grant's eyes narrowed. "Meaning?"

"Meaning the anarchists who caused all that trouble last year," Mackey said. "Meaning all of the unpleasantness that sprang up in town before your election. Meaning the recent arrival of the Hancock family in town and everything they bring with them."

Mackey leaned forward. "Meaning the three dead whores rotting as we speak in a house on River Street, including the body of the man who killed them and tried to kill Billy today."

Grant sat back in his chair as if slapped. "Those are all separate incidences you have chosen to bundle together to serve your personal dislike of me. I didn't ask you for an opinion on the state of Dover Plains,

Marshal Mackey, nor did I ask you for a summary of crimes that occur within town limits. I asked you to agree to protect Mr. Van Dorn. A simple yes-or-no answer will suffice."

Mackey didn't need to think about his answer. "No."

He noticed that Grant's expression changed slightly, the way a cat's expression changes when a mouse goes from being an object of idle curiosity to a possible meal.

Underhill looked surprised by the answer, too. "Why the hell not?"

"Because it's part of whatever plan he's cooking up." The image of Grant's plan came into focus as clearly as the painting that hung behind his desk. "Just like rushing to tell the world about those dead whores was part of your plan, wasn't it?"

Grant rubbed a thumb across his brown beard. "It appears that your elevation to marshal has made you paranoid, Aaron. In fact, I think a case could be made that you've completely lost your mind. I don't know where you're getting your information from, but I'd imagine it's from your deputy here."

"And from what I saw with my own two eyes." He looked at the police commissioner. "Underhill saw it, too."

All eyes went to Underhill, who clearly didn't like the attention.

"Walter?" Mayor Grant said. "Is there something you'd like to add?"

The chief shrugged. "Can't say I agree with everything Mackey said, but what happened with those women down on River Street is awfully fishy, James."

"I don't know what you're talking about." Grant said. "Three young women were butchered to death by a madman who was either a savage or had lived among them for so long he'd learned to kill like a savage."

The mayor looked at Mackey. "Given your experience among the redmen of the plains and the wild accusations you've made here tonight, I was thinking someone like you might be a suspect, Marshal. But, since you were out of town, I suppose that leaves us with your deputy, doesn't it?"

Then Grant looked at Billy. "Chief Underhill, I'm asking you to place Deputy Billy Sunday under arrest for murder."

Chapter 17

Mackey caught Billy's shoulder just before he sprang out of his chair and leapt at Grant. "You lying son of a—"

"Let him talk," Mackey said. "Let's see where he's going with this."

"I'm afraid the only one going anyplace is you, Billy. And that will be to jail. The one in this building, not the one manned by your best friend sitting next to you."

"If anyone's going to jail tonight," Mackey said, "it's you."

But Grant shook his head. "I doubt that. We don't put innocent men in prison in this country, at least not yet. But I'm afraid Deputy Sunday is as guilty as the day is long."

He opened his desk drawer and pulled out several sheets of paper that had handwriting on them and laid them out on his desk. He glanced at Underhill. "You may have wondered why I did not ask to meet with you this afternoon to hear the results of the investigation, Walt. I neglected to tell you that I was too busy solving it for you."

He tapped the papers on his desk. "For I have obtained sworn statements from a witness who reported seeing a Negro gentleman entering and exiting the murder house alone early this morning. Upon leaving the building, this same gentleman left the door ajar, whereupon the witness decided to go inside and investigate. That's when he reported what he saw to me. The witness said he thought the man bore a strong resemblance to the deputy here, so I brought in Commissioner Underhill to investigate. We decided to bring in Deputy Sunday to see if witnessing his own crimes would affect him in some way. Given his particularly strong reaction to the scene, he appeared to be overacting."

Grant continued, "Fortunately, our witness was hiding nearby and was able to positively identify Deputy Sunday as the man seen leaving the house on River Street earlier that morning."

Grant picked up one of the handwritten pieces of paper. "I have a sworn affidavit from one Mr. Dana King right here. I can personally speak for his character, as he has been a loyal employee of the Dover Station Company for some time."

He placed the paper back down on the desk and Mackey had to restrain Billy once again.

Grant continued, "Unfortunately, this statement is also a dying declaration, because Deputy Sunday killed this man—this witness to his crimes—only hours after he wrote it. Perhaps Commissioner Underhill let word of his statement slip during the course of his investigation, but the witness was, indeed, killed by Deputy Sunday, a fact the deputy does not dispute."

Billy grabbed onto the armrests of his chair until they cracked. "I only killed him because he was trying to kill me after I left the house."

"So you say," Grant went on. "But we only have your word to go on. The word of an accused murderer known to be handy with a knife."

Mackey glared at Underhill. "How the hell can you just stand there and go along with all of this? After everything we've been through together in this town?"

Underhill looked out the window and kept his silence.

"Commissioner Underhill is only doing his duty," Grant said, "as are other people in town. At this very moment, in fact."

"What are you planning, Grant?" Billy spat. "A lynching?"

Grant frowned as he looked down and swiped at an imaginary spot on his pants. "Hardly. I tried to keep these murders quiet in deference to your many years of service to this town, but I'm afraid my best efforts were unsuccessful. Word of the killings seems to have reached Charles Everett Harrington of the *Dover Station Record* just before you got here. He's champing at the bit to cover a juicy murder. Stories about new buildings and new jobs and petty bar brawls have bored him. He's looking forward to printing a story about a gory, scandalous murder. London has had their own horrific spate of murders recently, so why should Dover Station be any different? Could really put us on the map, you know?"

Mackey remembered reading about those murders. "Jack the Ripper. You sick son of a bitch. You want people to think that kind of thing is happening here?"

"What do you care?" Grant answered. "Murder's a town matter, not a federal one. Besides, once word gets out about your deputy's involvement, it'll only make the story even better. He'll be in jail, you'll be disgraced by association, and Commissioner Underhill will be seen as the man who brought a rabid murderer to justice. They'll probably write books about him. I can see the titles now. *The Great Detective of Dover Station* and *The River Street Ripper.*"

Grant folded his hands across his belly as he sat back in his chair, quite pleased with himself. "The tourism and attention we get in the papers will be something if it happens. And if the story doesn't catch on, no bother. Both of you will still be gone and I'll be in complete charge of all aspects of the town."

"You and the Hancock clan," Mackey said.

Grant smiled. "They have their uses."

"They going to help you run opium out of those houses on River Street?"

Grant's smile disappeared. "How'd you find out about that?"

But Mackey's smile returned. "I didn't until just now. Thanks for that."

Grant shrugged. "So you found out a bit early. It wasn't like I was going to keep it a secret for long. What good is an opium den if no one finds out about it?"

"And what good does an opium den owned by three whores do you if you have to split the profits with them?" Mackey concluded. "Best to keep it all to yourself."

Grant sat in his chair, swiveling back and forth, content with his own silence.

Mackey had to hand it to him. Grant had everything all worked out. "Think Mr. Rice will let you just take over like that? Van Dorn might be weak, but Rice is not."

"Rice is as irrelevant as Van Dorn," Grant laughed. "He has developed about forty-three percent of the town."

"It's a hell of a lot higher than that," Mackey said.

"He *thinks* it's higher than that, but a few unfortunate clerical errors on my part show that he actually owns much less than half of the available land in Dover Station. That leaves fifty-seven percent to the highest bidder. You think Mr. Rice is the only wealthy man in New York? Or in this country, for that matter? You don't think he has rivals that would love to take this place away from him and gloat about it later?"

"He still has the railroad."

"Which will continue to service this town because, unlike you, men like Rice and Van Dorn can't rely on petty indulgences like friendship and loyalty. They can still make money in this town as minority owners and will continue to do so. Casting you and Billy aside may give him a few anxious moments, but ultimately, business is still business, and he will abide. You know I'm right. Besides, how long do you think he'll remain loyal to you once word of Billy's arrest for murder gets out? He'll forget he ever knew you by this time tomorrow."

Grant and Underhill traded glances when they

heard a great commotion out in the hallway. Shouting and the sounds of boots echoing through halls. Running.

Mackey sat back in his chair and crossed his legs. "I wouldn't be too sure of that."

Grant glared at Underhill. "Find out what that's all about."

Mackey winked at Billy and gently nudged him to sit back in his chair.

As Underhill went outside, Grant caught the wink. "What? What have you done?"

It was Mackey's turn to smile. "Nothing. I'm just sitting here in a room full of witnesses."

Grant snapped forward in his chair. "Damn you. Tell me what you've done or I'll throw you in the cell next to him."

Mackey inclined his head toward the door. "Take a look for yourself."

Grant got up and ran out from behind his desk into the hallway. He stopped just outside the door.

From the windows in the hallway, he could see the large flames and smoke billowing high into the darkening sky just behind the Municipal Building.

"Looks like a house fire," Mackey called out to them as Billy got up and took Dana King's statement from Grant's desk. "Coming from River Street, near as I can tell. It look that way to you, Billy?"

His deputy struck a lucifer off Grant's desk, held it to Dana King's statement, and dropped the burning document into the steel trash basket beside the mayor's desk. He took the rest of the papers and dropped them in there, too.

Mackey cleared his throat and spoke loud enough for the men in the hall to hear. "I know this isn't a federal matter, Commissioner Underhill, but I think you might send your men out to maintain order and help the fire brigade. It'd be a shame if those flames jumped to those new buildings the company's putting up."

"And the den got destroyed with all that opium in the basement," Billy added.

Underhill motioned for his four men to go and they ran down the stairs immediately. The commissioner looked back at Mackey, over Grant's head.

The mayor was too taken aback by the sight of the flames to say much of anything.

"Quite a fire," Underhill said. "Kind of like what I always thought General Sherman's march through Georgia might've looked like."

"You know, my old man served with Sherman once upon a time," Mackey said. "I'll have to ask him about that."

Mackey could've sworn he saw Underhill smile as he followed his men out outside to deal with the chaos over on River Street.

Leaving Mayor Grant alone with them.

Before Mackey could stop him, Billy snatched Grant by the collar and dragged him back into the office. He threw the man against the wall behind his desk and pinned him there. The barrel of his Colt was jammed under his chin.

Mackey shut and locked the door.

Grant struggled, but Billy didn't let him move. "Guess tonight's ending a bit different than you figured it would."

"You crazy bastards," Grant gasped. "Do you know the trouble you've caused?"

Mackey took a seat on his desk. "I think the man who set that fire knew what he was doing. Too bad those bodies will probably be burned so bad, it'll be tough for anyone to tell how they died, much less poor old Doc Ridley." The marshal shook his head. "Should've let him see those bodies fresh right after you killed them."

"I didn't kill anyone." Grant squirmed as if a gun wasn't under his chin.

"Maybe not," Mackey said, "but Dana did. He was your enforcer in that part of town, wasn't he? Underhill already told us he did odd jobs for the company here and there. I'd bet he'd have no problem leaning on the whores who were smart enough to buy property near where the new sawmill is scheduled to go in. Bet you even had yourself lined up for a cut of the action."

Grant sneered, "You think you know everything, don't you? God, for a worldly man, you can be surprisingly ignorant sometimes."

Billy jammed the gun barrel harder into Grant's jaw. "Then how about you educate the man?"

"I had King lean on the whores, and they laughed at him. They threw him out, and he came back later and cut their throats without my permission. King came and got me, and I was furious. I wanted to make it look like it was more than what it was, so we arranged a scene the paper could use to grab headlines and attention. Make the most out of a bad situation. I thought Underhill would simply go along, but he wanted experts to look at the scene I described. That's my fault. I shouldn't have told him so much."

Billy jammed the pistol barrel hard enough under Grant's chin to make the mayor cry out. "What do you say, Aaron? Maybe the mayor here saw his town burning and got so sad over it that he went and shot himself right here in his office." He glanced up at the large painting of Dover Station over their heads. "Be a shame to ruin such a nice work of art like that, though."

"We wouldn't want to do that." Mackey grabbed Grant by the collar and pulled him away from Billy.

He turned the mayor around and held his head so he could see the painting. "Your motive for killing those women is right there. You never intended on letting them keep that land or those houses. That painting's based on those plans you showed all over town before your election. You didn't count on someone else owning the property, so you wanted them either to play along or get out of the way."

"You'll never prove it," Grant said, still struggling to get free of Mackey's grip on his head. "A painting won't stand up in a court of law. Won't convict anyone! I'll deny everything I just told you, and the people will believe me, not you, especially now that King's body is likely burned beyond all recognition."

Mackey held Grant's head tighter as he whispered into his ear. "Who said anything about court?"

Mackey released him with a shove as Billy aimed his Colt at Grant. "What do you think, Aaron? I still like the suicide idea. Easy to believe a man like Grant would take the coward's way out."

Mackey stood next to Billy as Grant stood alone in

the middle of his large office looking for a place to hide. "Let's look at this a different way. What does his suicide get us?"

Billy thumbed back the hammer on the Colt. "Peace."

His pistol tracked Grant as he inched toward the window. "You can't shoot me. Someone will hear the shot and come running."

"Not with all that ruckus out there on account of the fire," Billy said.

Grant balled up his hands into fists until the knuckles cracked. "I won't beg you bastards for anything. You want to shoot me, fine. Toss me the pistol in the top left drawer and at least give me a chance to die like a man."

"Same kind of chance you gave those helpless whores?" Billy said. "By stabbing them and scalping them afterwards? Like plain old killing them wasn't enough for you."

Billy's hand began to quiver, and Mackey decided there was a real possibility that he might actually kill Grant. He placed his hand on Billy's wrist and got him to slowly lower the pistol.

"Killing you would be more trouble to us than you're worth, Grant" Mackey said. "Underhill and his men know we were here. A lot of other people might know, too. They know we hate you. If we kill you, Underhill won't have any choice but to come after us for it." He looked at Billy. "We're lawmen, remember? It's different for us."

Grant began to breathe again when Billy holstered his pistol.

Mackey started walking toward Grant. "As of right

now, we're even. The death house is burned, the bodies destroyed, your opium den is in ruins, and your phony statements against Billy are gone. You've got nothing on us, and we don't have anything on you that'll stand up in court. If it stays that way, you stay alive. You keep pushing, we'll forget we're lawmen, because after what you tried tonight, it's personal from here on out. Understand?"

"Yes." Grant's eyes narrowed. "I understand quite clearly. I hope you're not expecting gratitude."

Mackey shoved him hard enough to throw him against the window. "I expect you to remember you almost died tonight."

Mackey walked out of the office first. Billy followed.

Grant called after them, "There's still the matter of escorting Mr. Van Dorn to Laramie, Mackey. I've got your word you'll do that, don't I?"

Mackey left the office without answering him. Grant's bellows echoed through the empty building he had built.

Chapter 18

Although Mackey wanted to go back to the hotel to see Katherine and Jerry, he knew he and Billy needed to talk now while everything was still fresh in their minds. Going to bed after all that had just happened didn't seem right.

Almost killing a mayor required some level of discussion.

Upon leaving the Municipal Building, Mackey and Billy had to struggle to make their way across to the jailhouse through all of the people and flatbed wagons full of buckets of water heading to River Street to fight the fire. River Street, despite its name, did not yet have a river flowing beside it.

Mackey and Billy normally would have helped, but they weren't local lawmen anymore. Underhill and his police force of thirty men or so were there to enforce order and let the fire brigade do their job.

Mackey looked back once they had reached the boardwalk in front of the jailhouse. The sheer size of the Municipal Building blocked his view of the fire, but not of the billowing smoke rising high into the Montana night sky just behind it.

"Think the fire will spread?" Billy asked as he unlocked the jailhouse door.

"Nope." Mackey eased himself down into his rocking chair. "Just about the only thing Pappy knows how to do, besides run his mouth and fight, is how to burn a building down. Sherman taught him that. He probably set the burn slow enough for people to see it in time to fight it. The house and all the bodies in it will be destroyed. Maybe the two houses next to it, too. But there's no wind tonight, and it rained a few days ago, so the ground won't burn. There's nothing close enough to the houses for the flames to jump to before the brigade puts it out."

That seemed enough of an answer as far as Billy was concerned. "Might as well start a fire of my own in the stove for coffee." He went inside. "We've got a lot to talk about."

Mackey began gently rocking the chair back and forth. He was surprised to see it was in exactly the same place he had left it days ago. Some of the folks who believed the nonsense that had been written about him in the papers liked to sit in his rocking chair just to say they had sat in the same place as the Savior of Dover Station.

The notoriety he had acquired since running down Darabont had never made sense to him. A bandit and his gang had attacked the town he protected, burned down a whorehouse, took some of the women, and ran. Mackey raised a posse, hunted them down, and brought the captives home. One of those captives happened to be Katherine, the woman he loved. Any lawman worth his salt would have done the same thing.

He didn't see why anyone would find that worthy of praise. But people did, and the old jailhouse on Front Street had become something of an attraction to people who found themselves in Dover Station for one reason or another. Many of those people liked to sit in his rocking chair when Billy wasn't around to run them off. Pappy ran a decent side business by agreeing to tell tall tales about the Siege of Dover Station and his role in defending the town against Darabont's horde. And with each retelling of the tale, Pappy's role in the events that had transpired grew, while the contributions of Mackey and the rest of the men diminished quite a bit. Pappy also tended to leave out the part about the posse and Darabont's death. Focusing on what he called a siege was much easier for the masses to grasp.

Mackey rocked back and forth in his chair as the smells of burning wood and worse from the house fire was mixed with the stove fire Billy had just set. He had left the oil lamp next to the jailhouse unlit, so he was able to sit in the darkness and watch the people run past him toward the fire. Some were going to help. Most were going to watch so they could later share lies about what they had seen.

He watched the dozens of faces that streamed past the jailhouse and recognized only two of them. He had grown up in Dover Station, back when his father and other veterans had founded a town called Dover Plains. The name had changed when the railroad came to town while Mackey was attending West

Point. A lot had changed since he was a boy. A lot had changed when the railroad had come to town and even more so since Frazer Rice had decided to make something of Dover Station.

Mackey had always held a healthy amount of disdain for wealthy men, but Mr. Rice had been different. He was a stern man who knew what he wanted and was not afraid of doing whatever it took to get it.

But even great men made mistakes, and Mr. Rice had made one in leaving his partner, Silas Van Dorn, in charge of the Dover Station Company. Van Dorn hated Montana and never left the grand house he had built for himself. That's why he had hired James Grant to do the job for him. The result had been at least four murders Mackey knew Grant had been responsible for, but could not prove. That didn't count the attacks he believed Grant had staged on the Great Northern Railroad to weaken it just enough for him to gain more power.

Now Grant sat in the fancy mayor's office inside the Municipal Building with the entire town in the palm of his hand. And now, with Van Dorn leaving, there was no one to stand in his way of turning Dover Station into his own empire.

No one, Mackey knew, except him and Billy. But this wasn't a federal matter. It was only a town matter.

At least for now.

Mackey was still ruminating the future of Dover Station when Billy came out of the jailhouse with two mugs of steaming coffee. Mackey gladly took one, but allowed it to sit for a while before drinking it. He enjoyed his coffee more when a bit of the steam was off it.

"Some kind of evening," Billy observed as he sat on the bench.

"Not a good kind of evening, either." Mackey watched a man trip in the muddy thoroughfare of Front Street before picking himself up and continuing to run toward the fire. The crowd was down to the stragglers now. He figured it would only be a matter of time before they began heading back the other way once the fire was under control.

"Shame," Mackey continued. "Jeremiah coming to town should've been a happy time. Should've had a dinner in his honor." He listened to the shouts and the clanging bells from River Street echo through the streets. He remembered the ugly scene in Grant's office. "Not this."

"We'll have a dinner for him when things calm down," Billy said. "He tell you he was in jail?"

"Yeah." Mackey took his first sip of coffee. The rich taste hit home. Billy always made a good pot. "Guess that's why we had so much trouble finding him after Sim's death. Said he'd been a lawman before it happened. We didn't talk much about that."

"He's certainly done his share of traveling since becoming a man," Billy said, "but he seems settled enough now. Must've ridden all of that wildness out of him. I don't think he would've come all the way up here from Texas otherwise."

"Underhill did," Mackey reminded him. "Look at how good he turned out."

Billy cursed and spat into the thoroughfare.

Mackey said, "Maybe Jerry just wanted to see his father's grave before moving on. Maybe he's got

He looked across the street at the staked-out lots where the sawmill was going to be built in a few weeks. "This place might not be the same as it was five years ago, but I'm not the same man who stepped off that train from the army, either."

He was about to stand up but stopped himself before he fell over.

Underhill rushed to keep him from falling off the back porch. "You all right, Billy?"

But Billy was better than all right. He had a feeling he was looking at the start of the answers to all of his questions. "Who owns these houses, Walter?" He saw the chief looked puzzled, so he put a finer point on it. He knocked on the wood he was sitting on. "Why did the company build these three houses before the saw-mill or the other buildings?"

"I guess because these lots don't belong to the Dover Station Company," Underhill told him. "They never have. I remember them from when I was helping Mr. Rice go over the survey maps. These lots were listed, but owned by someone else, so he decided to build around them."

Billy kept looking at the lots as he slowly got to his feet. "Do you remember the name of the man who owns these lots?"

"No, because it wasn't important," Underhill said. "I remember he said whoever owned them would sell out fast enough when they heard that saw going at all hours of the day and night. Figured we'd pick them up at a dirt-cheap price then." The chief looked at him. "Why?"

"I don't know," Billy said. "Think you can find out who owns these houses?"

Underhill nodded toward the Municipal Building.

make some sense. "You think they were being nice to you because they want to kill you?"

"They were setting me up." Mackey pointed at the hotel across the street. "The room they gave me takes up the entire top floor, and the balcony makes it easy for people to jump down from the roof and blast me while I sleep."

"So that's why you're over here. You think they're going to try something and you want to catch them doing it." He scratched his scalp. "That sounds like a good idea for you but not for me. If you shoot them from here, people will know it and they'll make trouble for me."

"I won't shoot them from here." Mackey doubted he could hit anyone from this far away in the dark, even with the Winchester. He'd have to get up close "Light as few lamps tonight in the livery as possible, Arthur. I don't want anyone knowing I'm here."

"Don't got to worry about that." The old black man padded off deeper into the livery. "Hell, I don't want anyone knowing I'm here, either."

It was not until about an hour or so later when Mackey spotted the man creeping across the flat roof of the Hancock Hotel. Another man soon followed. They carefully slipped over the side of the roof before allowing themselves to drop to the balcony below.

Since there was no way down to the street from the balcony, he knew what was coming next.

They kicked in the balcony door and opened fire on the bed where Mackey was supposed to be sleeping. The dark room lit up four times as each man unloaded his double-barreled shotgun. Four rounds of buckshot at point-blank distance. More than enough firepower to do the job.

Had Mackey been sleeping, he would have been dead by now. Instead, he had been watching the assassination attempt from the livery across the street.

And was very much alive.

Mackey saw the light from the hallway flood his room as the assassins opened it and ran toward the back stairs. None of the people in the rooms below would bother investigating what had happened, even if they had heard the blasts above the noise of the gambling on the first floor.

Mackey grabbed his Winchester and broke into a dead run toward the hotel. The street was eerily quiet except for the drunken cackles of the working girls that accompanied the tinny piano in the hotel lobby.

Mackey slid to a halt at the edge of the lamplight outside the enclosed back stairs. He took a knee and brought the rifle up to his shoulder as he waited for the men who had thought they had killed him to come outside.

The first gunman pushed open the door, quickly followed by the second one. They were both young, maybe twenty, but old enough to kill a man. And they both had the long faces and dead eyes of Hancock men.

Mackey waited until the stair door closed before he said, "Looks like you boys are empty."

The two men turned at the sound of his voice. Mackey fired and hit the lead man in the chest. He was knocked off his feet and crumpled next to the hotel.

The second one broke open the shotgun and fumbled to eject the spent cartridges.

Mackey chambered a round in the darkness. "Take your time."

The boy looked around for help as he dumped out one spent cartridge on the ground, then the other. But no help came, for the same sounds of pianos and laughter that had hidden his crime now drowned out any chance for his rescue.

No one had heard Mackey's shots.

The boy dropped a fresh cartridge from his pocket and threw the shotgun aside as he grabbed for something tucked in the back of his pants.

When he came around with a pistol, Mackey fired and brought the young man down.

The marshal remained in the shadow as he walked back to the livery. He ejected the spent round and fed two new bullets into the Winchester.

Arthur was standing inside the livery in a long nightshirt. He held an old Walker Colt at his side. "I woke up when I heard the shots. Surprised no one else did."

"I'm not," Mackey said as he walked past the hostler and back to the empty stall. "They were probably told to ignore anything they heard."

Arthur followed him into the livery. "Saw you kill those two boys. They the ones with the shotguns who shot up your room?"

Mackey laid the Winchester against the wall of the

stall as he lowered himself into the hay. "I wouldn't have shot them if they weren't."

Arthur looked outside, then at Mackey again. "You just killed two men who were trying to kill you and now you're just gonna go to sleep?"

Mackey slid his pistol out of the holster and held it across his stomach. "I would if you'll let me." He pitched his hat so it covered his eyes.

But Arthur didn't go away. "Ain't you afraid there'll be any more trouble?"

"Not from them." Mackey stretched. "Maybe from the other Hancock boys, but not until tomorrow. That's why I figure I'll need a good night's sleep."

Arthur mumbled to himself as he moved off back to bed. "Can't understand it. Man kills two men and can go to sleep right after. I just can't understand it."

Mackey twitched as sleep began to take him.

Because you're not me.

The following morning just after sunrise, Mackey collected his money for the five horses from Arthur. "Been a pleasure doing business with you, old man. Thanks for letting me sleep in your stall last night."

"I've seen the way you handle a gun, Marshal. I couldn't have stopped you even if I tried."

Mackey had almost forgotten about the business with the Hancock boys the night before. He looked outside at the hotel and saw no trace of the men he had shot. No bodies. No one looking around the area, either. It was as if two men had not died there only a few hours before.

But Mackey knew. And he knew why, which was even more important. The day he no longer remembered a man he had killed was the day to walk away.

He nodded over toward the Hancock Hotel. "Looks like someone cleaned up during the night."

"Saw that first thing this morning when I woke up." Arthur opened the door to Adair's stall to let Mackey lead her out. The mare had nipped at him and kicked the stall door last night when he fed her. "I'd say that means they know what happened and don't want to accuse you of it publicly."

Mackey laughed as he put the saddle on Adair. "What are they going to do? Arrest me for killing the men who thought they'd just killed me?" He cinched the saddle under Adair's belly. "Not even the Hancocks are that stupid."

"I hope you're right for your sake and mine," Arthur said. "I hope I'm still in business after you leave town."

"You will be, don't worry." He slipped his Winchester in the saddle scabbard. "If you need me, just wire me in Dover Station. I'm less than half a day's ride from here."

Mackey was checking his rig to make sure it was securely on the horse when Arthur grabbed his arm. "I'm awful worried about you, Marshal. I know you don't think much of them Hancock boys, but don't think too lowly about them, either. They're a nasty bunch, and there's a whole lot more of them than you. Hell, there's a whole lot more of them than anyone in these parts. You'd best watch yourself on the ride back home. They might've missed you last night, but today's a whole new day."

"Yeah, but I've got Adair." Mackey stroked the Arabian's neck. "This girl has gotten me through a lot worse than anything the Hancock bunch can throw at me."

"Don't be too sure," Arthur said as he laid the saddlebags across the mare's back. "What the Hancocks lack in brains, they make up for in pure meanness, and they know every inch of this country like the back of their hand. I'd stick to the open land if I were you. Ride far out of rifle range from anything that could serve as cover for them when you can, 'specially around the hills. No telling how many of them could be scattered out among the rocks between here and Dover."

Mackey pulled himself up into the saddle and took the reins from Arthur. "You've been a good friend to me, old man. If I live long enough, I'll pay you back."

"Don't go temptin' fate by talkin' like that." Arthur pulled Mackey's Winchester from the scabbard beneath his left leg and handed it up to him. "And don't forget to keep this brandished. Some of the Hancock clan are more easily spooked than others. The sight of a man like you toting a rifle ready to fire is apt to give him second thoughts before he takes a shot at you. Could help."

Mackey grinned down at the liveryman. "I'll wire you as soon as I get back to Dover. Let you know how all of this turns out."

"I ain't old," Arthur said, "just experienced. But I'll appreciate gettin' that telegram from you just the same."

Mackey kept the Winchester on his right hip as he brought Adair around and rode down Main Street at a good clip. He didn't want them to think he was running out of town. He saw the looks he drew from the people who had come to a stop to watch him pass. He wondered if half of them were just glad to see him go or if they were waiting for him to get shot.

When he reached the familiar corner of Norman Fong's café, he was glad to see the cook waiting for him, apron on and waving at him. Mackey tipped his black hat to him and continued on. At least he had made two friends in town.

As soon as he and Adair were out of sight from the town, he gave the horse its head and let her move at her normal, quicker pace. Dover Station was little more than half a day's ride from Hancock, and Adair could make the journey even quicker if he let her. Right now, speed sounded like a good idea.

Mackey was about an hour from Hancock when the first shot rang out. The report echoed across the flatland where he rode, making it nearly impossible for him to gauge where it had come from.

He brought Adair to a halt and listened. He knew he was well out of range of any rifle shot from the foothills in the distance. The flatland around him couldn't offer cover to anything bigger than a field mouse. Unfortunately, that also meant he was without cover as well.

He watched Adair's ears rotate toward something in the distance. It was only a moment later until he had heard it, too.

The unmistakable pounding of hooves moving fast along the ground. Dozens of them.

A moment later, a group of ten riders rounded a gap through the foothills and sped straight toward him.

Although he was still well out of rifle range, Mackey knew his time was quickly running out. The gang rode closer with every stride.

Mackey stood up in the saddle and looked for anything that might provide any kind of cover. He spotted a small copse of trees down the slope of the floor of the wide valley and snapped Adair's reins.

The whoops and hollers from his pursuers echoed throughout the valley as he rode toward the sparse outcropping of trees. It did not offer much cover, but it was better than taking his chances with the Hancock riders out on the flatland.

He brought Adair to a skidding stop once he had reached the trees. It was a small watering hole about ten feet in diameter that seemed to be fed from an underground stream from the foothills behind him. A few pines and firs sprouted up around it, casting the area in deep shadow. That alone could provide him enough cover from the ten men bearing down on him.

He dropped from the saddle and pulled the Winchester from the scabbard before moving to the farthest tree from Adair. He would not tie her down. He knew the horse would bolt to safety if too many bullets landed near her, only to drift back toward him once the shooting stopped.

He took a knee behind the thin branches of a sapling and took a closer look at the approaching horde. Ten riders in total, all running down toward him along the gentle slope he had just taken. He could see the nostrils of the horses were already open wide as they drew more air into their lungs. The men had already ridden them to the point of exhaustion and they were on the verge of faltering

And although they were out of range, he still might be able to help himself.

Mackey brought his Winchester to his shoulder, took careful aim at the lead rider, and fired. The bullet struck the ground well in front of the horse, throwing up a small cloud of dust and rock to make the animal shy away.

The lead mount bumped into the horse to its left. Their legs got tangled and both horses faltered, rolling over their riders as they collapsed to the ground.

He wished Billy was here with his Sharps. The whole group would have been easy pickings for the fifty-caliber long gun at this range. But wishing would not save his life. Only accuracy would.

He watched the eight remaining men stop their charge to double back and check on the two fallen riders.

One rider struggled to bring his excited horse under control as it skittered into the extreme range of his rifle.

Mackey levered in a fresh round, adjusted his aim for the great distance, and fired.

His target dropped from the saddle as the sound of the rifle shot echoed through the valley.

Three down. Seven to go.

He ignored the dead man's panicked horse as it ran down the slope, passed him, and kept running. Instead, he kept his aim on the remaining men scrambling out of their saddles as they tended to the injured men trapped beneath their fallen mounts. He could hear their screams from where he was hidden.

Six of the Hancock men were on the ground while the seventh struggled to keep the six other horses from riding off. The Hancock clan may have been cowpunchers by trade, but their mounts weren't used to gunfire. Not like Adair.

The man trying to bring the horses under control was well out of range, but another shot might scatter them. A man on foot was more likely to listen to reason than one on horseback.

Mackey fired and, as expected, the bullet fell well short of the group, but was close enough to spook all of the mounts. They broke and scattered as they ran back the way they had come, toward the distant foothills. Mackey could tell by their gaits that they were too tired to run far, but fear had caused them to run far enough away to make their riders vulnerable.

Three of the Hancock men were down. Six were on foot. Only one was still mounted in open country. Mackey was beginning to like his odds better all the time.

He took his rifle with him as he went back to Adair and pulled his field glasses from his saddlebags. He took a closer look at the scene up the incline and found it was as chaotic as he had expected.

Two men attended a man they had just freed from under his horse as he writhed in agony in the tall grass.

The others were trying to help the man still trapped under his horse. The animal looked too exhausted to even try to get up on its own. It seemed something else in mind. We don't know, and we'd be wrong to let our affection for Sim cloud our judgment. He's not the same little boy we remember from Concho. Can't forget that."

Billy sipped his coffee, too. "And he *did* do time."

"Doesn't make him a bad man. Not everyone we've hauled into jail were bad men."

"Most of them were," Billy said. "Especially the men we planted."

"Maybe," Mackey said. "Or just made a bad decision at the wrong time. Guilt doesn't mean a man is bad." He looked at his deputy. "Just means they let their worst inclinations get the better of them for a second."

"That was different." Billy looked down into his coffee mug. "You should've let me kill that son of a bitch, Aaron. We're going to have to do it eventually. You know that. Could've saved a lot of bother in the long run."

Mackey could not disagree with him. "Underhill never would've let it go. And he'd be wrong if he did. It would've cost us in the long run, maybe more than we know."

He took another sip of coffee and decided to change the subject. "The Hancock family is going to give us enough problems as it is. Didn't need Grant's death pointing more guns our way."

"I take it that you had to kill Henry," Billy said.

Mackey nodded. "Him and his whole gang. Fools holed themselves up in a box canyon after they robbed the bank in Titusville. Don't know what they were thinking staying put for that long. Had a good day's jump on me."

"Probably didn't think anyone would be coming after them." Billy set his cup on the bench and began to build himself a cigarette. "And I'd imagine you didn't get a warm reception when you rode into Hancock with Hank's body draped across your pommel."

"I used one of their horses," Mackey said. "And they didn't draft any proclamations in my honor. I didn't think going to Hancock was a good idea in the first place. But Mr. Rice wanted me to bring Hancock's body back home, and I felt like I owed it to him."

Mackey had always tried to avoid being in anyone's debt, but Mr. Rice was a different sort. He had pulled the right strings to get Mackey appointed as U.S. Marshal for the Montana Territory before Grant abolished the sheriff's department. Mr. Rice didn't ask much, so Mackey had no problems doing what he wanted.

"Besides," Mackey continued. "I had paper on him."

"That makes it legal, then. But not necessarily right."

"Killing Henry Hancock has been a good idea since the day he was born." Mackey took another sip of coffee. "Mad Nellie made a run at me as soon as I got into town."

Billy looked up from the cigarette he was building. "She try any nonsense?"

"Yeah."

"How'd that turn out?"

"There are a whole lot less Hancocks in Hancock now than before I got there."

"Sounds like good news to me."

"She admitted that her family is working with Grant," Mackey said. "Didn't seem to care who knew it, either. Told me she took Hank's death as an assassination on Mr. Rice's orders, but would be happy to let it go if Mr. Rice agrees to extend a branch line up to Hancock like Grant is promising. Since that's not going to happen, I expect her to throw all of her support behind Grant."

Mackey suddenly felt the enormity of all that had happened and what was to come begin to close in on him. He looked over and saw Billy was almost done building his cigarette. "Can you make one of those for me when you're done?"

"Certainly can." Billy licked the paper and sealed the smoke before handing it to the marshal. "Heard what you said in the Ruby earlier. 'Straight up or over the saddle. Makes no difference to me.' I remember that phrase."

Mackey knew where this was going. "Stop."

"Nothing to stop," Billy said as he handed Mackey a match. "Last time I heard you use that line was the last time I saw you smoke, too."

Mackey struck the match off the side of his chair and lit his cigarette. He drew the smoke deep into his lungs. It was his first cigarette in years and he'd forgotten how much he'd missed it. "This time is different."

"As I recall," Billy went on, "you were also drinking around that same time you used that phrase and smoked. Didn't drink while you were in Hancock, did you, Captain?"

Mackey shut his eyes and fought back the rush of memories that were darker than the night that now surrounded them. Memories of his last days in uniform.

Memories of screams and gunfire and blood. "Haven't touched a drop since we boarded the train back here, Sergeant Sunday, and I'm not starting now. Happy?"

"Just making sure." Billy went back to building another smoke for himself. "We both need to keep our wits about us now that Grant and the Hancock clan have us in their sights."

He held the tobacco pouch above the paper without tapping it. "You think Grant was serious about holding me for murdering those whores and King?"

"Anything's possible with Grant," Mackey admitted. "All I know is he would've lost a lot of men if he had tried to arrest you. Just like I know that if he wants us on that train with Van Dorn, something's going to happen to Van Dorn between here and New York City."

Billy resumed building his cigarette. "Because he plans on blaming us for it somehow. The only question I've got is why."

Mackey took a drag on his cigarette. "I don't care about why. I don't care what happens to Van Dorn, either. He let that snake Grant in here. If it rears up and bites him, then he deserves it as far as I'm concerned. I just want you and me to be as far away from it as possible. Let Rice hire Pinkertons to watch him. Get Lagrange on the job, not us."

"I don't know if we'll have a choice," Billy said. "Grant will write Mr. Rice, either as himself or under Van Dorn's name, and request our protection. Mr. Rice might not think much of his partner, but I imagine he wouldn't like it if he got killed on his way back to New York. The man's got a wife and family, and it wouldn't do Mr. Rice's reputation much good if his partner died on the way back home."

"If it happens on railroad property, Rice and the Pinkertons will be able to cover it up. Say he had a heart attack of some kind or a fever."

Mackey kept turning over the notion of took another quick drag on his cigarette as Billy lit his own. "Still can't figure out why Grant would want anything to happen to Van Dorn. He's running things here until Mr. Rice names a replacement. He's already mayor. It'll take Mr. Rice at least a month to get someone out here to take over for Grant, maybe even longer. Grant already has everything he wants. Why kill Van Dorn?"

"If he aims to kill him," Billy said. "He might be planning something else. A kidnapping maybe. Get more money out of Mr. Rice to get him back and scare off anyone else from coming all the way out here from New York."

Mackey could almost see the strands of possibilities race away from him like balls of string rolled across the floor. Anything was possible with Grant, and trying to figure out what he was up to ahead of time was pointless. He had learned all about strategy and tactics at West Point, but everything he had learned meant nothing in the field against the Apache. The same held true for James Grant. He felt the old pressure building in his chest again and took a deep drag on his smoke. The tobacco helped settle him down.

"Guess we'll just have to wait and see what happens."

Billy lit his cigarette and let the smoke drift from his nose. "Whatever he does, we'll be ready."

"Always have been so far."

The first group of stragglers from the fire began walking back along Front Street. Their faces were blackened, and they were shouting over each other about how grand a spectacle it had been. The legend of the Great River Street Fire was being born in front of their eyes.

Billy let the smoke drift from his nose. "Still think you should've let me just kill the son of a bitch, though."

Mackey just kept watching the people pass the jailhouse. He didn't have a good answer for Billy.

Chapter 19

The next day, the headline of the *Dover Station Record* blared:

FIRESTORM ON RIVER STREET!

Four Dead – Three Homes Destroyed

HEROIC FIRE BRIGADE SAVES TOWN

Brendan Mackey—Fearless!

From his table on the front porch of The Campbell Arms, Mackey snapped the paper open as he read the account of the fire written by Charles Everett Harrington himself.

It had been quite some time since the editor of the newspaper had written a story for the paper, especially after Mr. Rice's investment in the paper allowed him to hire a team of reporters to print stories that made the Dover Station Company look good. He was glad Harrington had taken up the pen again, as he had always enjoyed the newsman's articles. He had a gift for writing fancy prose and never allowed the truth to get in the way of a good story.

Anyone else who read the article wouldn't have seen James Grant's hand in it.

But Mackey wasn't just anyone and could practically see the town's mayor setting the type himself. It's probably why Harrington wrote it in the first place. One of his staff writers might accidentally tell the truth.

Harrington's account was as brief as it was fictional. It said a mysterious fire had swept through three new buildings on River Street the previous night. The culprit was a candle that had been lit too close to drapes. The burnt remains of three unidentified women huddled in a corner beside their beds had been discovered once the fire had been put out. A man was found dead in the parlor. He was undoubtedly a Good Samaritan who had been overcome by the smoke before he could rescue the doomed women. There was no mention of whores or Dana King anywhere in the piece.

But the article did manage to end on a positive note, praising Pappy for leading the fire brigade that combated the inferno. And that Mr. James Grant, in his offices as mayor and general manager of the Dover Station Company, had promised to purchase the blighted lots and make them part of the new sawmill that was to be built next to the site within the month.

Mackey set the newspaper aside in disgust. Grant had a hand in getting four people killed and came out looking like a hero in the papers.

Katherine touched his hand before his temper spiked. He had been so wrapped up in the article that he had forgotten she was there. "Please don't get upset," she said. "There's nothing you can do about it now, Aaron." She tried to put a good shine on it. "At least they said good things about Pappy."

That was part of Mackey's annoyance. "There'll be no living with him after this."

"At least the rest of the town didn't burn, though the loss of the four people was a tragedy."

He didn't have the heart to tell her the truth. He wasn't sure what good it would do, anyway. Maybe he'd tell her in time, but for now, he was glad the whole mess was finally over.

At least until Grant took complete control over the Dover Station Company.

He glared up at the Van Dorn House on the hill overlooking the town. It was a severe-looking building with steep pitched eaves and shuttered windows that seemed to scowl down on Dover Station. "I just hate seeing this town being taken in by that damned carpetbagger."

"Grant hasn't fooled everyone in town, Aaron." Katherine caressed his hand. "Why, I think you've beaten him every time he's come against you. You stopped the robberies he ran last year, and outfoxed him when he tried to run you out of town. You've even found out about his alliance with the Hancock clan."

Mackey blushed. He had told her too much in the dark safety of her room late at night. But he hadn't told her about Grant's involvement with the dead women in the fire. He hadn't told her about King. Some secrets he had to bear alone.

He looked around to make sure no one could overhear them, but remembered she had barred her guests from eating on the porch. Being the owner of the hotel had its privileges. "I don't know if killing Henry Hancock made things better or worse, and I don't care, either. Judge Forester signed a paper on him, so he got what he had coming."

"That's the man you should be worried about," Katherine said, picking up their conversation from the previous night, "not James Grant. I've read the judge's correspondence to you. He's very angry that you haven't relocated to Helena where you belong. He's threatening to complain to Washington, Aaron. To the president himself!"

Mackey knew she was right. "I'll send him a telegram and calm him down."

"A trip to Helena might not be a bad idea." Katherine sipped her coffee. "For both of us."

Mackey cursed himself for not thinking of it that way. A romantic week or so away with Katherine would be like a dream come true. Of course, it would be a scandal, but whispers and rumors had never meant much to them when Mackey was still married. Now that he was free, they mattered even less. "I like the way you think sometimes, Mrs. Campbell."

"Only sometimes?"

Mackey smiled the way only she could make him. "Don't want you getting too full of yourself."

She set down her cup and kissed him on the cheek before whispering, "As I recall, you like a lot of other things about me, too."

Mackey felt himself blushing again when he heard a man clear his throat from the bottom step of the porch. He saw it was the Pinkerton man—Robert Lagrange. Mackey was glad the detective was well out of earshot of what Katherine had just whispered.

He tipped his bowler to Katherine. "I hope I'm not intruding, Mrs. Campbell." He looked at Mackey. "Good morning, Marshal."

Mackey wiped his face with his napkin, hoping his blushing ceased before the Pinkerton saw it. "Morning, Lagrange. Come on over. You're not interrupting anything."

Lagrange swept off his hat before pulling out a chair and taking a seat at their table. "A beautiful morning, isn't it? Without a hint of the ugliness that happened only a few short hours ago. The fire, I mean. And those four unfortunates who were found in it."

He grinned as he tapped the newspaper next to Mackey's plate. "It appears that Mr. Harrington has missed his calling. With such a gift for fiction, he should have been a novelist. At least he made your father out to be a hero."

"Like you said, fiction." Mackey was interested in talking about more than his father's reputation. "I'm more concerned with how *you* write, Lagrange. Billy told me you were sending a report to your boss in Chicago by post."

"And to my client in New York City," Lagrange said. Katherine and Mackey knew he meant Mr. Rice without having to say the man's name. "I just dropped it off this morning. It's as complete a retelling of the murder scene as humanly possible. I took the liberty of including information that the Hancock family is working with our mutual enemy toward a purpose that remains unknown as of yet. I made it clear that it is our strong assumption that the new sawmill operation on River Street is most certainly part of it."

Mackey was sorry the news about the opium den hadn't made it into Lagrange's report, but there hadn't been time. After the fire, it didn't seem important anymore, even though Mackey knew it was. "That ought to catch Mr. Rice's attention."

"There's more to it than that," Lagrange said. "After the fire last night, I decided to earn my keep by doing a little detecting. People always love to talk after a big event like a fire, so I made my way to the Ruby, where the skin was still a bit thin from your altercation there earlier that day."

Mackey winced because he hadn't told Katherine about that.

"What altercation?" she asked.

"Just a dustup between me and one of the loudmouths of the Hancock family," Mackey assured her. "Go on, Lagrange."

"I don't know if it was because of the late hour or the excitement of the fire or the rotgut I paid to have poured down their throats, but I found quite a few acquaintances of the Hancock family willing to talk ill about them. The customers were upset the family has cornered the market on illegal activities on the outskirts of town without any fight from Underhill's policemen."

Mackey knew the Hancock clan was working with Grant, but he didn't know they had already begun to dig in. "What kind of activities?"

Lagrange glanced at Katherine before looking down at the table. "The kind a gentleman hesitates to discuss in front of a lady. The kind that cater to the basest appetites of the miners and loggers in the hills. And people right here in town."

"You mean whores?" Katherine surprised him by asking. "Or opium? Or whiskey? Perhaps all three."

She seemed to enjoy Lagrange's discomfort. "I'm a cavalry officer's widow and a trained nurse, Mr. Lagrange. I was already well acquainted with the results of life's basest appetites, as you call them, when you were still pulling pigtails in the schoolyard."

"Only if that school was college," Lagrange charmed, "for it is impossible that you should be that much older than I. And I apologize for attempting to talk around you."

Mackey admired the detective's ability to turn an insult from Katherine into a compliment to her. But he wasn't interested in compliments. "How long have the Hancock bunch been running the ragged end of things at the mines and the logging camps?"

"For about a month," Lagrange told him. "But I hear the family is planning on increasing their presence here in town over the next few weeks. They've already begun by quietly buying up some of the newer saloons that have opened up and will open up in the near future."

Mackey slumped back in his wicker chair. It was worse than he thought. "Grant's already making money hand over fist with the legitimate businesses in town. Why's he letting the Hancock bunch in town? He can't control them."

Katherine spoke before either of them. "But he thinks he can."

She acquired the far-off look Mackey remembered she used to get in the months after he had rescued her from Darabont and his men. The look she got when she had been too afraid to step off the front porch of her own hotel. A look he had hoped he'd never see again.

"Power is the only kind of currency a man like James Grant wants or understands," she went on. "Money means nothing to him. Neither does finery or fancy things. None of it means anything unless he can keep his boot heel on someone's neck and brag to the world about it. Grant is different. He'll go the long way around to getting it if he has to. He'll use a smile instead of a cudgel, but the result is the same. He wins. Everyone else loses."

Mackey took her hand and gently squeezed it to bring her back to him. She smiled and squeezed his hand in return.

Lagrange cleared his throat. "My new friends at the Ruby intimated to me that the Hancock men have also robbed several small banks in surrounding towns, as well as stagecoaches well out of Dover Station limits. A few wagons carrying goods to neighboring towns have also been victimized."

"I knew about that," Mackey said, "but I never thought the damned fool would let them into town."

"I don't think Walter will stand for that," Katherine said. "He has his faults, but he's a good man."

Lagrange said, "Even the best of men can be deceived when they chose to be. I don't think he's part of this, but he'd be a fool not to be aware of it. I'm certain some of the men on his police force must know about it, since they never accidentally run a Hancock man into that brand-new jail they have in the Municipal Building."

Mackey had sat down to breakfast that morning with an uneasy feeling in his stomach. What he had read in the paper and what he had just heard from Lagrange only made him feel worse. Having suspicions about something was one thing. Having them confirmed was something else.

He hadn't wanted to mention Grant's latest demands in front of Katherine, but now since she had already heard so much, there was no reason to keep anything from her.

"Billy and I had a run-in with Grant last night," Mackey told them. "He said Van Dorn has had enough of frontier living and is looking to move back to New York City. Grant will be running things until Mr. Rice sends out a replacement."

Lagrange pulled a telegram from the inside pocket of his coat. "Perhaps that is why Mr. Rice sent you a telegram this morning. The clerk saw me passing this way from the post office and asked if I would mind delivering this to you. The poor man seemed quite overwhelmed. Telegrams seem to be flying into and out of this place at a record pace."

Mackey took the telegram and opened it. It was, indeed, from Mr. Rice. And he didn't like what he read.

"It's bad news, isn't it?" Katherine said.

Mackey folded the telegram and tucked it into his shirt pocket. "Mr. Rice has asked me and Billy to escort Mr. Van Dorn out of the territory, at least as far south as Laramie."

"It makes sense to me," Katherine said. "Mr. Van Dorn is a very important man. It stands to reason that Rice would want you two guarding his business partner."

Mackey didn't want to take the time to rehash the

ugly scene in Grant's office the night before. It would take too long to tell and serve no purpose in the end. "Grant practically ordered us to do the same thing last night. This telegram makes it official."

Lagrange ran a hand over his carefully combed hair. "Sounds to me like Grant really wants you and Billy on that train for some reason."

"Which is exactly why you shouldn't put him on that train at all," Katherine said.

Both men looked at her. She smiled at the attention. "Well, it's obvious isn't it? If Grant wants Van Dorn on that train and he wants Aaron and Billy to guard him, then no good can come of it. Rather than worry about how to protect Mr. Van Dorn, change the way he's traveling entirely."

Mackey and Lagrange looked at each other.

"It's a brilliant idea," Lagrange said.

"If Van Dorn will go for it," Mackey said. "And it'll be tough to talk him out of taking the train without Grant hearing about it. If we make a change with the railroad, Grant's people will tell him about it. If we send a wire for more men at Chidester, Grant will read about it because he gets a copy of every telegram along the railroad lines." He looked at Lagrange. "He's probably already seen the telegram you sent Mr. Rice."

Lagrange seemed to have an idea. "How many men do you have at your disposal in the marshal's service?"

"Right now, it's just me and Billy," Mackey was sad to tell him. "Everyone else is either retiring, retired, or just quit. I've got one or two men in the far reaches of the territory, but none I could call in here in time for this. And Judge Forester would kill me if I pulled any men into Dover Station. He's annoyed with me about not being in Helena all the time as it is."

Mackey drummed his fingers on the table as an idea began to gel in his mind. He looked at Lagrange. "I've got a plan, but I'm going to need your people to help me do it."

The Pinkerton was all smiles. "Then enlighten me, Marshal."

Chapter 20

Over the next week, Mackey saw more members of the Hancock clan on the streets of Dover Station.

Neither he nor Billy had seen any of them ride in during the day, so they figured they must have ridden in after nightfall. He may not have known when they got there, but their presence was unmistakable.

They had taken to wearing black armbands to mark the mourning of the death of Henry Hancock. None dared called it murder around Mackey or Billy, but that's the reason they gave when neither lawman was close enough to hear it.

Underhill was sitting on the jailhouse bench next to Billy, sipping coffee, when a group of five of them rode past. Each of the riders was wearing their armbands with the pride of a new sergeant who had just ironed the chevrons on his sleeve.

Mackey stopped rocking in his chair when they rounded the corner on to Front Street. His rifle was in the rack inside the jailhouse, but the handle of his Peacemaker was within easy reach on his belt.

The pack of five riders slowed to a halt in front of the jailhouse. A bearded man who looked like the eldest of the youngsters called out to Underhill. "Kind of surprised at you, Commissioner. I'd have thought you'd keep better company."

Underhill set his mug on the bench and slowly stood up. His rifle was at his side. "I look like I give a damn about what you think, boy?"

"Not especially," the Hancock man admitted, "but that could change in the blink of an eye." He grinned at Mackey and Billy. "Just ask your two friends here. They went from being just a couple of town lawmen one minute to being federals the next."

The rider next to him leaned over his horse and spat a stream of tobacco juice into the thoroughfare. "Never had much use for federals, have we, Danny?"

"No," the one called Danny answered. "I can't say we ever have, especially after how they treated poor Hank."

Mackey lifted his head just enough so the flat brim of his hat allowed him to see Danny Hancock. "I went after Hank because I had a warrant signed by Judge Forester for his arrest. I shot Hank because he refused to come along peacefully. Shot his friends, too, for the same reason."

"Ambushed them while they were sleeping, the way I heard it," said another Hancock man. "Gunned them down like they was nothing but dogs."

But Mackey kept his eyes on Danny. He was the leader. If trouble came, it would start with him. "I had paper on him. I gave him the chance to surrender. He didn't. Straight up or over the saddle. Makes no difference to me. You'd do well to remember that." He tilted his head as he looked at Danny. "You got paper on you, son?"

"Kind of wish I did at the moment," Danny said, "so I could do what Hank never had the chance to do. Take you on in a straight-up fight."

Billy spoke before Mackey did. "Don't need any paper on you for that, Danny. You could do that right now if you've got enough sand to try."

Danny Hancock's horse fussed and tossed its head up.

All three lawmen drew on the Hancock family. Mackey's Peacemaker had cleared leather first, but not by much.

The riders flinched and galloped off toward River Street. None of them made a move toward their guns.

Mackey was the last to holster his weapon. "Guess they didn't have enough sand after all."

"Quick to ride off, though," Underhill said as he sat back down next to Billy. "More and more of them seem to ride into town every day. All of them blood kin, too. Normally, I'd write it off as a lie, but they all look alike. One just as nasty as the next. And now that they're getting numbers behind them, they're awfully cocky, too. That's a bad combination."

"Yes, it is," Billy said.

"And every time I think there's no more to come in," Underhill went on, "another five more ride in. How many of them could be living in that godforsaken town anyway?"

"Heard their grandparents had fifteen kids," Billy said. "Twenty if you count the ones that died."

Mackey had always been impressed by Billy's knack for finding out and remembering bits of information like that.

"Twenty kids," Underhill repeated as he crossed his legs. "Damn."

"They causing any trouble in town?" Mackey asked the commissioner.

"Some," Underhill said, "but nothing I can put them in jail for."

"You could put Danny Hancock in jail for spitting in the street like he just did," Billy reminded him. "That is, if you want to."

"I couldn't hold him long enough for a judge to see him. And in case you two haven't noticed, Mayor Grant isn't in any hurry to be inviting judges into Dover Station."

"Arresting them would send a message," Mackey said. "Remind them there are rules, even in a town they've been told they own."

Underhill glared at him. "No one owns this town, Mackey. The Montana Territory is still part of the United States of America. We've got laws here, and I'm paid to enforce them."

"Billy and I'll back you up whenever you decide to do that." He looked at Underhill until the commissioner looked away.

"I'll keep that in mind. Not many of my men want to cross the Hancock clan." Underhill picked up his mug and looked down into it as if seeking answers. "They outnumber us now, and even before they did, no one wanted to go up against them. Didn't seem to be much of an appetite for it."

"From the mayor, you mean," Billy said.

"It doesn't matter who from, Aaron," Underhill said. "Just matters that it's happening. In my town." He set the mug back on the bench and looked out over Front Street. "Hell, maybe I'm just fooling myself. This ain't my town and never will be. It's yours, no matter what badge either of us wears. There was a time not too long ago when two men could control it, but not anymore. Maybe it's Grant's town now."

Neither Billy nor Mackey could argue with that.

Underhill inclined his head toward River Street. "Tent City has given way to River Street, but it's still the same cesspool it ever was. Guess that's why a chunk of the Hancock family has moved in there."

Underhill looked right and nodded in that direction. "Got a whole bunch of new saloons opening up each week, one worse than the next. They make the old Tin Horn over there look like Buckingham Palace. A few respectable enough businesses are opening up on the far side of town near the *Record* building, but not enough to keep the bad element down."

"Won't be able to keep the bad element down with the men you have," Mackey said. "Or the mayor you have, either. He's bringing them in here to cement his control on the town as soon as Van Dorn leaves."

"You don't know that for certain. And just because your rich friend back in New York says it don't make it so." But the fire quickly went out of Underhill. "But I suspect you might be right."

Billy added more salt to the big man's open wound. "Grant will control the town's politics, the town's business interests, and the town's vices. He'll pay a man a wage for working in one of his offices or his mills, and his whorehouses and saloons will get most of it back. Even if he has to cut the Hancocks in for a share, it'll be worth it to him in the long run. And when he gets sick of them being around, he'll probably be powerful enough by then to bring the army in to flush them out."

Underhill squirmed like a kid getting his first haircut. "I don't like hearing the man run down like that, Billy. He's done a lot of good for this town." He gestured toward the Municipal Building across the street. "Even you have to admit that's a beautiful building. So are all of the others that he's put up. Finer than anything they have in Helena, I'd wager. That'll count once statehood comes."

"Fine buildings don't make fine towns," Mackey said. "People do. And right now, you're stuck in the middle between a crooked mayor and the thugs he's brought in to run the place when Van Dorn gets on that train back east tomorrow."

Underhill brought his big fist down on the bench. "And what about Mr. Rice? He's sitting back east making money off all of this. Van Dorn and Grant work for him. Why the hell isn't he sending someone out here who can run his company without Grant?"

Mackey knew why. Billy did, too. But they didn't dare share anything with Underhill. Mr. Rice knew James Grant was a corrupt, murderous thug. He couldn't prove it any more than Mackey could, but he knew it just the same. And, for better or worse, the Dover Station Company was making money. Quite a bit of it. Rice may be a powerful man, but even he had people to answer to. Investors, mostly, and investors didn't care how they earned returns on their money as long as they earned it.

Mr. Rice didn't go after James Grant, because Mr. Rice wasn't entirely sure he could beat him. There wasn't enough evidence to arrest him for anything and having him killed could threaten the success of the Dover Station Company. And with Silas Van Dorn going back to New York, Rice's weak grip on the company he had founded would be gone.

"Mr. Rice is a complicated man with complicated interests," Mackey said. "He's all the way back in New York City and we're way the hell out here. He might own the railroad, but owning it and having a say over how it's run are completely different things. We can get Grant if we want to, but we're going to have to be smart about it and we're going to have to do it publicly and legally. That's the only way to stop him once and for all."

He looked at Billy for a sign of encouragement, but his old friend did nothing. He knew his deputy had good reasons for distrusting Underhill. Good reasons. His instincts had always been solid, and Mackey had never gone wrong by following them.

But taking down James Grant would mean taking risks the marshal had never taken before. He decided to take one now.

Mackey decided it was time to finally put the question to Underhill. "Would you be up for that, Walter? For taking Grant down if we found a way to do it legally?"

Underhill drained the rest of his coffee and looked down into the mug again. "I took an oath to uphold the law, and no one's above the law. If he can be brought before a judge, then I'm all for it. I'll lose more than half my officers if I do it, but I won't care. Their loyalty is to Grant, not me."

"Might not be as clear cut as that," Billy said. "Might have to bend the law a bit in this case."

"Then you can count me out." Underhill stood up

to stretch and brought his coffee mug back into the jailhouse. "I'll help you take him down if it's legal or if you've got a paper with a judge's signature on it, but I won't abide anything else. Not even from either of you."

Underhill ducked his head as he walked out of the jailhouse the way he always did, even though he didn't have to do so. "Good day, gentlemen, and thanks for the coffee."

Mackey and Billy watched the town of Dover Station's commissioner of police touch the brim of his hat to some ladies passing in a carriage as he headed back to the Municipal Building. The ladies giggled and waved at the tall, handsome lawman with the broad shoulders and long, curly blond hair.

He had come a long way from being the disgraced drunk who had ridden into town the year before.

"Don't worry," Billy said. "I'll kill him when the time comes."

Mackey quietly cursed his deputy for practically reading his mind once again. "Let's hope it doesn't come to that."

He lifted his face to catch a slight breeze. "Never been hopeful men, you and me."

Mackey sipped his coffee and prayed his deputy was wrong.

Chapter 21

The day of Silas Van Dorn's departure was appropriately dreary.

A steady light rain fell at the station as Mackey and Billy loaded their mounts on to the stock car after stowing the rest of their gear on the train. Mackey didn't have to remind the hostler to be careful of Adair. He had loaded her onboard the Great Northwestern Railway before and knew her temperament.

With their animals secure, Mackey and Billy went back to Mr. Van Dorn's private coach. Billy produced the key that only he and Mr. Van Dorn had to open it. Not even the conductor could enter the car without their permission. Restricted access to the coach was one of the provisions that Mackey had insisted upon before agreeing to protect Mr. Van Dorn.

The second was that one of them, Mackey, Billy, or Lagrange, was to be in the rail car with Van Dorn at all times. No exceptions. Not even Mr. Van Dorn could refuse.

James Grant agreed to every condition on Mr. Van Dorn's behalf without the slightest hesitation.

That didn't make Mackey feel any better about the

notion of a plot. He had expected the man to have put up at least some kind of an argument, especially about having an armed guard with Van Dorn.

Grant had not even objected to Lagrange's demand that ten Pinkerton men be on the train throughout the entire trek to New York to give Mr. Van Dorn an added layer of security. Lagrange had also been allowed to choose the men personally.

Yet, despite all of Grant's agreement, Mackey knew the man was planning something. He knew it in his bones. He just had to figure out how he was going to pull it off.

Billy let out a low whistle as they walked through Van Dorn's private railcar. "This is finer than any house I've ever been in. A few churches, too."

Mackey knew it was typical of the kind of private railcar Mr. Rice offered on the Great Northwestern Railway. While Mr. Rice's personal car was far more ornate and completely encased in steel, this car had plenty of its own comforts.

It was adorned with deep red wallpaper and brass fittings. The windows had heavy drapery that hid iron shutters that could be lowered if the train was attacked.

The heavy wood furniture and brass chandeliers made the car feel small. There was also a private bedroom Van Dorn could use whenever he wanted. Mackey had seen to it the iron shutter in his room had already been lowered and locked into position over the window. Unlike the ones in Mr. Rice's personal car, these windows were not thick enough to be bulletproof. Since Van Dorn was most vulnerable when he was alone, Mackey decided the grand man would have to sacrifice scenery for safety.

The marshal sat in the plush chair next to the cabin's head door and checked the gold pocket watch Katherine had given him for the trip.

It was fifteen minutes until Van Dorn's coach was due to arrive at the station, which was exactly two minutes before the train was set to begin the first leg of its journey to Laramie, then on the long trek back east.

Van Dorn's effects had already been loaded into the car, so he only had to walk from his coach and into the private car.

Mackey would guard Van Dorn for the first eight-hour shift before Billy took over, then Lagrange. They would stay on that rotation until they reached Laramie and decided whether or not they should stay with Van Dorn farther on his journey.

At least, that was the plan he had submitted to James Grant.

What would actually happen was a different story.

He thought about that as he turned the watch over and read the words engraved on the back.

To the finest man
I've ever known.
With all my love,
KATHERINE.

He looked away before he welled up as he had when she had given it to him that morning. She always knew exactly what to say to him and how to say it.

Billy snapped him out of it by knocking on the wood paneling as he continued to look over the railcar. "This seems like this is a pretty solid set-up to me, Aaron. And with the extra guns on board, I can't see how Grant could get to Van Dorn. Maybe we're a bit too worried about this."

"It's Grant we're talking about." Mackey slid the watch back into his pocket. "You can't see him for what he is by looking at him straight on. You can only trust what you see out of the corner of your eye."

He stood up and motioned for Billy to unlock the door. "Let's get outside and wait for Van Dorn on the platform. I hear Grant and Underhill have a special send-off lined up for him."

"Probably a proclamation to his own greatness," Billy said.

Once again, Mackey saw there was no arguing with his deputy's logic.

From the station platform, Mackey watched the scene unfold with great ceremony. It reminded him more of a funeral than a farewell to the man who had helped transform the town.

Van Dorn's heavy black coach was pulled by two black drays with wild manes. The interlocking DSC emblem of the Dover Station Company was on the door. Twenty men from Underhill's police force formed a ragged honor guard that stretched from Van Dorn's black coach to the station platform. The ten remaining men formed a line from the platform to the private railcar, where Mackey and Billy awaited Van Dorn.

Robert Lagrange stepped out of the coach first and quickly walked through the cordon of men toward Mackey and Billy at the railcar.

"At least he's punctual," Lagrange told them as he joined them next to the railcar.

"I'd say that's Grant's doing," Mackey said. "He's probably anxious to see him leave town as fast as possible."

"There's nothing fast about Silas Van Dorn," Lagrange said. "If you haven't seen him in a while, prepare for a shock." He looked up at the gray skies. "Poor fellow looks like he might melt if it rains much harder than this."

Billy swore when the line of lawmen snapped to some form of attention when James Grant stepped out of the black coach first. He wore a top hat and black morning coat that made him appear slimmer than he was.

"They call that attention?" Billy snapped. "Looks like a bunch of damned rag dolls."

Mackey remembered Billy had been a stickler for ceremony when they had been in the cavalry. "At ease, Sergeant."

They watched Underhill step out next and heard the springs of the coach groan as he put all of his considerable brawn on one side of it.

Silas Van Dorn came out next. He had been a pale, skinny man of about forty the last time Mackey had seen him about six months before.

Now, he looked like he had aged twenty years since then.

His cheeks were sallow, and his skin was almost as white as porcelain. He was stooped over, even after Underhill reached up and practically carried him out of the carriage. He crept past the honor guard of gunmen with the aid of a cane. Mackey decided Lagrange hadn't been exaggerating. Van Dorn looked like he might shatter if he fell.

"Don't remember him being so delicate," Billy observed.

"Me neither," Mackey agreed.

"Don't bother trying to talk to him," Lagrange said. "He speaks barely above a whisper, if at all, and even then, only to Grant. We won't have many dealings with him on the ride east. He's even brought his own butler with him to tend to him, even cook for him."

Mackey didn't like hearing that. "A butler could complicate things."

"Don't worry about him," Lagrange said. "He's quite the dandy, and that means something coming from me. Goes to bed at ten o'clock each night, regular as clockwork. Doesn't appear to have much use for Grant, either, but that's just a hunch of mine. I don't think he'll be a problem."

But Mackey did worry as he watched Van Dorn stop every few steps as Underhill and Grant flanked him, with a man Mackey took to be the butler trailing close behind.

Mackey hadn't counted on Van Dorn being in such poor condition, and he began to wonder if they might have to scrap their plans to protect him. "But Van Dorn being so feeble could wreck our plan."

"Nothing we can't handle," Billy said. "Him being frail could make things easier."

"We'll see how he is once he's on board," Lagrange said. "He's not just feeble. He's downright brittle."

Mackey decided he was making everything worse by second-guessing himself. "Everything goes as planned until we know more."

The matter settled for now, they touched the brims of their hats as Mr. Van Dorn crept closer to the private car, guided by Grant.

"Marshal," he greeted, his voice barely above a whisper. "Deputy Sunday. Mr. Lagrange here says you have been charged with providing my protection?"

"Along with ten Pinkerton men spread throughout the rest of the train," Mackey told him while looking at Grant to make sure the point stuck.

"You're in the best of care, sir," James Grant said loudly. It was like he was speaking for the benefit of the people who had been drawn by the spectacle on the platform. "If Aaron Mackey could save Dover Station from the likes of Darabont, he's well-suited to take care of you on your journey, sir."

But Mr. Van Dorn seemed more concerned about navigating the steps up to his railcar than receiving any compliments from his former assistant. He grasped the railing with frail, thin hands and insisted on pulling himself up without assistance.

Underhill shook Mackey's hand, then Billy's. "Godspeed, gentlemen. Here's to an uneventful journey."

"Good luck with the Hancock mess," Mackey called after him. "Looks like it'll get worse before it gets better."

Grant quickly closed the short distance between them. He was almost as tall as Mackey, but the top hat made them look the same size. "Keep your voice down, damn you. We don't want people getting the wrong idea."

"Or the right idea," Mackey said, "depending on how you look at it."

Lagrange and Billy trailed into Van Dorn's private car, leaving the mayor and the marshal alone.

Grant looked at the policemen still standing at attention and motioned for them to move on. They hurried into the station, happy to be out of the rain.

When they were alone, Grant said, "I would have thought that after the fire, you would have learned that you and I are better off working together than against each other."

"We'll work together just fine," Mackey said, "as soon as you sign a confession listing all the people you've either killed or had killed since you've come to Dover Station. If Judge Forester acquits you, I'll give you a ride back to Dover Station personally. If he hangs you, I'll see to it they hire a hangman who knows how to tie a good knot."

"Normally, I admire determination in a man," Grant said, "but in this case, it's bordering on stupidity. You simply can't get over the fact that I've already won, can you, Aaron? I'm not only the mayor but the man who runs the Dover Station Company and therefore the town."

Grant shook his head in pity. "You can't live with the notion that another man came into your town and supplanted you as the favorite son. I can't say as I really blame you. Dover might not have been much before me, but it was all you had, wasn't it? The people here idolized you, didn't they? Now, you're just a story the newcomers tell in saloons. A legend your father spreads in the general store. And none of it would have been remotely possible if it hadn't been for me."

Mackey resented everything Grant had just said, mostly because it had the hint of truth.

But he thumbed the U.S. Marshal badge pinned to his lapel. "Whatever I have was enough to get me federal authority over the territory, Grant, and that includes Dover Station. That means you."

But James Grant smiled. "The only thing you've become is the worst thing that can happen to a man like you. You've become a legend in your own time. A legend I helped to build and one I'm going to enjoy tearing down."

The locomotive cut loose with the whistle, and Mackey climbed up to the lowest step on Van Dorn's car as the conductor yelled, "All aboard!"

Mackey leaned forward so Grant could hear him over all of the noise. "And just think about how famous I'll be when I'm known as the man who brought down James Grant."

Grant said something, but Mackey couldn't hear it. He hopped up onto Van Dorn's private railcar as the great wheels began to move and the train slowly pulled out of the station.

CHAPTER 22

Mackey sat in the chair next to the head door of the railcar and watched John, Van Dorn's butler and cook, fuss over his employer.

He watched John tie a large napkin around Van Dorn's neck before the wealthy man picked up the spoon to tuck into his soup. Pea soup. The smell and color of it, combined with the movement of the train, all served to turn Mackey's stomach.

The spoon trembled in Van Dorn's hand, and he gently set it back down on the desk. He told John to leave them. The butler frowned at Mackey on his way out of the railcar. He knew the frown wasn't directed at him. It was because of his employer's condition.

Now that they were alone, Van Dorn finally looked at the marshal. "Do you really need to sit that far away?" His voice was weak. "It's only the two of us in here. Why don't you sit closer so we can speak more comfortably?"

"No reason for us to speak at all," Mackey said. "Mr. Rice wants you protected. I can do that better by guarding this door and having a clear view of the rear door behind you."

Mr. Van Dorn's frown deepened. "There's no reason why this needs to be so unpleasant, Marshal."

"No reason for it to be pleasant, either" Mackey countered, "especially after what you've unleashed on my town."

"Forgive me," Van Dorn said. "I suppose you're right. Success and prosperity are bitter pills for a town to swallow."

"Nothing wrong with either of those things," Mackey said. "I'm talking about James Grant."

"Ah, there it is." The millionaire smiled, showing teeth that were as yellow and crooked as some Mackey had seen in the mouths of the Hancock family. "The green-eyed monster of myth finally rears its ugly head. Your jealousy of Mr. Grant's success is beneath you, Marshal."

"No jealousy," Mackey told him. "Just resentful as hell about all of the trouble he's caused since he got here. Resentful of you for letting him do it."

"I've heard this sort of nonsense before." Van Dorn pulled on his bib until the knot opened and he tossed it on the desk in disgust. He looked out the window at the blur of Montana countryside as the train sped along. "Progress is always difficult, Marshal, especially on the native born of a place. Just ask the savages who sold Manhattan Island to the Dutch. Or ask the Sioux or the Apache about their resentment of our manifest destiny. Given your experiences, I shouldn't think I would need to remind you about them."

"Comanche, too," Mackey added. "But the Sioux call themselves Lakota. 'Sioux' is an Algonquin term meaning 'enemy.'"

"Call them what you will," Van Dorn said. "I call them history. Recent history perhaps, but history just the same. And it is the winners who write history, Marshal. I'm surprised the Hero of Adobe Flats needs to be reminded of this."

Mackey had never accepted that term and resented Van Dorn for using it.

The millionaire went on. "The past is an enemy that needs to be conquered if the present is to triumph. America has always been a nation of the future, about that land just beyond the horizon. That next obstacle that needs to be overcome."

He grabbed his bib from the desk and tried to fold it properly despite his shaking hands. "People like James Grant understand that the past, no matter how quaint and comfortable it may be in our memory, only hinders progress. He is a man who understands that change is inevitable and is willing to do whatever it takes to see to it that said change occurs."

"By building up a town and ruining it in the process?" Mackey asked.

"Pulling down a few old, ramshackle buildings that were about to fall down anyway is hardly destroying a town, Marshal."

"But leading bands of criminals looking to feed off what he has built *does* destroy it," Mackey said. "No one in town minds progress. My father and his friends didn't just wander in to the wilderness to start Dover Station on a whim. They knew life would be hard, but the risks were worth it. They don't resent Mr. Rice or you for making the town better, but they do resent you for giving Grant a free hand to do whatever he wants."

Van Dorn tucked a withered hand under his chin and looked out the window again. With the natural light hitting his pale skin, his hand looked almost transparent. He had never been a robust man, but Mackey could see his health had failed a great deal since he had first come to Montana.

Or since James Grant came to Dover Station.

That made Mackey think of something. "It could be said James Grant has even ruined you, sir."

"Rumors," Van Dorn murmured. "Scandalous innuendo. Rubbish and nothing more. Successful men are always the objects of such rebuke if they dare to rise above the rabble. Look at what happened to you when you returned home from the army. I've heard all of the stories about you and the fetching Campbell widow who chased you all the way out here only to find you had married another."

Van Dorn caught himself and stuck a bony finger in the air as if he had just remembered something. "Forgive me. Unlike your slander against James Grant, the rumors about you were actually true."

Mackey refused to take the bait. "Every bit as true as the rumors about Grant. You're either too blind or too busy to see it."

"Then why haven't you brought him before a judge?" Van Dorn countered. "Probably because you haven't the slightest bit of evidence against him, which is why Mr. Grant is free to serve the good people of Dover Station and you are simply a bitter, forgotten young man."

"Just because I don't have any proof doesn't mean Grant is innocent," Mackey told him. "And any man who has gotten as rich as you have should know that."

Van Dorn scoffed and went back to looking out the window while his soup continued to get cold. Mackey could not understand how a man's health could fail so much in only a few months.

Unless it had help.

"When did you start getting sick, Mr. Van Dorn?"

"I don't see how that is any of your concern." He looked at his hand, which shook despite his obvious attempt to control it. "I'm just not feeling particularly well at the moment, nothing more."

But Mackey wouldn't let it go. "In fact, you haven't been in good health since you got to Montana, have you?"

Van Dorn kept looking out the window. "I know what this is. You can't question James Grant in a courtroom, so you're turning your frustration on me. Well, you can just forget it. I refuse to be interrogated on my own train car."

But as the pieces began falling into place, Mackey was certain. "I think we're talking about a matter of life or death, Mr. Van Dorn. Your life and death."

Van Dorn glared at him from across the room. The man may have appeared weak and gaunt, but he still had a fire burning somewhere within him. "Don't be so dramatic."

"Then answer my question. Did you get sick after you came to Montana or after James Grant came to work for you?"

Van Dorn folded his bony, quaking hands across his stomach. "Damn you, Marshal."

That was the answer Mackey had been looking for. "It was after, wasn't it?"

Van Dorn looked out the window again and brought a trembling hand to his mouth.

He was not angry. He was frightened. And he had asked himself these questions already.

Mackey got up out of his chair and began to approach Van Dorn's desk. "You started feeling sick after Grant came to work for, and you've been slowly getting sicker ever since, haven't you? How bad is it?"

Van Dorn gestured toward the window. "It's the infernal air out here, I tell you. There's no character to it. No buildings or people to absorb it and filter it like in a large city. Nothing to keep the impurities of nature from my lungs. Country living has never held much appeal to me, and now I see my constitution is simply ill suited for this climate."

But Mackey ignored his defense. This was too important. "Did you start getting sick before or after Grant hired your servant?"

"Grant didn't hire John," Van Dorn snapped. "I brought him out here from New York after—" He looked back out the window again.

Mackey finished the sentence for him. "After you already started feeling sick. Isn't that what you were going to say? That's why you sent for him, isn't it?"

Van Dorn responded with silence.

Mackey knew the harder he pushed him, the more likely Van Dorn would ignore him. He would have to go at him another way. "I'm only asking questions you've already asked yourself, sir. Or should have."

Van Dorn finally looked at him. "I began feeling much better when John prepared my meals," Van Dorn admitted. "I had even stopped taking the elixir Mr. Grant had been giving me to improve my health. But when my headaches became so unbearable, I began to feel worse. That elixir proved to be invaluable to me. I don't think I could have lived out here this long without it."

Mackey knew there was something more going on here than Van Dorn had allowed himself to believe. "Did you ever have Doc Ridley take a look at you?"

"You would have known if he had," Van Dorn said. "So would the rest of the town. The man is an insufferable gossip."

Mackey took that as a no. "Did any other doctors look at you? Maybe one who worked for the railroad?"

"There was no need," Van Dorn insisted. "I abhor doctors, and my health suffered from the climate. Nothing more. That's why I'm heading back to Manhattan where I belong."

"Was going back your idea?" Mackey asked. "Or did James Grant tell you that, too?"

Again, Silas Van Dorn's silence said it all.

"I believe there's a doctor on board this train," Mackey said. "I'm going to bring him back here so he can examine you. We're going to get to the bottom of what's wrong with you once and for all."

"How dare you treat me like a child on my own railroad!" Van Dorn glared up at him with all of the menace a sick man could muster. "You will do no such thing. I forbid it! Get out of my car this instant!"

But Mackey held his ground. "Mr. Rice practically ordered me on this train to keep you alive, Van Dorn. Not just from bullets and bandits, but from everything that might kill you. The doctor is going to examine you right now if I have to hold you down while he does it. And you're going to answer every one of his questions truthfully or your butler will."

Van Dorn broke off the glare and looked down at his desk, defeated. "He would, too. He's been worried."

"Sounds like he's had reason."

Much of the fire that had burned in the wealthy man had gone out. "It's this damnable climate, I tell you."

But Mackey knew it was much worse than that.

Mackey and Lagrange stood up when Van Dorn's butler, John, and Dr. Eric Goodman from the Great Northwestern Railway stepped out from Mr. Van Dorn's bedroom and quietly closed the door behind them.

The butler lowered himself into a chair. He looked almost as bad as his employer.

Lagrange asked the doctor, "What did you find out, Eric?"

"I'm afraid it's not good news," Dr. Goodman said.

John stifled a sob and buried his face in his hands.

Mackey knew that couldn't be a good sign. "What is it?"

"His condition hasn't been caused by the harsh

Montana climate, but from a rather nasty addiction to opium."

"Opium?" Lagrange said. "Are you sure?"

"No," Dr. Goodman admitted, "but based on what John has told me, combined with the patient's recollection, I would say that someone was giving Mr. Van Dorn regular doses of opium seemingly without his knowledge. My guess is that it's most likely laudanum in his daily tea or coffee. It's normally given to help women with their monthly pains or to babies to quiet colic, but it is also regularly abused by people of all classes of society."

Mackey was not surprised. He had seen his share of dope fiends in towns that had sprung up in the various posts he had been assigned to in the cavalry. He knew the signs and should have seen them in Van Dorn this morning.

Now he understood why Grant kept Van Dorn locked away in that dingy house for months at a time. He didn't want anyone to see how much Van Dorn had failed. He didn't want anyone to see that Van Dorn had lost complete control over his own life.

"He's hooked, isn't he?" Mackey asked.

"I'm afraid so," Dr. Goodman said. "To the point where eliminating it from his system may prove enough of a shock to be fatal." He looked back at the butler. "I was quite surprised John didn't bring any laudanum for his employer on this trip. But when I saw the look on his face, I realized—"

"I didn't know," the butler sobbed.

"You took care of him every single day," Lagrange

said. "If you didn't know, it's because you didn't want to know."

"I never would've allowed him to use that poison. The man doesn't even drink spirits and only smokes a pipe on the rarest of occasions. If I had known what Grant was doing to him, I would have put a stop to it immediately."

"You might've tried," Mackey said. "But its claws were too deep into him then."

John continued, "Mr. Van Dorn told me his condition was due to a poor response to the elements. Of course, I asked permission to allow Doctor Ridley to examine him, but he said Mr. Grant was handling the matter. I even had the doctor come to the house one afternoon, but Mr. Van Dorn refused to see him. The man was only on the other side of the door and he wouldn't agree to see him."

"Mr. Van Dorn mentioned getting headaches," Dr. Goodman said. "That is a primary symptom of withdrawal, akin to the headache one receives the next morning from imbibing in too much alcohol the night before. The effects can be quite severe, so I can understand why Mr. Van Dorn would want to avoid them at all costs. It's easier to take whatever elixir James Grant provided rather than face the pain. He may not have realized he was addicted at first, but after a while, the body knows."

Mackey imagined that was why Van Dorn had stopped arguing. Mackey had hit too close to home. He had uncovered Van Dorn and Grant's secret. The dirtiest secret of all.

His addiction. The addiction James Grant had given him.

James Grant hadn't just assumed control of Dover Station when Mr. Van Dorn left town. He had been in control for much longer than that, only now, it was out in the open. And no one could stop him anytime soon.

No one, Mackey knew, except him.

"I don't care about what's been done to him before," the marshal said. "I care about how he is now and how he'll be for the rest of the trip back."

"In his present state," Dr. Goodman explained, "he won't be in good spirits. He's already going through massive withdrawal symptoms, which explains his gaunt appearance and involuntary spasms. But I've given him a dose of laudanum to help him rest. There are sanitariums he can go to back east to treat his addiction if he chooses. But if he maintains his current course, he will most certainly die by the end of the year. The drug has already robbed him of his appetite, which only serves to make him weaker. For now, the only way to ensure his health is to continue giving him regular doses of the same drug responsible for his ruin."

Dr. Goodman looked again at John, the butler. "Do you have any idea how he consumed it? Many people inject it into their veins, but I saw no such marks on his person."

"Mr. Grant must have added it to his afternoon or evening tea," John said. "It's the only meal I never prepared for him. And I never saw any bottles in his room or in his pockets like the one you used today."

Mackey gestured toward the doctor's medical bag. "Show me."

Goodman dug out a bottle of laudanum from his

bag and handed it to the marshal. "As I said, it has valid medicinal purposes, but only in controlled doses and not for a prolonged period of time. I'm afraid Mr. Van Dorn's dependency is at a level where he must continue to receive regular doses of laudanum or his body will react violently. Were he in a better physical state, I would be confident he could weather the storm of withdrawal. But given his weakness, I simply don't think his system could stand the shock."

Mackey held the brown bottle up to the light. "It's almost full."

"I only gave him a small dose," Goodman said. "Just enough to calm his nerves."

Mackey made sure the cork was firmly in place before pocketing it. "Good, because we're going to need to give him a whole lot more of this before the night is through."

Chapter 23

The train stopped outside of Chidester Station just as the last hint of sunlight disappeared from the western sky.

The conductors passed the word among the nervous passengers that all was fine and the delay was due to a slight problem with the boiler engine. They would be underway shortly. The passengers were justifiably nervous about any unscheduled stop as the Great Northwestern Railway had been the target of horrific robberies and holdups the previous year. The conductors told them they had nothing to worry about because the man who stopped those robberies was on board. Aaron Mackey, United States Marshal. The Savior of Dover Station. This news eased the nerves of some of the more nervous passengers.

Everyone felt even better when the whistle blew and the train was moving once again.

According to the pocket watch of the assistant conductor, the delay lasted less than five minutes.

The consequences would last much longer.

* * *

It was Lagrange's turn to sit in the chair by the door and guard Van Dorn's railcar. After lighting all of the lamps in the car, he sat on a sofa and settled in to begin reading the latest edition of *The Dover Station Record.*

He was impressed by how the paper had grown from a tawdry, local broadsheet rag into a respectable newspaper filled with advertisements from businesses throughout the territory. The editorial section had changed, too, from little more than a gossip column to a proper page giving voice to the concerns of people who would soon play a role in the territory's bid to become a state.

Lagrange thought the paper had certainly benefited from the new ownership of the Dover Station Company.

Lagrange had finished reading the paper by the time the train had completed its scheduled stop at Chidester Station, loaded new passengers and freight before resuming its long trek down to Laramie, then on to Chicago and finally New York.

He checked the clock on the wall and saw it was time to begin getting ready.

He set the paper on Van Dorn's desk and began lowering the iron shutters on the windows. He walked over to the large cabinet at the end of the car and hummed a vaguely familiar tune he couldn't quite place as he found the key to unlock it.

The cabinet had been installed by the railroad to serve as a discreet bar for the railcar's guest. However, since Mr. Van Dorn did not drink, Mackey, Billy, and Lagrange had decided to put it to better use.

As an armory for five Winchester '86s and one Greener shotgun with the rest of the space stocked up with boxes of ammunition for each. He knew the rifles and the shotgun were already loaded, for he had loaded them himself earlier that day. He figured he'd only need one of the Winchesters and the shotgun to handle the coming attack.

An attack that was bound to happen soon, as it would allow the Hancock clan to operate under the cover of darkness.

Lagrange had left strict instructions with the other Pinkerton men on the train to forget about the private car. Their concern was to protect the rest of the passengers at all cost. The attackers only cared about Mr. Van Dorn and his car. The Pinkertons were asked to make sure the fight didn't spill into the rest of the train. Lagrange was afraid that if he did too good a job in repelling the Hancock clan, the battle might spread to the rest of the train, resulting in a bloodbath where innocents were sure to get killed. He had no doubt his men would ultimately prevail, but the loss of life among customers would devastate the railroad. He was paid to protect the railroad, not to hurt their business.

Lagrange had just taken down the double-barreled shotgun when he heard the rattle of someone fiddling with the chain blocking the platform to the private railcar. The sound was unmistakable, even over the low rumble of the train wheels along the tracks.

He thumbed back one of the hammers on the Greener, aimed it at the back door and waited. He heard a clanging sound of metal on metal and knew someone must have been working on the link-and-pin coupling that attached the railcar to the rest of the train.

Their plan became obvious to him then. They probably wanted to let the railcar pull loose, then drift back down the track on its own before it hit the Weaver Tunnel southeast of Chidester. The grade began to incline there and, without an engine to keep pulling it along or a break to stop it, the railcar would slowly roll back to even ground, where it and its passenger would be easy pickings for the Hancock clan.

Lagrange and Mackey had expected that. They had even counted on it.

The detective heard the unmistakable sound of the pin being removed and the clanking of the coupling mechanism opening. He knew that the railcar would follow the rest of the train until the incline and gravity forced them apart.

He gave the kidnappers credit. It was a good plan.

But it wouldn't be good enough.

Lagrange doubted any shooting would start until the car was separated. Whoever they had sent to uncouple the car must have realized the railcar door was too thick to be shot through, which gave Lagrange some time. He spent it extinguishing the lamps in the car. He'd likely have enough trouble on his hands without worrying about a fire breaking out. Before extinguishing the last flame, he made sure the sliding door to Van Dorn's room was locked. He knew the lock could only stand a couple of rounds, but it would be enough to slow them down for a bit.

That was the point of all of this.

Most passengers could not feel the gradual rise of

the train as it began the climb toward Weaver Tunnel, but Lagrange was not most passengers. He had been a railroad detective long enough to notice such things, and it helped him get in position well in advance. He made sure the doors at both ends of the car were locked and bolted to make it just that much harder for the raiders to breach the car. He knew they would eventually, and when they did, Lagrange's work would begin.

Lagrange heard the coupling clank, then the motion of the lock giving way as the railcar slipped back from the rest of the consist. His fellow Pinkertons onboard the train would have felt it, too, but Lagrange had ordered them not to investigate under any circumstances. The main play likely wouldn't happen until the railcar was alone, miles away from the rest of the train.

Until then, Lagrange pulled his chair behind the corner of the railcar entrance and set the Winchester on the floor against the wall. He kept the Greener in hand and blew out the lamp.

He shifted his weight to account for the gradual movement of the railcar as it rolled downhill. He knew it was only a matter of time before they came to rest.

Al Brenner leaned against the platform railing as he pulled up his kerchief to mask his face. He wanted his identity hidden in case someone opened the door to see why the car was moving backward. If he was lucky, Van Dorn was the only one inside. If not, then whoever opened that door was in for one hell of a surprise.

He pulled his Colt and waited for someone to come out so he could keep the door open for when Carl and the others rode there. Carl and the others were still plenty hot over Mackey leaving them afoot the way he did, and Al wanted to look like a hero in his cousins' eyes. He hoped the marshal was inside. The man had thrown him a beating at the Ruby a few days ago, and he wanted to hurt the lawman more than Carl did.

Al's cousins always saw the Brenners as nothing more than dirt farmers who were dumber than the pigs they raised. Grabbing Van Dorn and killing Mackey before they got there would show them he was more than just a big, dumb hick.

But after waiting on the car platform for several minutes, he realized no one was coming outside. His hopes of revenge changed to the hope that meant that anyone inside the railcar was already asleep. The rest of the train had pulled well out of sight already. He figured it would take whoever was on board about an hour or more to stop the train, unload their horses, and come riding back for Van Dorn. That should give Carl plenty of time to get there and pry Van Dorn out of his car.

The railcar rolled to a stop, and Al knew it was time to signal the others.

Al holstered his Colt and searched his pockets for the matches Carl had given him before he'd ridden away from camp to board the train at Chidester. Brenner remembered he wasn't supposed to call his cousin Winslow anymore on account of him changing his name back to Hancock after his run-in with Mackey outside of town, but some habits were tougher to break than others.

Brenner would have changed his name to Hancock, too, but given how his daddy was still alive and had no love for his in-laws, Al did not want to feel his father's wrath.

Al found the matches in his pocket, struck one, and managed to light the lantern that hung beside the railcar door without burning his fingers.

He took the lantern off the hook and held it high, swinging it back and forth so Carl, Flint, and the others might spot it in the darkness and ride to his position. He didn't like being on this creaking old bucket alone. The railcar felt like a house on wheels, and he didn't trust something that made this much noise and wasn't living.

He felt better again when he heard the jangle of spurs and the sound of men riding along the Montana prairie, not along the track bed. His cousins had seen his signal and were on their way.

Brenner hung the lamp back on the hook and grabbed hold of the doorknob. He slowly tried to turn it, but found it was locked. No surprise there. Maybe the other door would be open. It had been at the very end of the train, after all, and they probably hadn't expected anyone to try to board a moving train from the rear.

With the lantern leading the way, he climbed down from the platform and walked beside the tracks to the back of the railcar. He stopped several times and listened, hoping he could hear something from inside, but all he heard was the sound of his cousins approaching carried on the night wind.

Brenner gingerly climbed up on the rear platform as quietly as a man his size possibly could. He knew Carl had told him to get clear of the car once he'd lit the lantern, but the notion of earning his cousin's respect outweighed any orders he may have been given.

He tried the knob of the rear door, hoping it would turn, but it didn't budge. Not an inch. Frustrated, he wanted to try to kick it in or, if that failed, shoot the damned thing, force his way inside, and drag the old man out of bed before Carl got there.

But there was no telling who might be waiting for him on the other side of the door, and Carl finding him dead would be an indignity he would have to carry with him through eternity.

Al waited at the side of the car until Carl and Flint showed up with the seven other Hancock men who rode with them. He was glad they had thought to trail another horse with them. It was a long walk back to Chidester from here.

"What's going on, dummy?" Carl whispered from the saddle.

"Don't call me dummy," Al said. "I was smart enough to unhook the railcar like you told me to, wasn't I?"

Carl didn't apologize. He looked at the railcar. "Anybody come out of there yet?"

"Nope," Al told them. "Not a sound or sign of anyone being in there. Hell, I'd have thought the thing was empty if we weren't told different. I think the old man is still asleep."

The men all laughed, Carl the loudest. "You hear that, Flint? The pig farmer here thinks they're all still asleep in there."

"Let him alone," Flint said. "He's not used to this kind of work like we are."

Carl drew his pistol, signaling the rest of them to do the same, including Al Brenner. "Then he'd best get used to it right quick, 'cause it's about to get awful loud in a second."

Carl fired first and the others joined in, sending a withering barrage of pistol fire into the windows of the railcar at near point-blank range. All of the men, except for Al, were carrying two pistols, so when one ran dry, they switched to the second gun. By the end, all nine men had pumped twelve rounds apiece into the car. The ground around the track was shattered with glass from the windows. The carriage was pockmarked with holes.

But even accounting for this being his first raid, he knew something was wrong.

Things were quiet again when the men stopped shooting, and there was still no sound from the railcar. He forgot all about reloading his pistol like the others were doing, but instead raised his lantern toward the window. He expected to be able to see into the car but instead saw only a large plate of iron in each of the windows.

He was about to point this out to Carl, but he never had the chance.

The rear door of the railcar opened and the outline of a man appeared on the rear platform.

Al couldn't see him clearly, but heard him say, "Looks like you gents are empty."

A shotgun blast tore through the night sky, pouring buckshot into the line of riders behind him.

Horses and men screamed.

Instinct and fear made Al throw the lamp in the general direction of the man on the platform before he dove under the railcar. The shotgun roared again. More screams from his family followed.

As he rolled to the track under the car, Al could tell the lamp had shattered on impact, for flaming bits of glass covered the ground at the back of the train. He wondered if he had struck the shooter.

Al fumbled for his Colt in the cramped confines beneath the train and dumped the empty rounds from the cylinder. His hands were surprisingly steady as he drew fresh rounds from his belt and fed them into the gun.

The sounds of men and horses screaming in the night almost rattled him. Lit by the shattered lamp, he saw four Hancock men and horses were down. It was impossible to tell more than that.

Smart.

He heard someone drop to the railbed and begin moving away from the railcar. Hurried pistol shots from the remaining Hancock men rang out from the darkness, hitting the car and the iron plated windows. But the legs of the man Al had seen drop from the back of the car kept moving. A single rifle shot—not a shotgun blast—answered the pistols. Another horse screamed and a man cried out, followed by the sound of another horseman hitting the ground.

Al turned away as an errant round struck the ground to his left, kicking up dirt and dust into his eyes.

He realized he'd filled all six holes in the cylinder and shut it as quietly as he could despite the gunfire erupting all around him. The battle had assumed a horrible rhythm: a pistol shot followed by the rifle shot, then a scream or a curse, then another pistol shot.

Al realized he was lying flush with the rail and scrambled over it to get onto his belly. He kept expecting to see more feet dropping to the ground from the railcar, or more rifles join in, but all he heard was the one rifle firing into the darkness.

One man had done all of this. He assumed it had to be Mackey. Only he could do so much damage on his own.

Al had an idea. He scrambled over the second rail and rolled out from under the car on the far side of the tracks. The firing continued, but he wasn't in that fight. Nellie had told them to grab Van Dorn or die trying and that's exactly what he intended to do.

The rifle answered more pistols, though the conversation was becoming more one-sided now as the rifle did most of the talking.

Al reached the back of the car and saw the lamp had, indeed, shattered on impact. The remnants of the lamp still burned and cast an uneasy light on everything he could see. But the door to the car was open, giving him a clear shot at Silas Van Dorn. If he couldn't grab the man, he'd shoot the old fool. Nellie would have to be content with that.

Al pulled himself up onto the platform one handed while he let the Colt lead the way into the car. The unsteady light from the shattered lamp burning on the platform cast his shadow over a fancy rug and the biggest desk he had ever seen.

And while his vision wasn't perfect, he could tell there was no one else inside, except for the door on his left. He tried the handle and found it locked, too.

He moved to the side several steps, aimed in the general direction of the lock, and shut his eyes to avoid being blinded as he fired twice. He opened his eyes and saw the lock and knob were ruined.

Al Brenner shoved the sliding door open and aimed his pistol into the darkened room. "Get up, you old bastard. You're coming with me!"

But the room was entirely dark, save for the flickering triangle of weak light from the burning platform that revealed an empty, unmade bed.

Silas Van Dorn was not on the train. They had been fooled.

But that was impossible. Al had kept an eye on the car until the train had begun to leave Chidester Station. He had waited so long, he had almost missed the train when he jumped on board. He had been in the last car before Van Dorn's car and knew that no one had left that way. Since Nellie's people confirmed that the old man had gotten on the train at Dover Station, that meant Van Dorn must have gotten off the train before Chidester.

Nellie did not like being wrong. She liked disappointment even less.

Al Brenner was wondering how he was going to break the news to her when he heard something strange from outside.

Silence.

He had turned just in time to see a man with a rifle enter the railcar. Al backed up as he raised his Colt, but hit the bed and fell backward, firing as he fell.

He had no idea if his shot had hit its mark as the man with the rifle cursed and struggled to raise it in the cramped confines of the car. Al heard it clatter to the floor as he fired once again into the darkness where he thought the man would be. Al knew he had used four of his six bullets and only had two left. Clay might have been right about him being just a dumb pig farmer, but even he knew that two bullets could be the difference between life or death in a gunfight.

A single pistol shot rang out from the darkness and struck the pillow just behind Al's head. Al fired again as he saw a shadow dart past the doorway. He had just one shot left and vowed to hold it until he thought he could hit something.

He sat up and cried out when he felt an intense, burning in his left shoulder. The pain made him collapse back onto the bed and he realized he had been shot. The bullet that had hit the pillow, sending feathers into the air, must have gone through him first.

He quickly holstered his pistol out of fear that the pain might make him squeeze the trigger and waste his last shot. He was panting as pain coursed through his shoulder. When he thought he had gathered enough strength, he cried out as he eased himself off the bed and staggered out of the room.

Even though the remnants of the exploded oil lamp were beginning to burn out, there was still enough light for Al to confirm he was the only one around.

There was also enough for him to see the bullet hole in the paneled wall and the streaks of blood along with it. The man with the rifle may have shot Al, but Al had shot him, too. That made him feel a little better. No one crossed the Hancocks without the Hancocks crossing back.

He moved outside but collapsed against the platform railing. He did not know if he had tripped or collapsed from blood loss. The reason did not really matter. He was down and knew he did not have the strength to pull his considerable bulk back up. He knew the hole in his shoulder had to be tended to, but he did not have the strength to do anything about it.

The last thing he saw before he passed out was the four dead horses and men heaped on the ground next to the railcar. How many Hancock men had survived, if any had survived at all?

Weakness took him as all went dark.

Chapter 24

The first signs of sunrise had just begun when Jerry Halstead pulled back on the reins and brought the four horses pulling the prairie schooner to a complete stop. As if on cue, Mackey and Billy Sunday rode back to him from their outlier positions.

"What's wrong?" Mackey asked. "Daylight's just starting."

"And a long night's just ending." Halstead set the wagon break and laid the team's reins aside as the horses began to eat the grass at their feet. "We've been running these girls at a good clip all night, Aaron, and they're mighty tired. Figured they could use a rest. Your mounts look like they could use it, too."

That was why Mackey had always hated riding at night. It was easy to lose track of time and distance without the benefit of the sun and the shadows to help him keep track of where they were going. The high moon had helped show them the way across the rough country when they'd taken Van Dorn from the train the night before, but he found it difficult to remain centered in the darkness.

He was glad Jerry had not fallen into the same trap.

"Maybe stopping for an hour's not such a bad idea." Mackey began to dismount. "Best use the twilight to rest. I don't think anyone's on our trail, anyway."

"I've been keeping an ear out for anyone riding out after us," Billy said as he climbed down from the saddle, too. Like Adair, there was no reason to hobble her because she wasn't going anywhere. The grass was too plentiful. "Didn't hear anything, so we should be safe for a few hours."

"Sounds good to me." Jerry jumped down from the jockey box. "My backside could use the rest."

Mackey climbed up on the tailgate and took a look at their charge hidden beneath a blanket. The wagon was actually a stripped-down prairie schooner with the bows and cover removed to make it less conspicuous.

Inside the wagon bed, Silas Van Dorn slept on a mattress as peacefully as a newborn baby. The man had just spent the night being bounced across a landscape that wasn't meant for a wagon, but the last bit of laudanum the doctor had given him had served to keep him asleep the entire time.

Mackey had always had doubts about the wisdom of taking Van Dorn off the train, but doubted they could have held off an attack for very long. He didn't know how many men the Hancocks would send to take Van Dorn or if they might use dynamite. Taking him via wagon was longer, but safer in the long run.

At least that's what he had told himself when he devised the plan.

That was before he knew Grant had hooked Van Dorn on opiates. It had been too late to call off the plan by then, but after what Lagrange had told them, he still thought he had made the right move. Fending off gunmen from a railcar in the middle of nowhere would've been madness. At least they had a chance on the trail.

But he was beginning to wonder if reaching Laramie would prove too hard a task.

Billy was waiting for him when he stepped off the tailgate. "How's the patient?"

"Still out of it," Mackey said. "I don't want to give him another dose unless we have to. I know the doc said a tablespoonful would do the trick until Laramie, but I plan on giving him more if he wakes up before then."

"Shame," Billy observed. "All that money and power and he's still no better than a Tent City drunk."

"Grant got him hooked on it without him knowing," Mackey said. "I'd like to see him answer for that, too, but after we get old Silas here to Laramie."

Billy leaned against the wagon and looked off in the general direction of the train. They had ridden well south of Chidester, but were still a good day or so away from Laramie.

They were too far away to hear anything, much less see anything, especially at night. "Wonder how Lagrange fared against the attack."

Mackey said, "I'd say the chances of him still being alive are pretty good. Lagrange might be a dandy, but the man knows how to fight. Same can't be said about the Hancock boys. Hell, I took them down in the open when they tried to run me down. I'm sure he's just fine."

"Still, bet they outnumbered him at least ten to one. That'd be tough for anyone, even us."

Mackey looked off in the same direction. "We've been through worse."

Billy dug out the makings of a cigarette and began to build one. "Think we'll be through even worse before all this is done."

"I believe you're right." He looked at Jerry, who was stretching his back after a long night's ride driving the schooner. It had been a tough ride, even for a young man. "You sure you didn't see signs of a camp when you brought the wagon to pick us up outside of Chidester?"

"I didn't see one," Jerry said. "That doesn't mean one wasn't there. But this wagon isn't exactly quiet, and since no one rode out to give it a look, I'd say there wasn't anyone in earshot of me. That might tell us something."

"Something," Mackey agreed, "but not enough." His mind told him one thing, but his instincts told him another. He wanted to send one of them back to see what had happened to Lagrange but knew it would be a waste of time. Lagrange knew what he was doing when he had volunteered to handle the train. That part of the plan was his responsibility. Van Dorn was Mackey's.

"We'll need to be ready if the Hancocks track us down when they find out Van Dorn's not on that train."

"Assuming they even care," Billy added. "Assuming they tried to kidnap him in the first place. There's a lot of land between here and that tunnel. Car could've stopped anywhere if it got uncoupled at all. They could be waiting to hit him in Laramie."

"That's a Pinkerton problem," Mackey said, "not ours."

Jerry Halstead seemed confused by the conversation. "If this man Grant is so bad, why doesn't someone just shoot him and get it over with?"

Mackey felt Billy's eyes on him but didn't look back. "Not one word, Deputy Sunday."

Billy smiled and kept building his cigarette.

Back in Dover Station, Joshua Sandborne had just finished cleaning the last Winchester in the rack when he heard a great ruckus out on the jailhouse porch.

His first instinct was to investigate, but the memory of Billy's final words to him before he left held him back. "We're deputizing you to keep an eye on the place while we're gone. Nothing else is your concern."

He took down the Winchester he had just finished cleaning and leveled the rifle at the door. He did not have to rack a round into the chamber. The marshal wanted the rifles kept fully loaded and Sandborne had obeyed his wishes.

Now was the time to wait and listen. The time to aim and fire might never come. Mackey had taught him the difference.

As Sandborne listened, he heard the unmistakable sound of splintering wood. He knew it wasn't coming from the heavy wooden jailhouse door, for the wood was still intact. It was coming from outside. He saw a chunk of dark wood pass by the window and knew the attackers must be breaking up Billy's bench and Aaron's rocking chair.

But why? Didn't they know the lawmen would be

back and, when they were, would not be happy to find their seats ruined.

He braced himself when he heard a key in the lock and it began to open. He took a step back behind the desk for cover and dropped to one knee as he raised the Winchester to his shoulder.

The door swung open and three men walked into the jailhouse. The gold stars on their brown dusters showed they were Dover Station policemen.

"Don't move," Sandborne shouted from behind the desk.

The three men saw the rifle and stopped just inside the doorway. All three had pistols on their belts. None of them threw up their hands, but none of them reached for their guns, either.

The policeman in the middle peered into the jail. "That Joshua Sandborne from The Campbell Arms I see hiding behind the marshal's desk? What are you doing here, boy?"

Another one, who Sandborne recognized as a man called Harry, laughed, "I know what he's doing here, Sam. He's trespassing. Playing marshal while the big man's away."

The third man, Leonard Penn, did not laugh. "Best put down that gun, boy, before you get hurt."

But Sandborne remained exactly where he was, and the gun did not move. "Looks to me like you three are trespassing on federal property."

He stood up slowly so they could see the Deputy Marshal star Mackey had given him before he left on the train to Laramie. The Winchester remained aimed at them. "You back out of here right now, and I won't tell Mackey or Billy what you did to their chairs."

Sandborne was glad he had managed to keep the fear out of his voice. He thought he sounded downright serious, just the way the marshal always did.

Only none of the men backed up. None of them even moved.

Only Leonard Penn spoke. "You think you'll run us off just by pointing a gun at us, boy?"

The man in front, who Sandborne now remembered was called Steve Edison, said, "We've lost count of how many times we've had guns pointed at us. And we're still here to tell the tale."

From his spot on the right, Harry said, "We didn't run then and we're not running now. We've got a writ signed by Mayor Grant himself authorizing us to take this building, and that's exactly what we're going to do."

"A writ?" Sandborne had spent most of his life on cattle ranches, not in jailhouses. He had a vague idea of what a writ was but knew it sounded official. Official enough to give these three the notion they had a right to come into the jail and take it over. The fact they had a key, too, only strengthened their claim in young Sandborne's mind. "What kind of writ and from whom?"

Edison slowly dug into his coat pocket and brought out a folded piece of paper with fancy typing on it. "An order signed by the honorable James Douglas Grant, mayor of the town of Dover Station, Montana Territory. Said this here is a federal facility that has sat vacant for too long and, as such, is now property of the municipality."

"That'd be us," Penn added.

"Damned surely would be," Harry agreed.

Edison continued. "Now, I'll be happy to lay this

right on your desk there, *Deputy*, and maybe even agree to step outside while you read it over. Assuming you can read, of course."

Sandborne didn't know if that was meant to be an insult, but given the number of illiterate people he had worked with over the years, he could understand the concern. "I can read just fine. The marshal can read even better than I can."

Edison shook his head. "We've been given orders by the mayor to seize this property today and that's exactly what we're going to do. We'll be damned before we let some damned waiter stand in our way."

"He's not a waiter," Walter Underhill said as the big man easily pushed his way past his men and into the jailhouse. He snatched the writ out of Edison's hand and stood between Sandborne and the others as he began to read it.

Without looking at the young deputy, he said, "You lower that Winchester now, Joshua. There won't be any gunplay today."

Sandborne did as the police chief said, but kept the rifle at his side. He was fairly certain that Underhill didn't want gunplay, but he wasn't so sure Harry, Edison, and Penn shared his opinion.

He watched Underhill hold the paper up to the window so the sunlight could come through it. "Looks official enough, but I'm not sure it's legal."

"The hell you talking about?" Edison asked before a glare from Underhill reminded him to add, "sir." "I mean, the mayor signed it. You can see so yourself. If you don't believe us, we'll wait right here while you go check it with him."

Underhill crumpled the writ as he faced his men. "I'll wait anywhere I please in this town, including right here if I choose to, just like you three go wherever I say. And I'm telling you to get out of here right now and head back to the office until I come get you. That's an order."

It was an order he only had to give once, because, unlike young Sandborne's order, the men immediately obeyed it.

Underhill eyed them until all three had gone back inside the Municipal Building across the street before turning his attention back to Sandborne. "I can't give you any orders, especially with that federal badge on your shirt, but I'd appreciate it if you'd put that rifle down. You've got nothing to fear from me."

Sandborne had almost forgotten he was holding it. He eased down the hammer and set the Winchester back in the rifle rack where it belonged. He wouldn't lock the rifles in place until he was ready to leave the jailhouse. Doing otherwise would only leave him at a disadvantage. A locked-down gun wasn't much good to a lawman. Mackey had taught him that.

Underhill handed the writ to Sandborne and he took it. "Lots of legal language in there that I'm not sure I understand. It claims the federal marshals that are supposed to be stationed here aren't here enough to keep the property from being vacant and becoming town property. I don't think they were counting on you being here, much less being deputized. Guess there's got to be something to the law if Mackey posted you here."

"He didn't tell me why he deputized me and sent

me here." After a few sentences, Sandborne gave up trying to make sense of the writ and handed it back to Underhill. "Guess that's the reason why. Could've gotten me killed, come to think of it."

"Don't look at it that way," Underhill told him. "I've seen how you can handle yourself in a gunfight. You'd have held your own against those three just now. Better than any other available man in town, under the circumstances."

Sandborne took some pride in that. "Even better than you?"

"Don't go getting carried away," Underhill admitted, "but I'm not available. Still, this writ doesn't look legal." He looked back out at the remnants of the shattered chair and bench on the porch. "Too bad I couldn't get here before those three idiots wrecked the bench and rocking chair, though. But that's the ruckus that brought me over here in the first place, so at least their destruction served a purpose."

Sandborne walked out onto the porch and took a look at the damage for himself. The bench looked like it had been caved in by a rifle butt and smashed to pieces. The rocking chair looked like it had been kicked apart and thrown into the thoroughfare. Some people had recognized it as belonging to Mackey and scrambled to take pieces of the chair while the getting was good.

Sandborne saw a boy dart out from their side of the street, grab a chair arm, and run down the alley of the Municipal Building toward River Avenue. "Why would anyone want a piece of a busted chair? Even a kid?"

Underhill leaned his big frame against the porch post. "Guess maybe he thinks it'll be worth money someday, seeing as how Aaron's managed to get himself famous." He nodded at the Municipal Building. "And I'd wager he's about to get himself even more famous after his fight with the mayor comes to a close."

"I sure hope it doesn't come to that," Sandborne said. "I've got no love for Mr. Grant, but if Aaron and the mayor go at it, it just might tear this town apart."

"Hoping won't keep it from happening," Underhill said as he patted Sandborne on the back before stepping off the boardwalk. He had meant it as a friendly gesture, but it had almost knocked the young man over. "You just keep that star pinned to your chest and your gun on your hip. You've got nothing to fear from me, but Edison, Harry, and Penn might have revenge on their mind. I'll have a word with them, but they're a testy bunch, so be careful."

Sandborne knew he was young, but he didn't like being taken lightly. "And you tell them to mind their step around me, Commissioner." It didn't come out as forceful as he had hoped.

Underhill glanced back at Sandborne, amused. "I'll do that. And while we're giving each other advice, I'd suggest you send a telegram to Aaron. Tell him what happened here today and what the mayor tried to do. It'd be best if he knew what he was riding into before he came back here, whenever that is. Be sure to lock down the rifles and the front door when you do. Might even want to take one with you, just to be safe."

Sandborne hadn't thought about sending a telegram to the marshal about all this, but figured it might be a good idea. He'd get to writing it now so he could cut down on the extra words. He had never sent a telegram before, but was pretty sure they charged by the word, so the shorter it was, the cheaper it would be.

"Thanks for the advice," Sandborne called out to Underhill just as the commissioner reached the front steps of the Municipal Building.

Underhill waved back at him without looking around and walked inside.

Young Sandborne had a horrible feeling that would be the last time the two men would ever see each other alive.

Walter Underhill's mind was busy as he threaded his way through the crowded boardwalk toward The Campbell Arms for an early supper. He imagined Katherine would be missing Aaron something awful and decided she could use some company. Underhill knew he could use some.

He had never been able to understand her attraction to the marshal. She was so refined and polite, while Mackey was usually reserved to the point of being downright nasty at times. But there was no doubt that the two of them loved each other, and love was rare in this world and should be cherished when found.

Cherished in the way he valued his place in Dover Station. There was no denying that the place had changed since the day he had ridden into town looking for the Boudreaux boys over a year ago. The amount of building that had taken place then would have been impossible to comprehend had he not been there to witness it. Money was an amazing thing.

Almost anything was possible if you threw enough of it at something you wanted done fast. That and owning your own railroad certainly helped.

Money and a railroad had been the reasons why Mr. Rice had been able to transform the sleepy town of Dover Station into a main attraction along the Great Northwestern Railway. Walter Underhill was proud to have played some part in it all.

That pride did not necessarily extend to his association with James Grant or many of the accusations that had been leveled against him, but at least Underhill had gotten something out of it. He would always be the first police commissioner in town history. Whether the town flourished to be the London of the Northwest or got buried under sand like one of those old cities in Egypt, no one could change that he had been part of history.

He wished his success had not cost him Mackey's friendship, but if there was one thing he had learned in his forty-five years of living, it was that time waited for no man. Every man had his day and, if that man was not careful, the day would pass without his notice.

Besides, Mackey had sensed what Grant was going to do and finagled himself a federal badge out of Mr. Rice before Grant had the chance to drop the hammer on him by abolishing the sheriff's office. A smart move.

Which led Underhill to question once again why Grant had done something as shortsighted as issuing a writ to seize the jailhouse. He must have been looking for a way to pick a fight with Mackey when the marshal returned home. Directing the men to smash his prized rocking chair was evidence of it. The act wasn't enough to bait Mackey into a fight, but the intention behind it certainly was.

It showed Grant was now in control of every aspect of life in Dover Station. He was the mayor, the acting head of the Dover Station Company, and quite possibly, the man who had brought the Hancock clan into town. If so, that would make him responsible for a vast majority of the crime that happened within town limits.

Given that Grant had directly ordered Penn, Harry, and Edison to enforce the writ proved to Underhill that not all of the men in his department were loyal to him. Underhill had known that since the beginning, but now Grant didn't seem the least bit interested in allowing Underhill to even think he was in charge.

Underhill wondered if he should do something about that. He was not interested in only being an honorary police chief. He may have his flaws, but he was a lawman, and by God, he was no one's puppet, either. Perhaps throwing whatever influence he still had behind Aaron Mackey might be the best thing for the town?

Perhaps it was because Walter Underhill's mind was as crowded as the boardwalk he walked on that he did not see the short old man with the missing teeth and bad leg waiting in front of The Order of the Garter Saloon on Front Street. The chief of police had been too deep in thought to notice the man was watching him through the bobbing heads of the men and women going to supper, going to work, or just going home.

Underhill hadn't even noticed when the man dove through the crowd and drove a dagger deep into the left side of Underhill's belly.

The big police chief staggered back as the men and women around him screamed at the sight of the attack. The old man's bad leg gave out, and he stumbled into the street as people rushed to restrain him.

But Underhill drew his Colt and fired three shots into the old man's chest before anyone could reach him. The Texan fell back against the wall of The Order of the Garter Saloon, the handle of the dagger still protruding from his belly. He felt himself sink to the boardwalk as his legs grew numb.

He laid his pistol on the boardwalk and looked at the belly wound. The dagger was still in his stomach, but had been driven down at an angle that he knew could only be fatal. He shoved away the hands of well-meaning townspeople who offered to pull it out. He knew he was already a dead man, but pulling out the knife would only hasten the inevitable.

He glanced up at the sign for The Order of the Garter Saloon with its fancy red cross on a shield and garter design. His mother had been from England and would have been proud. "Well," he said out loud, "at least it ain't a whorehouse."

Despite the earnest attentions of the people who had come to his side, Walter Underhill allowed the darkness to take him.

Chapter 25

Robert Lagrange brought his mount to a halt and climbed down from the saddle before he fell from it.

He staggered to the closest tree and used it for support as he slid down to the ground. He opened his shirt and got a better look at his wounds. The bullet had struck him in the right side, nicked a rib on the left, and came out through the right side of his chest. He could breathe normally, so he didn't think his lung had been hit. The wounds had even clotted some since he had cut off the sleeves of his shirt and made makeshift bandages from them. But he was still incredibly weak from the loss of blood and knew his chances of infection were high unless the wounds were treated quickly.

Fortunately, nature provided some benefits to a man in his predicament.

He took his knife from his boot and dug around the base of the tree he had chosen. He drove the blade deep onto the green moss until he cut out a wet square of dirt and slapped it on the bullet hole at his side. The cold sod on his flesh made his skin crawl, but he knew the Indians had faith in the healing properties of tree moss. And although he did not like the savages, only a fool would discount their ways. Besides, he had seen the remedy work on men who had been shot in the field and knew there was something to it. The fact that there wasn't a doctor anywhere in sight only helped make his decisions that much easier.

He wrapped the strip of shirtsleeve to tie the mossy square to his side. Then he dug out another square and tied it to the exit wound on his chest. He hated having the unwashed earth so close to his skin, but he knew it was his best chance for survival out here. In fact, it was his only chance.

After using the second strip of shirtsleeve to tie the moss to his chest, Lagrange tucked the knife back into his boot and collapsed back against the tree to rest.

He cursed himself for the hundredth time about walking into that railcar blind and with the awkward rifle in his hand. Close-quarters action dictated a pistol, not a long gun. That small lapse in judgment had cost him a hole in his side and one in his chest. Next time, he'd be more careful, if he lived long enough for there to be a next time.

He knew he had put a hole of his own into the Hancock man who had shot him. The only question was whether or not he had killed the man. Lagrange hoped he had. He knew he had not been able to wipe out all of the Hancocks who had fled in the night, but he had killed most of them. At least four of them were still on the loose.

He had no idea about who the men were or the kind of men they might be. He did not know if they would keep riding after Van Dorn or if they would turn tail and head back home to lick their wounds the whole way.

That was the problem with the Hancock family.

Other than knowing Mad Nellie was the matriarch of the clan, it was impossible to get a handle on who the other leaders were, especially now that Mackey had killed Henry Hancock. Some of them were meaner than others. Some did exactly what Nellie told them to do or died trying. Others talked big but chose to feed off the family name instead of enlarging it.

In short, Lagrange decided they were no different than any other family. Some good, some bad, and some just plain lazy.

He hoped the remaining Hancock men back at the train were the lazy type. He hoped he had killed all of the strong men and left the cowards and shiftless men behind.

Lagrange had a general idea of the location of the trail Mackey, Billy, and Halstead would use to take Van Dorn to Laramie. And while tracking was far from his strongest skill, Lagrange did not consider himself a tenderfoot, either.

He was enough of a field man to know there was no way to push past the pain or danger of a gunshot wound this early in the game. He needed to give his wounds time to heal and for the medicinal properties of the moss to do their job.

He also needed to rest, as he and the horse he had grabbed following the battle had ridden all night and needed rest. He grabbed the reins of the animal and wrapped them around his wrist just before passing out.

His last thoughts before sleep were about whether the crude hobbling would be good enough to keep the horse in place or the animal would simply drag him to death.

When sleep took him, he found himself not caring one way or the other.

Al Brenner woke with a start. The sunlight on his face felt warm before the pain from the hole in his shoulder burned through his body, causing him to collapse back on the bed.

Yet even through the pain, he wondered what he was doing in bed in the first place. Especially this bed. It was the bed on the railcar. And why did his wound feel different?

He began to paw at the hole in his shoulder, but rough hands eased his hand away. "Easy now, cousin Al," said a voice that was unfamiliar to him. "Let that hole heal for a while longer."

Al Brenner blinked open his eyes and found his cousin Nick's face swim into view. Unlike Al, Nick was a Hancock in name and in the way he lived. He had ridden with both Clay and Henry for years and had lived to tell the tale. The other two cousins had a lot of newspaper ink spent on them over the years, but the one common link between the two outlaws—besides blood—was that Nick had ridden with each of them. That meant something.

"Take it easy," Nick said as he set Al's head back against the pillow. "You'll be just fine as long as you take it easy."

But Al had no intention of taking it easy. "How'd I end up in this bed?"

"Farley, John, Robert, and me doubled back after the shooting ended," Nick told him. "We wanted to see if anyone was still alive. Glad we came along when we did or you might've died out there in the elements come sunrise."

Sunrise. "What time is it?"

Nick looked around Van Dorn's bedroom and saw a fancy wind-up desk clock. "Near as I can tell, around half past seven. Why?"

Al sat up despite Nick trying to hold him down. Al might not be a cowpuncher like the rest of his family, but he was the biggest and strongest Hancock man alive. He'd gotten that part from his daddy's side. "We've got to get riding."

"Damn it, Al. You're in no shape to be bouncing all over God's creation on a horse. I've been shot once or twice in my time. I know how much getting shot can take out of a man. You can play it risky with a posse riding down on you, but we've got time yet for that. Best take the rest while you can get it."

"And rest up for what?" Al said, sharper than he would have liked. "Heading back home where Nellie will whup us for allowing one man to kill so many of us? Or are we going to take a whipping because we don't have Van Dorn like she wanted?"

Nick stroked his craggy, gray-streaked beard. "Can't say as I've thought that far in advance. We saw you out there bleeding to death and wanted to get you inside. With so many of the others dead, I didn't think we had enough to ride up against the likes of Mackey and that colored deputy of his, assuming they've even got this Van Dorn fella. I've heard tell of those two cutting down thirty hostile Apache when they were in the army. Just the two of them. Now, we Hancock men ain't nobody's idea of a bargain, but we ain't Apaches, neither. And I've seen what Mackey can do to a man your size. There ain't a lick of fear in him. So, given our number, I suggest we take our chances with Nell and come at Van Dorn another way."

Al forced himself off the bed and snatched his bloody shirt off the top of the dresser. "We're not staying here any longer than we need to. We're getting out of here right now."

Nick was now up and standing with him as Al cried out as he pulled his shirt over his head. "You're in no shape to travel, and we're not leaving you, so we're staying right here for a while."

But despite the pain, Al did not see it that way. "You think those railroad men are going to let a car like this holding a man like Van Dorn just slip off the back of one of their trains? They've probably already sent people back to look for it and for Van Dorn, and I don't want to be here when those hard cases show up."

Nick didn't argue with that. "Then we'll get you on a horse, but set a nice easy pace back home. It'll take a couple of days, but—"

"Days we could spend tracking down Van Dorn like Nellie told us to." Al checked his belt and was glad to find his pistol was still in his holster. "We've lost a lot of our kin going after that rich old man on Nellie's say-so. Might as well make their deaths count for something."

Nick looked at Al as if seeing him for the first time. "All right, cousin. We'll do it your way."

Now that he was moving around, Al felt the fog over his mind begin to clear. "You said you rode back here with three others. Plus me means five, don't it?"

Nick nodded.

"There's not enough of us to bury our dead, but I don't want to leave them here for the stragglers to pick clean. Take whatever guns or ammunition we need from the bodies and move on as soon as possible."

"But move on to where, Al? It looks like they took Van Dorn before the train reached Chidester, but we don't know where their trail is. Or where they're going."

"They're going to Laramie," Al said. "It's the only place Van Dorn can catch the train to New York. So that's where we're headed, too."

"But they could go to Laramie any number of ways," Nick said. "And we could be in front of them and would never even know it. We could be out there for days and all we'd be doing is leaving a trail for them to follow and avoid."

But Al had a little more faith than that. He inched out into the hallway and saw a bullet hole in the corridor wall. "You see that?"

Nick said he did.

"I put that there," Al said. "But it went through the fella that gunned down our family first. The same man who was working with Mackey to get Van Dorn off this train before we hit it. I know I didn't kill him, but I wounded him plenty. And I'd bet that if he knew enough to protect an empty car just to buy his friends time, then he probably knows where they are and how to meet up with them."

Al rapped a knuckle on the bullet hole. "We can't track Van Dorn or the men who have him. But we can sure as hell track a man bleeding his way clear across Montana."

Nick bent over and took a closer look at the bullet dug into the wall. He wasn't sure it had gone through anyone, but he appreciated his cousin's thought just the same. "I'll see if I can't find a trail while the others loot our cousins for guns and ammunition. We're going to need every bullet we can get if we go up against Mackey and his men."

"That's where you're wrong, Cousin Nick." Al Brenner wiped beads of sweat from his brow. "We're not going up against the marshal. He's making the mistake of going up against us. And he won't even know it 'afore it's too late."

Chapter 26

Later that afternoon, Mackey rode drag while Billy took point and Jerry kept the wagon on a steady line between the two along the trail. His deputy had offered to relieve him every once in a while, but Mackey didn't mind bringing up the rear. Besides, Billy was a better tracker than he could ever hope to be. He wanted his eyes out front in case they ran into something ahead.

He was glad Van Dorn had been quiet since the moment they had placed him in the wagon. Aside from a few moans here and there, the millionaire had remained in an opium stupor for the entire trip. It had allowed the men to concentrate on what they saw and heard on the trail, as well as what they had not seen. And he was glad they had not seen any sign of Hancock men on the trail.

But as the miles toward Laramie rolled slowly by, Mackey wondered if Lagrange had made it out of the railcar alive. He hoped so. The Pinkerton man may have been too much of a dandy for his taste, but Lagrange had a knack of growing on him. His tenacity in battle and his usefulness in other times made him a good man to have around. He was glad Mr. Rice had asked him to stay on in Dover Station to observe the ways of James Grant. Mackey knew Lagrange had been placed there to protect Rice's business interests in the town, not just to protect the town itself, but he was glad to have another man on his side against Grant just the same.

He hoped the detective had survived his run-in with the Hancock family. He hoped he would remember the path they had told him they would be following and would be able to catch up to them soon with news of the battle.

But Mackey's hopes faded when he saw Jerry rein in the horses and bring the wagon to a sudden halt.

Mackey brought Adair to a full gallop and quickly caught up with the wagon. Having agreed to use sign language instead of speaking, Jerry used two fingers to point to his own eyes, then one to point farther up the trail to where Billy rode. The silent message was easy to decipher. Billy had signaled him to stop the wagon.

Mackey rode toward Billy, who was already off his roan and out of the line of sight. Not a good sign. He pulled his Peacemaker and slowed Adair to a slow walk as he approached the scene.

He brought Adair into a wide arc around Billy's horse, Peacemaker ready, as he scanned both sides of the trail for any sign of his deputy.

He found him just off the right side of the trail tending to a fallen Robert Lagrange.

Mackey holstered his pistol and waved at Jerry to bring the wagon team forward as quickly as possible.

Mackey dropped from the saddle to help Billy attend to the detective. "Is he alive?"

Billy had opened Lagrange's shirt and was examining a hole in his right side covered in moss. "Looks like he passed out from these holes he's patched up for himself." He checked the chest wound next. "Did a pretty good job of it from what little blood I can see. Looks like he lost consciousness, though, and most likely fell off his horse." He held the back of his hand to Lagrange's forehead. "No fever, but he's in no condition to have walked this far from the tracks, so he must have ridden, then fallen off his horse."

Mackey looked around for signs of a horse, but saw none except for those left by their own. "Must've taken off after he fell."

Lagrange's eyes sprang open and he looked at Billy and Mackey. "Good morning, gentlemen."

Mackey knelt beside him. "Think you can stand?"

"I'm not sure," Lagrange rasped. "My horse threw me, though I don't know why. Did I break anything in the fall?"

Billy felt under Lagrange's head and neck. "Don't have any broken bones, and your neck feels fine to me, but I'm not a doctor. Just a sergeant who knows a bit more about fixing people up than I'm supposed to. You feel like standing up?"

"Can't just lie around here all day, can I?" Lagrange accepted the help from Mackey and Billy and let them help him to his feet. He was a bit dizzy at first, but quickly regained his balance. "After all I've survived these past few hours, it would be a shame to be killed by a bucking horse."

"What have you been through?" Mackey asked.

"Would help us know what might be waiting for us ahead."

Lagrange told them about the gunfight outside the private car as Jerry brought the wagon up beside them. "I was lucky they all had to reload at once," he said when he was finished, "otherwise I would have had to wait for them to breach the car, which would have been bad for me."

"The whole idea was bad," Mackey said. "You should've just let them raid the car and protect the train with the rest of your men. Then, you could've led them to ride out to meet us from Laramie."

"Never would've worked," Lagrange said as he limped toward the wagon. "They had a man on the train watching everything from Chidester Station onward. He watched me go inside the car to keep guard. If we hadn't carried the ruse all the way through, they would have known Van Dorn wasn't on that train and they'd still be out there somewhere. Now, there are six fewer Hancock men in the world."

"But we still might have some Hancock men on our trail." Mackey quickly added, "No offense, Lagrange. I know you did everything you could."

Billy looked over the ground where Lagrange had fallen. "Bad news. Looks like Lagrange's mount caught wind of the other horses and began riding back to them. Means they're not as far as we thought."

"Looks like I got here just in time." Lagrange pulled out his Colt to check if he had reloaded it, but got dizzy when he looked down at the cylinder.

Mackey grabbed him before he passed out. "Just in time to get in the back of the wagon and keep Van Dorn company until you're better."

While Billy climbed back on his horse, Mackey dragged Lagrange to the back of the wagon, pulled down the tailgate, and helped the Pinkerton man climb up. "A bit of sleep and you'll be as good as new in a few hours. Until then—"

A rifle shot echoed through the forest as a bullet slammed into the head of the lead horse of the team. The poor animal dropped where it had stood, throwing the others in the team into a panic.

Billy brought his roan under control and made her run into the woods in the direction of the gunfire.

Mackey broke as fast as he could for Adair, who was so accustomed to gunfire that she tended to stand stock still when the lead began to fly. It had made her a great horse during a gunfight, but it also tended to make her an easy target.

Bullets kicked up dirt all around him and smacked into trees as he barreled for the mare. He barely caught a foothold in the stirrup before he leapt into the saddle and snapped the reins, bringing Adair to life and into a full gallop away from the clearing. Now that she knew a fight was on, she would know what to do.

He looked back at the wagon and saw Jerry had dropped from the jockey box and had taken up a position in the wagon with his Winchester to cover them. A few rounds struck the wagon, but none seemed to have penetrated the sides. Mackey knew the wood was not thick enough to be bulletproof, but it was better than no cover at all.

Like Adair, Jeremiah Halstead knew what to do in battle, too.

Mackey brought his horse around and rode toward the sound of the guns.

As he and Adair bounded through the forest, he had no idea where Billy had gone. He did not need to worry about his friend. The two men had been in more fights than either of them cared to remember and some they wish they could forget. They would find a way to locate the enemy and devise a strategy, the way they always had before.

Knowing this would be an up-close battle, he kept the Winchester holstered under his left foot and drew his Peacemaker instead. He imagined these were the same men who had survived the run-in with Lagrange the night before, which meant there were probably five of them. Not impossible odds for Mackey or Billy alone, but seeing as how the Hancock men were already dug in and under the cover of the dense forest, it would be difficult to find them.

Rifle shots rang out from his right, which were quickly answered by more distant shots, probably from Jerry. His bullets must have hit close to someone's position, because the air was filled with curses, followed by, "Shut up, you idiot. Don't mark yourself."

The voice was less than ten feet in front of Mackey. With all of the firing, the wounded man had not heard Adair approaching.

The wounded man cried out again and the other man tried to quiet him as he reloaded his rifle. "I told you to shut up before you mark us."

"Good advice," Mackey said before killing him with

a single shot to the head. He urged Adair on through the line, not knowing where the others might be until they began firing at him. The bullets were all either too high or hit trees he had already passed.

Mackey ducked as he rode, firing when he could at the tufts of smoke that rose up in the blur of the wilderness. Unfortunately, he did not think he had hit anything, either.

He reined in Adair when he knew they were well clear of the line and spotted Billy Sunday's horse tied to a tree about a hundred yards ahead of him. Knowing better than to mark his friend's spot by riding straight toward it, he broke left and took the roundabout way until he stood right next to it.

Adair wasn't breathing hard. She didn't fuss, and she didn't nose the plentiful grass of the forest floor. She stood with her head up, stock still. She wasn't grazing now. She was waiting to get back into battle.

But Mackey used the lull in the action to see the scene clearly since the first shot had been fired.

This area of the forest was on a slight, densely wooded incline that gave the attackers an excellent vantage point to strike the wagon. Lagrange's horse had likely drifted back to join the others, whose tracks had led them here.

Now, the Hancock men were dug in under deep cover. Their horses had been picketed well behind their lines, as he saw no sign of them here. They had attacked the wagon on foot and upwind so the horses would have a harder time catching their scent. *Smart.*

Billy would be somewhere off to the left under thick cover by now. Probably between the shooters and the wagon. He'd have his Sharps with him, and Mackey's run-in with the shooters had probably allowed him to fine-tune his sights on his targets.

He had to peer through the trees to get a good look at the wagon. Jerry's head full of black hair was barely visible above the flatbed wall, but he was still alive. He was glad the young man knew better than to fill the woods with wild shots, especially with him and Billy out among the enemy. The boy had been through this kind of thing before.

He was giving his eyes time to adapt to the weak light in the dense forest when he heard a voice barely above a whisper carried on the wind.

"Four of them to the left." It was Billy. "Closer to the trail than the man you just killed."

Mackey tried to find their positions, but could not. "Can't see them well."

"I can," Billy whispered. "You ride and draw their fire. I'll shoot from here."

Mackey knew it had worked for them before. There was no reason why it would not work now. And there was no man he trusted more with his life than Billy Sunday.

Mackey opened the cylinder of the Peacemaker and dumped out the empty brass onto the forest floor. Normally he saved his shells, but there was nothing normal about this. He fed six rounds into the pistol and snapped the cylinder shut. He repositioned the Winchester under his left leg so it rode a little higher, giving him an easier chance of grabbing it quickly if he had to.

Things would have already fallen apart if he had to

go to the rifle, but it made him feel better knowing that it was there.

Billy's whisper reached him again. "Go, Aaron. Go now!"

One of the men broke cover and began crawling down toward the wagon.

Billy's big Sharps boomed. The buffalo round turned the man's head into a ball of red mist.

Mackey picked up Adair's reins.

He didn't have to snap them for her to begin riding in that direction.

The hillside erupted with gunfire in all directions. Mackey aimed across his body at the movement that seemed to be everywhere on the forest floor. The shooters had covered themselves in branches and leaves, which had made it difficult for him or Billy to have spotted them.

One man rolled over on his back and aimed a double-barreled shotgun up at Mackey. The marshal fired and hit the man in the center of his chest. The impact rocked the shooter flat on his back, but he was still in the fight. Mackey brought Adair around and fired once more. This time, he hit the man in the left side of the chest. He was dead before he hit the ground.

In his mind, Mackey counted three down, leaving one or two still out there.

"That all of them?" Jerry called out from the wagon.

"Not yet." Mackey scanned the forest floor for

signs of shooters as Adair galloped. "Still got a couple out here."

He cried out when a bullet grazed his back before sinking into a tree to his left. The pain almost made him drop his pistol, but he held his grip and heeled Adair to get him out of there.

Jerry rose to a knee and fired from the wagon. A man cried out, and Mackey looked back to see a man stagger backward into a tree, holding on to his leaking belly.

Mackey brought Adair around and quickly closed the distance between him and the gut-shot man. He finished him with a final shot to the head as he galloped by.

He rode hard past Billy's position and quickly dropped from the saddle. The fire that tore across his back when he hit the ground almost made him pass out.

He bit off the pain and yelled into the forest, "You're the last one. Throw down your rifle and come out. You won't be harmed."

Billy had crept silently beside him and whispered, "You sure there's someone else out there?"

He kept searching the dense forest for movement as he pointed to the tree that had been struck by the bullet that had grazed his back. "I got shot from the right side. They've got someone deeper in the forest to cover them. Close enough to get a bead on me as I rode by, but far enough away to stay covered."

Billy looked into the forest, too. "Want me to go in after him?"

But Mackey had already made up his mind against it. "No. We could waste a day or more looking for him and still never find him. We need to get moving and hope we can outrun him."

"We won't be outrunning anyone with a wagon carrying two sick men," Billy said.

"And we won't be finding anyone in forest cover that thick," Mackey added. "We need to protect Van Dorn and keep him moving. We'll worry about this sharpshooter if we have to, but he's only one man. For now, we move."

Mackey kept an eye on the woods as Billy grabbed his roan and walked it back to the wagon trail. He listened, hoping the shooter would make some kind of noise that would pinpoint his location. But all he heard was the wind blowing through the trees.

When Adair began to fuss, he decided it was time to go.

Chapter 27

Al Brenner may have been a pig farmer, but he had spent a good portion of his childhood hunting in the woods around Hancock. He knew how to stalk prey and when to go home.

That same instinct was why he was sitting in Mr. James Grant's office, talking to the great man himself.

"And why on earth should I trust you, Mr. Brenner?" the mayor asked. "You seem to have failed at every turn."

Al Brenner had never met Mr. Grant before, but he had heard his family talk about the man. Nellie said he liked to put on airs to impress people like Van Dorn and the rest of the town elders, but that he was really no better than the Hancocks. Nellie said he had done his share of dirt in his life, from being a pimp in Abeline to running a stagecoach stop for Wells Fargo to somehow weaseling his way into the good graces of the Dover Station Company.

Al didn't think he looked soft like a man who had spent his life in an office. He looked exactly as Nellie had described him—like a man who was trying very hard to impress someone, maybe even the world.

"On account of me living through every run-in I've ever had with that bastard Mackey and his men."

Mayor Grant raised an eyebrow. "Is that so?"

"Yes, sir," Al was glad to tell him. "Once in the Ruby and twice out on the trail while doing that business you don't want to talk about. Even put a bullet across the marshal's back."

"After you say you tracked down Lagrange, who led you to Mackey and the others," Grant said. "After you got everyone else killed except for you."

"And that's the way it happened, Mr. Grant. As true as the given word. I shot that son of a bitch for you and for all of my kin he killed, too."

"If true, that would be a quite a feat," Grant told him. "I've never heard of Aaron Mackey being shot before."

"Then I guess that makes me kinda special," Al said. "Kinda like being the only man to go up against the marshal so many times and live to tell the tale."

James Grant seemed to consider it for a moment. "Of course, I could be forgiven for thinking you're lying. That you turned tail and ran at the first sign of trouble and everything you just told me is a lie."

Al felt the fire of rage rise within him. "I'm no liar, Mr. Grant."

"So you say, but I don't know you, Mr. Brenner. I don't know a damned thing about you."

Brenner knew he had been a fool to expect this man—this stranger—to believe him without proof. Mr. Grant had risen to his station in life by being someone who knew how to get things done.

So had Al Brenner.

"I bet a man like you can spot a liar from a mile off when he sees him," Al said.

The mayor shrugged. "People are often less than truthful around people of authority."

Brenner drew his Colt and aimed it at Grant's head. "I'm ready to blow your damned head off right now if you call me a liar again. So, since you're supposed to be so damned smart," he thumbed back the hammer, "tell me if I'm lying right now."

Grant looked at the gun with more curiosity than fear. "People are always pointing guns at me in here. If I didn't know better, I'd think the damned place was haunted. Perhaps I should move offices."

Al kept the gun pointed at the mayor. "That ain't no form of answer to my question."

"I believe you're telling the truth, Mr. Brenner. I think you'd kill me this very instant on the slightest provocation."

Al didn't know what a provocation was, but kept it to himself. "You think I've been lying to you since I came into this fancy office of yours?"

"No, Mr. Brenner. I believe you're telling the truth about everything."

Al looked at him closely. "Been known to be able to see if a man was lying to me a time or two myself. You lying, mister?"

Grant held out his hands. "Why would I? You're either going to shoot or put the pistol away. If you shoot, my men will kill you before you get two feet out the door. If you put the gun away, we can talk about the reasons why I believe you."

Al decided he did not have anything to lose by listening to what the man had to say. He could always kill him later if he lied. "I'm no man's fool, Mr. Grant. There are other members of my family who have better reputations with a gun, but they're all dead and I'm still here. That's got to count for something."

"So does evidence that supports your story." He picked up a piece of paper from his desk. "I just received this telegram this morning. It reports that Mr. Van Dorn was escorted to Laramie safely this morning by ten Pinkerton men. I would say you were wise to break off your pursuit of the wagon when you did, Mr. Brenner, for if Billy Sunday didn't kill you with that Sharps rifle of his, then one of the Pinkerton men would have finished you off for certain."

Al didn't see any good fortune in it, just common sense. "How does any of that support my claim of wounding Mackey?"

"It doesn't." Grant picked up a second telegram. "This does. It tells me that Robert Lagrange is being treated by a railroad doctor for a bullet wound that did significant damage to his upper torso." The mayor looked at him. "Looks like you shot him in the railcar just like you told me earlier."

Grant went back to the telegram. "It also says here that Aaron Mackey is being treated for a bullet graze across his back." He set the telegram back on his desk and pinned it there with a finger. "That's why I believe you, Mr. Brenner, not because you sound honest or because you pointed a gun at me. I had the proof in my hand before you ever walked in here."

Al was as relieved as he was embarrassed. "Sorry for acting the way I did just now, Mr. Grant."

"Never apologize," Grant told him. "You did what

you thought was right in the moment. If you ever point a gun at me again, I'll have your hands broken, but you followed your instinct. In this case, it served you well."

He tilted his head at the big man standing in his office. "You interest me, Mr. Brenner. You came to me before you went to see your Aunt Nellie. Why? Do you think I'll be more merciful than she would be about your failure?"

"Nope," Al said. "I figured you wouldn't see what happened as a failure."

"I certainly hope you don't view nine dead men spread across Montana as a symbol of success for the Hancock clan."

"No," Al admitted. "But I see them as one hell of a problem for you."

Grant's smug expression soured. "Explain yourself, Mr. Brenner."

Al had never considered himself a great thinker, but he had given himself plenty of time to think about what he would say to Grant on the ride back from his run-in with Mackey and his men. "We were already late before Van Dorn's train even pulled into Chidester. The man you hired us to kidnap or kill was already miles away before I even touched the coupling pin and is now with the Pinkerton Detective Agency."

"And your kinfolk died for nothing," Grant added for spite. "And I hope Mad Nellie doesn't come around here rattling her tin cup looking for a handout, because I have nothing to give her."

"I wouldn't know about that," Al said.

"Well, let me educate you, Mr. Brenner." Grant

slowly rose out of his chair. "My arrangement with your aunt or whatever the hell she is to you was contingent upon the successful murder or kidnapping of Silas Van Dorn. His death or abduction would have terrified the investors back home, and it would have been nearly impossible to find a suitable replacement to run the Dover Station Company. But now that Van Dorn has safely reached Laramie, he is under a doctor's care, which complicates matters in ways that don't concern you. But Mackey and his companions are alive and well. They will testify that I was behind the attempt on his life and other things." Grant glared at him from behind his desk. "Surely even a simple farmer like you can grasp the severity of the situation."

Al tried very hard to not take offense at the way Grant spoke to him. "Means you're sucking hind teat when it comes to the company."

"A wise perception from a farmer," Grant admitted. "It means I'm done as far as the company is concerned. The company I have spent the last year or so building and shaping into my own image. The company whose investments have been crafted in such a way that they have financed my endeavors here in Dover Station. Endeavors that have profited the Hancock family handsomely."

Al had never fooled himself into believing he was an intelligent man. Some of his cousins had, which was why they were dead and he was still above ground. Most of what Grant had just told him went over his head, which was probably what he had intended.

But the gist of it was plain enough even for Al to see. "Aunt Nellie takes care of the family problems, Mr. Grant. Problems she's never seen fit to involve me in unless there was dirty work to be done. People who needed to disappear, never to be heard from again. Bad work, Mr. Grant, but it was the only kind of work she thought I was fit for. Fed my pigs an awful lot of awful things over the years, but I did it because I'm loyal."

"So is a dog," Grant spat. "I don't need dogs."

"No," Al allowed, "you need men you can trust. I came here today to tell you I'm not just a Hancock man. I'm big and I'm strong and I can handle myself when things get thick." He pulled open his shirt and pointed at the ugly red hole in his shoulder. "If this doesn't prove it, I don't know what will."

Grant glanced at the wound. "Getting shot doesn't take much talent, son."

"But shooting the man who shot you does," Al said. "Tracking them down after they've done it takes even more talent. You need someone like that, Mr. Grant. Someone who's tough and loyal and knows how to make problems go away. You need someone who sees a problem and don't quit hacking at it until it's out of the way. That's why I'd say you need yourself a pig farmer right about now, especially since your chief of police got himself killed."

"He's not dead," Grant spat. "Just close to it. He's lying on a cot in Doc Ridley's office with a knife wound to the belly. A knife that managed to avoid hitting anything vital. Another sterling achievement your family managed to pull off." He ran his hands over his brown hair. "Good God, man. If your family had to live by their wits, they'd starve."

"Maybe they would," Al said, "but not me. I'm smart enough to be a dumb pig farmer, remember."

Grant looked at him. "You're getting at something, aren't you? Spill it if you are or get out."

Al had never been an elaborate man anyway, so he got to the point. "Looks to me like it might be good if you had someone who knew the way the Hancock clan thought and who wouldn't mind working for you in the bargain. Maybe you lose your job with the company, but you're still mayor and you've still got my family working for you. What if you had a man who could play on both sides of the fence, making sure it came out in your favor every time?"

Grant clapped. "Let me guess. You're just the man I need."

"A blind man could tell you what you need, Mr. Grant. I'm the only one who can give it to you."

"The Israelites had Moses. The apostles had Jesus and I get a pig farmer from Montana to grant me salvation in my hour of need." Grant groaned as he dropped back into his chair. "Though I must admit that I find your confidence impressive. I didn't think pig farmers were known for their ambition."

"We're not. We're known for our being stubborn. And if you're going to keep what you've built for yourself here, you're going to need someone who knows how to tend to things. To make them grow. To get rid of the weeds that choke the crops and kill the wolves that come around looking to eat the sheep."

Al noticed Grant's expression change. He didn't know the man well enough to know if it was for the better or the worse, but it had definitely changed.

Al continued. "The Hancock family's my kin, but they're nearsighted and greedy. Always have been. Guess that accounts for why so few of them ever left town and made something of themselves. Guess that's why they think your offer's the best thing that ever happened to them, even though there's no way in hell you're going to extend the railroad up to Hancock."

Grant's brown eyebrows rose. "You're a railroad man, too, I take it?"

"Nope. Just a man with common sense. You won't extend it that far because you don't need it that far. But you do need Nellie and her family to help you run the crooked side of your dealings here in town, and that's something my family's good at. So you figure you'll just keep stringing her along until she's so wealthy off your saloon and opium trade that she'll quit caring about her town and let the railroad dream go."

Grant shook his head slowly. "You see a lot for a farmer."

"The back end of a mule can give a man a lot of time to think if he's of a mind to put it to good use," Al said. "I know what you need and I know how to make sure you get it. What's more, I know my place and won't ever try to challenge you like I heard Underhill liked to do from time to time. I've been taking orders from Mad Nellie for a good chunk of my life, so I figure you and me can get along just fine."

Grant threw open his hands. "And here I am without a job to give you. Once again, fortune frowns upon me and I must reject your generous offer."

"You've got a job just waiting for me," Al said. "Walter Underhill's spot is open."

"Is that so?" Grant threw his head back and laughed. Al could hear his laughter echo throughout the great halls of the Municipal Building. It was a sound that was quickly getting on Al's nerves.

After he had finished, Grant wiped his eyes. "Let me get this straight. You and your family fail at the one task I gave you, so you ride back here and have the gall to ask me to give you the most plumb position in the territory." Grant shook his head. "And I thought Mackey was arrogant."

"Mackey's wounded," Al said. "And I'm the one who did it. I put lead to him, and I'll do it again if I have to. He whupped me in Ruby's and he got away from me out on the trail, but I've faced him twice now, so a third time won't scare me none. And you'll be needing someone to face him, Mr. Grant. Someone who won't run on account of his reputation. Because I've seen through that reputation. I've made the man bleed."

Grant stopped laughing and grew very still.

Al watched Grant's eyes look around his cluttered desk as he turned over everything he had just been told. He didn't blame him for being cautious, maybe even thinking Al was a liar. He'd be a fool to take everything he had been told without seeing it for himself.

But Al knew he'd given him an awful lot to think about. He was talking to the first man to ever put a bullet in the great Aaron Mackey. And he could give him the leverage he needed with the Hancock family.

But Al also knew he couldn't tell all of this to a man like James Grant. He had to come to his own decisions before he accepted them.

Grant looked up at him as he drummed his fingers on his desk. "If I give you that job, I'll be turning a lot of men on the force against me. Some of them think they're in line for Underhill's job, though I can't think of a man jack among them who has earned it."

"I have earned it," Al said. "And what's more, I've got the family to back me up whenever I need it. Let me make a few of them my deputies and we'll bring the rest into the fold easily enough."

He saw Grant pull a watch from his vest pocket and check the time. "It's just after noon now. Be back here at eight o'clock sharp. I should know much more by then. Head over to the Ruby and see your kin. Get yourself something to eat, but don't get drunk and not a word to anyone about what we've discussed here today or you'll get nothing. Understand me?"

That sounded fair to Al. He picked up his hat from Grant's desk. "It ain't complicated, Mr. Grant."

Al felt Grant watch him as he walked out of his office. "Let's just hope it stays that way," Grant said.

Chapter 28

In his office at the train station in Laramie, Frazer Rice winced as Mackey finished telling him all that had happened since leaving Dover Station. Rice had given in to his determination to come west.

"You've had a hard trail, Aaron." He looked at Billy, who was building a cigarette. "You too, Deputy."

"I've had better times," Billy said, "but we're still here to tell the tale."

"Indeed," Rice agreed. "And thank God for that. How's your back, Aaron? I hope you've had a doctor tend to it."

"Some of your Pinkerton men were handy with a needle and thread on the trail," Mackey said. "I'm fine. I'm more worried about Mr. Van Dorn and Lagrange."

"Mr. Lagrange is having his wounds tended to as we speak by my personal physician," Rice told him. "Unfortunately, Silas's wounds are deeper and will require more intricate attention. How he allowed himself to become addicted to such a substance is beyond me."

"Likely wasn't his doing," Mackey said. "Sounds like Grant fed it to him without his knowledge. Doesn't take long for a man to get hooked on it. A couple of times usually does the trick."

Rice pushed himself away from his desk and walked around his office. "I'm awfully tired of hearing that name, Aaron. James Grant has become the bane of my existence. He has caused more trouble for my company than anyone else I have ever employed, and yet I can never seem to be rid of him. He always manages to somehow evade getting caught red-handed."

"Not anymore," Billy said. "You've got that report Lagrange sent you a week or so ago. You know Grant had a hand in those three dead Chinese women. You know that man I killed was working for him. Now, with Mr. Van Dorn's testimony that he got him hooked on laudanum, we'll have enough to swear out a warrant for his arrest."

"Multiple warrants," Mackey added. "I can head to Helena straight from here with signed affidavits from all the witnesses. All of that, combined with a letter from you to Judge Forester, should be enough to put an end to Grant once and for all."

Rice cast a nervous glance at Billy, and Mackey felt his stomach drop.

Some bad news was coming their way.

"Deputy," the wealthy man said, "I was hoping you might be good enough to give Aaron and I a few moments to speak privately."

Mackey said, "No need for that. Anything you can say to me, you can say in front of Billy."

"Not everything, Marshal, I assure you."

"And I assure you that you can," Mackey persisted. "I almost got killed out there, Mr. Rice. If I had died, then you would've lost the only man in the territory who knows your mind in full. Now is not the time for secrecy, especially now that we've got Grant ready to fall. I'm not saying our conversations need to be transcribed and printed in the *Record*, but it's safer if Billy knows as much as I do."

Mr. Rice hesitated. "I'm not sure I agree."

"You don't have to," Mackey said, "because it's not open to discussion. Either you tell Billy now or I tell him after I leave here. Either way, he's going to know everything we speak about in this room today."

Mr. Rice did not appear to like it, but he also seemed to understand he did not have much of a choice. "Fine, Aaron. I'll try someone else's way for once in my life. You see, going after James Grant has become far more complicated than I had first believed."

Mackey knew that explained the look that had given him a pit in his stomach. "Meaning?"

"Meaning that Montana's statehood is just around the corner," Mr. Rice explained. "Statehood will mean a lot for this territory. It'll mean a lot for you, as well as for Deputy Sunday here. There's a big difference between being a frontier marshal and the marshal of one of the United States of America."

"It'll also mean a lot for you, too," Billy observed. "And your company."

"Of course," Mr. Rice admitted. "Why do you think I invested in Dover Station in the first place? For my health? You both saw how I increased my investment after witnessing what the town endured during Darabont's attack. I was impressed by the way the townsfolk rallied together in defense of their town. But I'm also not given to investing millions of dollars in a place just because nice, brave people happen to live there. Surely, both of you knew there were other factors involved."

"Never thought otherwise," Mackey said. "I still don't see what it's got to do with letting Grant go."

"Then I'll explain it to you." He inclined his head toward the office door. "For one, there is no way Silas Van Dorn will press charges against Grant for getting him hooked on laudanum. He'd have to admit it in public, and that's something I know his pride won't allow. Addiction is too shameful a shortcoming for a man in his position to admit, no matter the circumstances."

Mackey hadn't thought of that. "Then his butler will attest to it."

"Not if he wants to continue working for Silas, he won't," Mr. Rice said. "Besides, without Silas's testimony, no judge in their right mind would issue a warrant. Not even with my backing."

Mackey felt himself sitting forward. "And what about those three dead Chinese women Lagrange told you about in his report?"

"You mean the corpses of the three foreign whores and their murderer in the house you admit to having burned by your father to protect Billy here?" Mr. Rice asked. "I'm not blaming you for doing it. Why, if it was a choice between Deputy Sunday facing difficulty and letting James Grant go free, I would have done exactly the same thing. But the destruction of those bodies also took away the only leverage we had against Grant concerning those murders. According to you, the man who killed them also went up in flames, so we can't ellicit a confession from him or even prove his identity, much less his association with Grant, now can we?"

Mackey grabbed his stomach. He had walked into Mr. Rice's office believing he had just served James Grant to him on a silver platter. Now that he looked at the platter, he saw it was empty, for everything Mr. Rice was saying was absolutely true.

"Damn it," Billy said, "there has to be something you can do. Fire him. Or call him to New York on business. Something!"

Mr. Rice thought it over for a long moment. "It just so happens there is something we can do. I'm afraid it's the only thing we can do, but you gentlemen are not going to like it."

Mackey couldn't speak, so Billy spoke for him. "What is it?"

"We can allow James Grant to have Dover Station."

Mackey almost came out of his chair but remained right where he was.

Because although it was difficult for him to admit, Mr. Rice may be on to something.

Mr. Rice sat on the edge of his desk. "I'm not taking his side over you, gentlemen. I'm trying to be practical. You're a federal marshal now, Aaron. Your place is in Helena now, not Dover Station. You're the marshal for the entire territory. Judge Forester and the governor have been making a lot of grumbling back in Washington that you have spent too much time in your hometown and no time at all in the capital."

"I went after Henry Hancock first because you wanted me to," Mackey reminded him.

"Which is why I've given you suitable cover in Washington. So far, they've turned a deaf ear to the governor and the judge, but they won't ignore them forever and especially now that statehood is gaining momentum. They can't afford to ignore them, and even the slightest oversight will be magnified."

"Scandals, too," Billy said. He set his cigarette in the ashtray. "You're worried about a scandal affecting your company too, aren't you?"

"Not just my company, but the bid for statehood itself," Mr. Rice said. "What do you think will happen if word gets out that one man was not only able to turn my partner into an addlebrained puppet, but to also take over my investments and the mayor's office of the town I built? Every company I own would be at risk from ridicule and stockholders questioning my authority. And they'd be right, too. I know we tried to stop Grant at every turn, but he always managed to stay just one step ahead of us when it really counted. I believe he's guilty of every crime we've accused him of. But we cannot prove it. And even if we could, no one would really care."

"Because all it amounts to," Mackey said, "is three dead whores and a town no one's ever heard of in the middle of Montana."

"That's where you're wrong, my friend," said Mr. Rice. "There are plenty of people who have heard of Dover Station. More and more people hear of it every day. That's why my plan works in the long run. Allow Grant to continue to run the town. Let him think he's won. You marry the lovely Katherine and take her with you to Helena. You belong there anyway, and I'll see to it you're well provided for. After a year or two, new blood will flow through Dover Station. The same appetite for change that created James Grant will ultimately become his undoing. Maybe then, with the formality of statehood in place, the opportunity will be right to wrest Grant from power."

Mackey spoke through clenched teeth out of fear he might be sick. "He could have the whole town ruined by then. He's got your company in one pocket, the police in the other, and the criminal element tucked in his belt. The Hancock family aren't much now, but they will be in a year when they have some of their own money behind them. Maybe they'll have enough to buy off Underhill's men and turn them against him. I don't know what you've read about that family, Mr. Rice, but they're not just a bunch of ignorant hillbillies and rustlers. They're mean and stupid. And when you give people like that money and power, you're looking at a world of trouble. Not just for Dover Station, but for the whole territory."

Mr. Rice began to speak, but Billy cut him off. "I might not have your head for business or Aaron's head for tactics, but I know how to handle people. I know trouble when I see it and I'm telling you this Grant problem will get a whole lot worse before it gets better. And so will the Hancock family. You think they're bad now? What happens when they start looking at Helena as their next target?"

Mr. Rice clasped his hands behind his back and looked at the floor. "What do you propose, Deputy?"

"I say we go at them now while we've got some

support in town. Wipe Grant out forever, then go about our marshaling business in the rest of the territory or the state, if statehood happens. What you say might go all right if Grant just cared about Dover Station, but he doesn't. Tomorrow, maybe he'll look at another town to take over north or south of there. And when that one falls, maybe another, then another until he becomes a real problem for the governor. Hell, he might even be governor by then or have his hooks so deep into him that it won't matter who's in office."

Mackey knew everything Billy was saying was true, but he also knew Mr. Rice had a point. Becoming federals had saved them from Grant's chopping block when he had become mayor, but it had also expanded their responsibilities well beyond Dover Station. He did not like the idea of giving up, especially to Grant. He did not like letting go just to get a better hold of him later on.

But there was a time when a man had to know when to give up the chase. Just like they had decided against hunting the sharpshooter in the woods. Sometimes, enough had to be enough.

"Billy, maybe he's—"

"Don't you say it, Aaron." Billy was on his feet now. "Don't you dare say he might have a point, because he doesn't." He looked at Mr. Rice. "I know you're a good man and you think you know what you're talking about, but you're wrong. Aaron and I saw what happens when you let a problem go on for too long while we were in the army. When you see the warning signs all around you and just hope it'll go away or die down. We saw it when people hoped the Apaches would just calm down and go along peacefully, and we saw what happened when they didn't. A lot of people got killed later on when only a few in the right places would have done the trick. The same thing is happening in Dover Station, sir. Just because Aaron and I happen to be from there doesn't mean we're partial to the place. If we turn our back on Grant now, we'll regret it in the future. And so will you and your company."

Mr. Rice frowned as he returned to his desk, picked up a newspaper, and tossed it down in front of Mackey and Billy. "I'm afraid Dover Station may already be lost, gentlemen, as Grant seems to have made his boldest move yet."

It was a copy of *The Dover Station Record* that bore the screaming headline:

UNDERHILL CUT DOWN
ON FRONT STREET

Is Dover Station a Lawless Town?

MAYOR APPOINTS TEMPORARY CHIEF
AL BRENNER

Mackey read the headline aloud for Billy's benefit. He looked at the date of the newspaper. "This is two days old." He quickly read through the article, written by Charles Everett Harrington. "It doesn't say if Underhill is alive or dead."

"No, it doesn't," Mr. Rice said. "Grant wired me about what had happened a couple of days ago. The weasel hides these kinds of events from me, but he probably figured this was too big a development. I've come to rely on Mr. Lagrange to be my eyes and ears in town, but with him here, I have no idea what's really going on in town. I have no idea if Underhill is alive or dead and, what's more, I don't think it matters."

Billy looked up from the paper he couldn't read. "That's a cold way of looking at things, mister. He helped you in those early days when you were looking at Dover Station."

"Yes," Rice allowed, "and he also helped Grant solidify power and take the town from me." Rice waved down the arguments before Billy or Mackey made them. "Yes, I know he seemed reluctant about it, but he could have thrown in with you once he realized what Grant was up to. I would have seen to it that he would have gotten his federal badge back, but he didn't do that, did he? No. Instead, he had his nice title and big office and enjoyed Grant's good graces. I know he's your friend and you like him, but his vanity has caused us almost as much difficulty as Grant's. I know it's unpleasant to hear, but you know I'm right."

He looked at the lawmen from behind his desk and waited for a response.

Mackey sat back from the newspaper and ignored the pain webbing through his body from the wound in his back. "Damn."

"I don't know if Chief Underhill is alive or dead," Mr. Rice admitted. "And I no longer think Dover Station is worth the trouble of taking it away from Grant. And neither do my investors."

"That's easy for you to say, mister," Billy said. "It's not your home."

"No, but it is my property," Mr. Rice countered, "at

least most of it is, anyway. Grant has been wise enough to see to it that it pays a handsome dividend each and every month, which further weakens my position in having him removed. My board is happy with his progress and would protest if I tried."

"You're willing to let him get away with all of this," Mackey said, "because he's making your company money?"

"And because we can't prove anything," Mr. Rice countered. "We suspect him of much but can prove little, if anything at all. I think he's guilty of everything you've said, Aaron, and probably of some sins you don't even know about. But there's only so much I can do at this point to stop him without pulling everything down. And for what purpose?"

Mr. Rice held up a hand to stop Billy from interrupting. "Not because of my profits, but because of what he's done for the town. He's popular because he's been prosperous and, as for the rest of it, no one really cares, not even in Dover Station." He looked at both of them. "You know I'm right."

Mackey lowered his head and slowly ran his hand over his hair. Billy sat quietly, looking at the paper.

Both men knew Mr. Rice was, indeed, right.

"I know the way you view the world, gentlemen. You view everything as either a victory or a defeat. A man is either guilty or innocent. In this case, I recommend you make the tactical decision to delay the battle until such time as you have sufficient resources to wage it." He tried a smile. "Go to Helena, Aaron. It's a lovely city, I assure you. Enjoy your position and expand your influence. And, when the time is right and Grant has become complacent, we'll oust him from power. Please. It's the only practical way."

Mackey could not open his eyes or raise his head. He was not angry at Mr. Rice. He did not even disagree with him, because the man was not wrong. He had followed the man's direction for quite a while now and had always done well by it. He had done good work, too. Henry Hancock was dead because of Mr. Rice's suggestion, and they had tried to stop the Hancock family from coming to Dover Station the best way they had known how. They had saved Silas Van Dorn's life and had rid the world of a lot of Hancock men.

No, Aaron Mackey was not angry. He was exhausted. It was a feeling that seeped through his bones and into his soul. His mind hurt from all of the twists and turns and steps it took to chase James Grant from one rabbit hole to the next only now to finally wind up in a dead end.

He knew Grant would hurt himself eventually, but that could take years. If Montana was ever going to be a state, then it needed to have laws, and those laws needed to be enforced. They needed to be enforced by men like him and Billy if the state had any hope of surviving.

Mackey looked at Mr. Rice. "What if I just kill him?"

Mr. Rice considered it. "That would technically be against the law."

"Doing right doesn't always follow the law," Billy said, "especially where Grant is concerned."

Mackey decided to make it easy on the man who had become his patron, maybe even a mentor. "I'm not asking your permission, Mr. Rice. I'm not asking for your help, either. I'm asking you to let it go if it comes to that."

Mr. Rice kept his hands clasped on his desk as he appeared to give it some thought. "Were you to ask my investors, most of them would tell you that James Grant is an indispensable part of the Dover Station Company."

Then Mr. Rice looked at the lawmen and smiled. "But cemeteries are filled with indispensable men, aren't they?"

Chapter 29

As soon as his train arrived in Dover Station, Mackey walked back to the livery car to retrieve Adair. She had nipped at the hostler when he had tried to put her in the stall back at Laramie, so they decided it might be better for all concerned if Mackey got her instead. He had set the saddle on her personally and led her out of the stall and down the ramp.

The hostler was cradling his bandaged hand. He still managed to catch the gold piece Mackey had flipped to him. "Sorry about the hand, mister. She's not a friendly animal, especially around strangers."

"She's a demon if I ever saw one," said the Scotsman. "A demon, sir."

Mackey climbed up into the saddle and tipped his hat to the wounded man.

He rode behind the train and across the tracks, intending to see Katherine over at The Campbell Arms before checking on Walter Underhill's condition.

But his path was blocked by five men on horseback. Each of them was wearing the brown dusters and badges of the Dover Station Police Department. Each of them had a Winchester resting on his hip, pointing at the sky.

None of them looked familiar, and Mackey wondered if Grant had hired on new men after the attack on Underhill. The bastard probably already had a plan ready to go before Underhill was stabbed.

Adair stood stock still at an angle from the five horses. Mackey crossed his hands on the pommel. His right hand casually near the handle of the Peacemaker on his belly holster. "Morning, gentlemen."

The man in the center spoke first. "No sudden moves, Marshal. You're under arrest for the attempted murder of Police Chief Walter Underhill."

"That'd be a pretty neat trick," Mackey said, "seeing as how I was out of town when it happened."

"Had it done, then." The man held out a piece of paper to him. "Mayor James Grant has issued a warrant for your arrest and ordered us to bring you in for questioning."

Mackey ignored the paper. "The mayor doesn't have the authority to have anyone arrested, so what you're holding in your hand is useless."

Given their obvious ignorance of the law, he decided to try a bluff. "I'm also the United States Marshal for this territory, so you can't arrest me without a formal writ from a federal judge. Any attempt to impede my movement can result in an obstruction of federal law charge, which would land you boys a nice cell in Helena for a couple of years." He looked them over, especially the big man in front. "You boys look like you'd be right at home in a cell to me. How much time have you done?"

The men's mounts grew restless and had to be brought under control.

Adair hadn't moved.

The lead officer put the phony writ back in his pocket. "We have orders to take you by force if you fail to obey our lawful command."

"I don't know what's more impressive," Mackey said. "You buying what Grant's telling you or your ability to repeat all of those fancy words he's feeding you." There was something familiar about the man he couldn't quite place. "What's your name, boy?"

"I'm not a boy," the policeman said. "I'm Acting Commissioner Al Brenner."

The name had not meant much to Mackey when he had read it in the paper, but now that he saw the man, he remembered him. "You and I danced at the Ruby a couple of weeks back. Bad balance on your part, as I recall."

"Nothing wrong with my balance now." He gestured to the men flanking him. "I'd say I've got just the right amount of balance to take you in or take you on."

Mackey acted as if he had not heard a word of what Brenner was saying. "You're part of the Hancock clan, aren't you? Cousin or something. Pig farmer, right?"

Brenner flicked the badge on his duster. "Acting Commissioner of the Dover Station Police Department. I'm taking over while Chief Underhill is indisposed."

"Indisposed?" Mackey laughed. "You call taking a knife to the belly 'indisposed'?"

Brenner's beady eyes narrowed. "You coming peacefully, Marshal, or do my men and I have to rip you from the saddle and take you in?"

One of the men on the left of the arc of horses began to lower his Winchester.

A clacking sound that could only be a round being chambered in a rifle came from the warehouse behind him.

"I wouldn't do that if I were you," Mackey said. "I don't think Deputy Marshal Halstead will appreciate that."

They looked around to see Jerry walk just close enough to the warehouse entrance to be seen.

Mackey continued. "You're new here, aren't you, son? I'd wager these four are new, too. Hancock men from the looks of them. And the smell of them. They pig farmers, too?"

He saw Brenner's Winchester flinch downward, but Mackey's Peacemaker cleared the holster in time to stop him. "I wouldn't do that, either, Acting Commissioner Brenner. See, if you had been from around here, you'd know I don't travel alone often. So, not only are you covered by Deputy Halstead over there, you're also covered by Deputy Billy Sunday from the top corner room of The Campbell Arms just behind your right shoulder."

Brenner swallowed hard and looked in that direction. So did three of his men. Billy was clearly on the porch of the top floor, aiming his Sharps down at them.

Brenner faced Mackey once more. "Fair distance to hit someone."

"With a Winchester," Mackey agreed. "But not with a Sharps. You ever see what a fifty-caliber bullet can do to a man's skull, Acting Commissioner Brenner?"

The involuntary flinch that went through him told

Mackey he had. He wondered if he had seen it along the wagon trail outside of Chidester Station.

Mackey decided he'd had enough talk. He raised the Peacemaker so it was aimed squarely at Brenner's face. "I've had a long train ride and I'm hungry, so if you and your men plan on doing something, do it now. If not, take that paper back to Grant and tell him to come find me himself if he wants to talk."

Mackey could see Brenner didn't seem to know what to do. He was a big man, maybe as big as Underhill, but he was much younger and unsure of himself.

And Mackey didn't plan on allowing him to gain any experience on his behalf. "I'm getting real tired of this. Best get moving." He thumbed back the hammer of the Peacemaker. "Right now."

Brenner sneered as he brought his mount around and led his men back to Front Street toward the Municipal Building.

Mackey eased down the hammer on his Peacemaker and holstered it. He looked up at the balcony of The Campbell Arms and touched the brim of his hat to Billy. His deputy responded in kind before stepping back inside.

Jerry Halstead rode out of the warehouse atop his dappled gray. "Gotta give you credit, Aaron. I've never seen a lawman back down like that before."

"That's because they're not lawmen," Mackey said. "They're hired guns with badges. Cut-rate hired guns at that."

Halstead turned his mount so he could watch the last of Brenner's men disappear along Front Street. "They're not going to be happy about what we just did to them. Neither will the mayor."

Mackey knew it would take Grant a few hours to figure out what to do next. Until then, he had other things to do. "Let's head over to the Campbell and find out about Underhill."

Since Underhill was resting, Mackey had no choice but to talk to Doc Ridley, who was attending to the police commissioner's injuries.

"It's a miracle he's still alive," Doc Ridley said in the dining room of The Campbell Arms. "If he had been in the hands of any other doctor, he most likely wouldn't have made it. I just thank God that my training on the field of battle saw him through."

Doc Ridley had been one of the men who had founded the town when Mackey was a child, so he had grown up hearing Pappy and the doctor trade lies about their time in the War Between the States. He also knew the doctor could never pass up an opportunity to gossip or remind anyone that he had once been a surgeon for the Confederate States of America.

"At least something good came out of that damned war," Mackey said.

"For the people of this town, anyway," Doc Ridley said. "The last time I saw an injury like Underhill's was at Sharpsburg." He looked down at his flat stomach and pointed at a spot just below the right side of his rib cage. "His assailant lunged forward and plunged a dagger right here, which traveled downward at an odd angle. The assailant lost his footing in the attack and stumbled into the thoroughfare, where Underhill shot him dead. The dagger was long enough to hit any number of vital organs that could have proven fatal. Instead, the blade punctured his gallbladder and remained stuck there."

Doc Ridley sipped his tea and marveled again at Underwood's good fortune. "One inch in either direction and the blade would have punctured his liver or his stomach or even an intestine. Damage to the gallbladder is quite serious, of course, but in the hands of a skilled surgeon such as myself, not entirely fatal."

Katherine poured the doctor more tea. "We're all grateful for your skill and bravery, Dr. Ridley. Walter surely would have died if it hadn't been for your efforts."

Mackey made sure he didn't roll his eyes. She wasn't complimenting Ridley out of kindness. She was also doing it to give Mackey a bad time.

Mackey decided to change the subject before the doctor's ego got big enough to force them all from the room. "You sure he'll make it?"

"No one can be sure of anything with a stab wound to the belly, Aaron. You know that. A tiny nick to any of the nearby organs could rupture at any time. I didn't see such damage when I operated, but that doesn't mean it isn't there. So let's just say I'm cautiously optimistic for the moment, but I wouldn't advise him to resume a career in law enforcement."

That was not the news Mackey wanted to hear. "I thought someone could live without a gallbladder."

"They certainly can, and I have every confidence that Walter will do just that," Doc Ridley said, "but he'll never be the man he once was. He's been attacked,

Aaron. Stabbed in the belly and came within a whisker of dying. Men in your profession don't often rebound from such a setback. It preys on their mind and for good reason. I've seen many a soldier damaged for life from being confronted with their own mortality, and I judge Walter Underhill will be no different."

He looked around the dining room to make sure he wasn't being overheard before whispering to Mackey, "We both know he was more bluster than ballast anyway. Texans are like that, as you know well, my Yankee friend."

Mackey wasn't in any mood to discuss Doc Ridley's opinions about his fellow southerners. "Did you tell Underhill this?"

"Of course not," Ridley said. "But he is aware that the mayor has already appointed a new man to take his place. One Alfred Brenner. Kin of the Hancock clan, I believe."

"I had a run-in with him at the Ruby a couple of weeks ago," Mackey said, "then down at the station just now. Had four others with him who had that Hancock look."

"He brought them onto the police force with him when Grant gave him the job," Katherine said. "The boys who were already on the force are none too happy about the changes, but they like the paycheck, so they put up with it."

"Looks like Grant's allowing the Hancock family to take over the police force as well as all of the other godless vices in town," Ridley said. "Pretty soon, I fear we'll find ourselves pining for the good old days when we only had James Grant to worry about."

Mackey had to enjoy the irony of the situation. "I can remember a time when you held a couple of rallies to get me fired back when I was sheriff, Doc."

"Prayer meetings can hardly be called rallies," Ridley said. "And besides, that was a different time. I never questioned your intentions, Aaron, just your methods. Even a broken clock is right twice a day, you know."

The doctor had not meant to do it, but his words sparked an idea in Mackey's mind. *Times may change, but people do not.* Mr. Rice's words from his office in Laramie came back to him, too. *Maybe the change Grant embraced will also lead to his undoing.*

He had not realized he had trailed off into his own thoughts until Katherine touched his hand and snapped him out of it. "Are you okay, Aaron? I know you've been through the mill with Mr. Van Dorn and all. Why not have Doc Ridley take a look at you while he's here?"

He knew she would be upset when he told her about the bullet graze across his back. He also did not want an old gossip like Doc Ridley telling the town about his injury.

Part of the legend that had grown up about him was that he had never been shot before. The scars in his thigh and his right shoulder from his cavalry days proved otherwise, but he did not see any reason to explain himself to anyone. Any threat to whatever legend he had around him now might only make the Hancock men seem even tougher than they already were.

Doc Ridley took the cue to excuse himself as he

had other patients to tend to. Neither Katherine nor Mackey dissuaded him from leaving.

When they were alone, Katherine asked, "What's wrong, Aaron? I know it's something."

Mackey glanced around the dining room and was glad to see they were the only people there. He decided there was no easy way to speak his mind other than to say what he was thinking. "Mr. Rice wants us to give up on the town. He wants us to let Grant take it over. Says his company won't support removing Grant because he makes them too much money. He wants you and me and Billy to move on to Helena so we can concentrate on our marshaling duties."

"Mr. Rice has always been a very reasonable man." She stroked his hand. "You've got more responsibilities than just Dover Station now, and Judge Forester would be a lot happier with you in the capital."

"No one cares what Forester thinks except Forester." Mackey didn't want to sound bitter or angry, especially to Katherine. He knew Forester had a point. So did Mr. Rice.

He had every valid reason to just let Grant take over the town. But for some reason, he hated the idea of allowing the schemer to even think he had won.

He covered her hand with his, mostly to cover the trembling of his own. "If we go to Helena, I want you to come with me." He raised her hand to his lips and kissed it. "And I want you to be my wife when you do."

Mackey dared to look at her, expecting tears of joy. He was not expecting her to laugh in his face.

"What's so funny?"

"Aaron, I left my life in Boston and traveled across the country to be with you." She caressed the side of his face. "When I got here and found out you were married, I stayed just so I could be in the same town as you. And I've never regretted a day since, not even when Darabont took me, because I knew if he killed me, at least I'd been given the chance to see you every day. And I knew if he let me live, you'd come to rescue me. And you did, and you've helped me and the girls get past what those animals did to us."

She eased his face toward her when he looked away. "A lot of men are good at riding in and rescuing a woman, but they're scared to death about truly saving her. You did both."

He began to deny it, but she held his head in place with both hands. "You held me through my nightmares. You helped me become brave enough to stand on the porch of my own hotel again. You helped those girls we rescued find a better life than they had before. You stayed when most men leave."

"You were here," he said. "Why would I go anywhere else?"

She smiled up at him. "I loved you from the first moment I saw you, Aaron Mackey. And I love you even more today. Of course, I'll marry you. I just can't believe you'd think any different."

He looked at his coffee. "Didn't work out so well for me the last time, Katie. Mary left. Maybe I'm a lousy husband."

"We've been living together since she left," Katherine said. "I know what you are and what you're not. And what you're not is a bad husband."

They stood up together, and she let him take her in his arms. She was not as tall as he was, but she always felt warm and glowing whenever he held her. She pushed away all the troubles that preyed upon his mind and allowed him to just be happy for a change. She was his only weakness and she knew it, and she never used it against him.

They kissed, standing alone in the middle of the dining room of the hotel she had purchased when she had come to town to find him all of those years ago. He remembered seeing her on the front porch of her hotel for the first time since their affair in Boston and the warm feeling that had spread through him just from looking at her, and all of Mary's yelling and cursing didn't seem to mean as much to him as it used to.

She was wrong when she said he had saved her life. She had saved his life many times, simply by giving him one.

Neither of them broke off the kiss. They simply stopped at the same time as they always did.

She held his face in her hands. "But we're not getting married yet."

He felt his stomach drop even further than it had in Rice's office. "Why not?"

"Because you have a job to do," she said. "You have to take care of Grant once and for all, and I know that look you just had meant you've figured out a way to do it and do it the right way."

He tried to answer, but she gently covered his mouth with both hands. "Don't try to explain it. Just know I'll be here for you, no matter what. And when the time comes for you to go to Helena, you'll know it and I'll be honored to go with you as your wife. But you'll know when the time is right. Not Mr. Rice or Judge Forester or anyone else. You know this town.

You know your mind, and you know what needs to be done. I don't care if it's tonight or next year, I'm not going anywhere except with you. But you leave when you're ready or you'll end up regretting it for the rest of your life. I've seen what regret did to you before, my love. I won't let it happen again."

He eased her hands away from his face and kissed them. He did not know why he was so relieved she had agreed to come with him. But hearing the words made all the difference.

"I'll let Billy know, and we'll figure out the particulars."

She smiled and smacked him on the backside to go. "And tell him I want to see more of him in here. He's getting too skinny."

Mackey smiled as he gathered his hat and walked out of the dining room. Billy would be happy to hear that.

He would be happy to hear how they were going to pull down James Grant, too.

Chapter 30

Mackey was not expecting to see Billy leaning against the jailhouse where his rocking chair ought to be. It took him a moment to understand why.

His rocking chair was not there.

Billy held up his hands as Mackey drew nearer. "Don't get upset."

Mackey looked down at the grooves that had been well-worn into the boardwalk's wooden slats by the rails of his chair. "What happened?"

"Sandborne said a couple of Grant's men tried to seize the jailhouse while we were gone," Billy told him. "Sandborne managed to hold them off, but they kicked your chair and my bench to pieces before he did."

"Seize the jailhouse?" The words did not make any sense to him. "It's federal property. He can't just seize it."

"His men claimed they could on account of us abandoning it," Billy explained. "Fortunately, Sandborne was here and held them off until Underhill pulled them back. The kid hasn't left since it happened. He takes that deputy badge we pinned on him real seriously."

Mackey had done it as an afterthought before they left. He wanted the kid to keep an eye on the place to make sure no one thought to break in and steal the rifles. He never thought he was putting the young man in any danger. "They hurt him?"

"He's fine," Billy said. "Hasn't left since they tried to take the place. Not that he's been wanting for company."

Mackey figured he meant the girl who had been sweet on Joshua after they had saved her from Darabont, but he didn't care about that just then. He didn't even care that the old rocking chair had been busted up.

He cared about how he could use all of this to his advantage.

Without looking, he asked Billy, "How many men does Grant have watching us from across the street?" He knew someone would be there. Grant had them followed from the moment he had stepped off the train. He wouldn't let up now.

"Same five Hancock boys we ran off at the station earlier today," Billy told him. "Standing around the entrance of that building like a bunch of jackals, just waiting to see what we're going to do."

"Good. That idiot Brenner with them?"

"Out front like he's always been there," Billy said. "Boy was a farmer before he came here, now he's taken Underhill's place."

"Doesn't make him a bad man."

"Doesn't make him a lawman, either," Billy countered.

"And him being a Hancock man probably doesn't

make him too popular with the rest of his men," Mackey said.

Billy looked down and smiled. "I know that look. You've got something cooking."

Mackey would not be sure until he heard it himself. Many's the idea that sounded good in his head only to sound like garbage when he aired it out. "A lot of Underhill's boys may not have liked him much, but they respected him. I'll bet anything that his men won't like being stepped over for a Hancock man, much less five of them. Do you?"

"No," Billy said. "I'd imagine not. You plan on using that resentment against Grant, don't you?"

"I plan on giving it a try." He glanced over his shoulder. "Right now."

Mackey looked over and saw all five men grinning at him from the entrance of the Municipal Building. He turned so the barrel of his holstered Peacemaker was aimed in their direction. It would cut down on the firing time if it came to that.

Al Brenner saw Mackey looking at him and called out to him from across Front Street. "You look like you're missing something, Marshal. Like maybe that famous rocking chair of yours."

"As a matter of fact, I am," Mackey answered back as a wagon moved past them along the thoroughfare. "But the chair can wait. I was hoping you might be able to tell me where Mad Nellie is."

Al began walking down the steps of the Municipal Building. "That's a name she doesn't much care for, mister."

"Didn't ask you what she likes to be called." Mackey moved his hand to his belt, close enough to draw the

Colt if needed, but not enough to provoke him. "I asked you where she was. And I don't like repeating myself."

"Can't rightly say." Brenner kept walking down the stairs. "But I wouldn't head back up to Hancock if I were you. You'll find it a lot less friendly toward you this time around."

Mackey could see he was itching for a fight, and this was his chance to goad him into one. "Never had a problem handling your people before, Al. Just like I didn't have a problem cutting you down to size at the Ruby. Just like we had you pinned down in the woods outside Chidester. Quaking in the branches all alone like a scared rabbit."

"Closer to a bunny, I'd say," Billy added. "His teeth were chattering so loud, scared all the game away."

Al Brenner stopped at the bottom step of the Municipal Building. His hands balled into fists and he shook with rage.

It was almost too easy, Mackey thought. James Grant had made a mistake putting this youngster in charge, and Mackey was going to make him pay for it.

Mackey glanced back at Billy. "See that? Still quivering."

"I'd say quivering is just about the only thing he's good at."

Brenner bellowed before charging at him across Front Street in a blind rage.

His four relatives thought about joining him, but the sight of Billy's Colt clearing leather made them think better of it. He stepped aside as Brenner came running.

Mackey didn't move.

Brenner leapt up on the jailhouse porch, showing surprising agility for such a big man.

But he wasn't agile enough to stop in time to avoid Mackey's punch to the throat.

The blow brought Brenner crashing to his knees. His eyes bulged as he struggled to get air into his lungs.

Mackey drew his Peacemaker, kicked Brenner in the ribs, and brought the handle of the big Colt down on the back of his head, laying him out cold.

Mackey stepped on Brenner's back and aimed the Colt at the Hancock men across the street. "Any of you boys want some while it's hot, come and get it." Out of the corner of his mouth, he spoke to Billy. "I'll cover them while you go inside and get the shackles. Have Sandborne help you drag Brenner into a cell."

Billy went into the jailhouse and Mackey kept the pistol aimed on the men. They were pitched forward and wondering if they should try to save their kin or wait for a better time.

"Any of you boys tired of living can either jump off that porch or go for your pistols. The result will be the same either way."

The men stood upright and seemed to change their mind. The one with blond, scraggily hair beneath a faded bowler yelled out, "You're a dead man, Mackey."

"So you say." The marshal grinned. "But what are you going to do about it?"

But neither the man in the bowler hat nor his kin had a chance to do anything before three of Underhill's men came running out of the Municipal Building, rifles at the ready, only to come up short when they saw Mackey aiming the Peacemaker in their general direction.

The one he remembered as Edison yelled, "Whoa, Mackey. Put the gun down. What the hell's going on out here?"

"You promise you'll keep those boys covered?"

Edison looked around at the four Hancock men and shoved one of them back up the stairs. "Get inside before you damned fools get yourselves killed."

Only the blond man in the bowler resisted. "You can't talk to us like that, you damned piker. Al is the chief now. You do what we say."

Edison shoved him even harder up the stairs. One of the other policemen gave Blondie a boot to the backside for good measure.

Mackey holstered the Colt before the policemen turned around. Edison kept his hands visible and his rifle at his side. So did the men with him. "You mind telling me what the hell that was all about?" He looked closer at the man Mackey had pinned to the boardwalk. "Is that Chief Brenner?"

Mackey stepped aside as Billy and Sandborne came out, clapped Brenner's hands in shackles and dragged the big man inside. Billy heeled the jailhouse door shut behind him.

"That's Al Brenner," Mackey called back, "but he's not the police chief anymore. You are."

Edison took a step back. "You might be a federal now, but you don't have a say. Only the mayor does."

"Only as long as he's the mayor," Mackey said. "Because I'm on my way in there to arrest him right now on conspiracy to murder a peace officer. That peace officer was me. He so much as admitted it before he charged at me."

The three policemen looked at each other. One of them called out, "You'd better be able to prove that."

Mackey inclined his head toward the jail. "Brenner's all the proof I need. He was one of the men who tried to kill me while me and some others were escorting Mr. Van Dorn to Laramie. And he did it on Mayor Grant's orders."

"That's awful thin," Edison said.

"It's thick enough to make you police chief if you want it," Mackey said. He had intended on using the resentment against the Hancocks to his advantage, but he hadn't figured out who the new chief would be. Edison would be as good a choice as anyone else on the force who was not a Hancock. "Unless you're happy taking orders from those inbred sons of bitches Grant put in front of you, then Brenner can remain chief."

Edison looked at the two men on either side of them, and from even at that distance, Mackey could see they had reached an agreement. If there was one thing a lawman could always bank on, it was the self-interest of other people.

"The mayor's been acting a mite squirrely lately," Edison called out. "Made us serve a writ to seize your jail. That boy you've got in there held us off before Underhill told us to go away. Come to think of it, the mayor might not be in his right mind."

Mackey liked where this was headed. "Sounds like a question of competency. Something for a judge to decide."

"Certainly does." Edison ran a hand across the

stubble on his chin. "We also kind of busted up the bench Billy likes to set on sometimes. Your rocking chair, too."

Mackey hid his anger about his chair. "That was then. Today's a different day, isn't it, Chief?"

Edison's face broke into a wide grin. "Glad to hear it. But I'm afraid you can't arrest the mayor here today."

Mackey felt the good will the two had built up between them across the thoroughfare melt away. "Why not?"

"On account of him not being here, is why." Edison pointed toward the Van Dorn House. "He's just finishing up moving in there, all right and proper like. If you want him, you'll find him there."

Mackey tipped his hat and went to go inside the jailhouse to fetch his Winchester when Edison added, "Might look better if you had a proper escort while you were going about the execution of your duties. The three of us would be happy to join you."

"Much obliged." Mackey knocked on the jailhouse door, and Billy opened it. "Hand me my Winchester, will you?"

Billy stood at the half-opened door. He had the Greener cocked and at his side. "You really going to let them back you?"

"I'd rather it was you," Mackey admitted, "but I need you and Sandborne here in case the Hancocks try to spring Brenner. Edison and his men might not be much, but they'll keep the rest of the force off my back."

Billy ducked back inside, pulled down a rifle from

the rack, and handed it to Mackey. "Bring that bastard back alive and let's end this thing once and for all."

"Lock the door," Mackey said, "and shoot anyone who isn't me."

Billy locked the door, and Mackey looked across the street at Edison and his men. "You ready, Chief?"

Mackey looked down the alley beside the Municipal Building and cut loose with a stream of Spanish words.

"What the hell was that about?" Edison asked, "Who you talking to?"

"Doesn't concern you." Mackey began walking toward the Van Dorn House. "Let's go to work."

Chapter 31

Mackey had hoped Pappy wouldn't be holding court in front of his store, but he was. And Pappy noticed his son across the street with his Winchester and the three policemen walking toward him.

He interrupted his conversation and came to the edge of the boardwalk. "What are you up to, boy?"

"Nothing, Pappy. Best get back to your guests."

"I know that walk," Pappy persisted. "And I know where you're headed. Wait for me!"

But Mackey didn't wait for him. Neither did the others. If anything, Mackey picked up the pace to put as much distance between him and his father as possible. His father was the bravest man he had ever known, and maybe the most fearless. But he had a way of getting under a man's skin that could make a bad situation worse, and Mackey didn't want Grant's arrest to turn into a shoot-out if he could avoid it. He had no qualms about killing the man if he had to, but he did not want to risk turning him into a martyr.

He also knew Grant's death would look like a lawless coup orchestrated by a lawman known to hate him.

He needed this to look as official as possible.

And he didn't need Pappy's mouth turning it into a bloodbath.

He rounded the corner in front of The Campbell Arms and walked up the hill. He didn't look to see if Katherine was on the porch.

He noticed Edison had about ten policemen with him now. None of them were Hancock men. His mind told him the men were capable of betraying him, but his instinct told him these men had no intention of serving under Hancock rule.

They had tolerated Underhill because he knew how to treat them.

Edison would want that loyalty for himself.

Mackey saw that all the drapes of the former Van Dorn House had been opened, and every window was up. Light poured into the dour structure that was only about a year old but already looked ancient.

He spotted a wagon with a fancy oak bed in front of the former Van Dorn House. Two movers were in the process of carrying down an old headboard from the house when one of them spotted Mackey and the ten men behind him. The movers quickly set the headboard against the wagon and ran down the hill.

Two policemen who were standing guard on either side of the door began to bring up their rifles when they saw Mackey approaching. He was glad they stepped aside when Edison motioned for them to stand down.

The front door was open, and Mackey had no intention of waiting for Grant to come outside. Every second that passed risked this turning into a shooting match.

He paused just long enough to let Edison catch up

to him. "Might be best if you and your boys surround the house while I go in. Don't shoot anyone unless you have to. We're here to make an arrest, not a martyr. Understand me, *Chief*?"

"I understand just fine," Edison said. "Just make sure you don't go and kill the son of a bitch yourself. Kinda hard to prove that competency thing you mentioned if he's dead, ain't it?"

Mackey began walking up the steps to the house when James Grant appeared in the doorway. His shirtsleeves were rolled up, and it was the first time Mackey could remember seeing him without a fancy vest and tie. He looked like less of a dandy and more like the hired hand he really was.

Mayor Grant looked over the crowd of men gathered in front of his house like Caesar reviewing his adoring public.

"What an odd procession," he said to Edison. "I see you've finally managed to bring him in. Good work, boys. I'm sure Chief Brenner will be pleased." He looked at the man to the right of his doorway. "Take his pistol and rifle and run him over to the jail. I'll be there as soon as my new bed is in place."

But the officer did not move.

No one did, except Mackey as he slowly walked up the stairs. "They didn't bring me to you, James. They came with me to bring you in for conspiracy to commit murder."

Grant laughed. "And just who did I supposedly conspire to kill? And who with?"

The police men began to fan out in a circle around the house as Mackey reached the top step and stood only inches from Grant. "For conspiring with the

Hancock family to murder Silas Van Dorn, Robert Lagrange, Deputy Billy Sunday. And me."

Grant looked up at Mackey. "I sure hope you can prove that nonsense, Marshal. Because Chief Brenner isn't going to be happy about this."

"Brenner's got nothing to say about it," Edison said. "He's in jail. And he already confessed to everything the marshal here just said."

Grant looked around Mackey at Edison.

Mackey had no idea why Edison had lied about that last part, but it might be enough to push Grant over the edge.

"That's right." Edison smiled. "Me and two of my deputies heard Al say he was in them woods shootin' at the marshal here under your orders. Best come along peaceful like before there's trouble."

Grant sneered up at Mackey. His hands balled into fists. The rage began radiating from him. "You're not taking me anywhere, you son of a bitch."

"Sure I am." He set his rifle against the banister. He was too close to use it now. "Straight up or over the saddle. Makes no difference to me."

Grant turned and bolted back inside as a gunshot rang out from inside the house. Mackey realized he must have another gunman in there with him, possibly one of the Hancock boys.

He snatched his Winchester from the railing and dove to the left of the doorway. More shots rang out as Mackey called to Edison. "Stay outside and have your men surround the house."

The two guards were crouched on either side of

the door. He asked them, "Any idea about who's in there with him?"

Both men said no. The man next to him said, "He never lets us in the house. Most of his private visitors come in the back. Got no idea who's in there or how many there might be."

Another shot rang out and smacked into the right side of the doorframe. The guard jerked his head back and said, "I think there's only one in there with him. Maybe two at most. People have been in and out of there all day, moving and such."

Another couple of rounds hit the back of the door, which caused it to begin to swing closed.

Mackey stuck out the barrel of his Winchester to stop it from shutting.

"You boys do this kind of thing before?"

The man behind him admitted, "From the other side of the door."

Mackey had known most of Grant's policemen had been criminals, but this was no time for grudges. "If you follow me in, follow my lead. If you'd rather stay outside, that's fine, too."

He didn't wait for the men to answer before pushing the door all the way in with the barrel of his rifle. More shots rang out, peppering the floor and the right side of the door.

That meant the shooter was to his left behind the staircase.

As the door swung open, Mackey crouched in the doorway, brought up the rifle to his shoulder, and snapped off a shot to the left. The bullet sailed into the hallway without hitting anyone.

Mackey remained where he was and didn't move a muscle. Whoever was hiding in the hallway was obviously waiting for them to rush inside, guns blazing.

When the rush didn't come, the shooter stole a quick look around the corner to see where they were. He revealed just enough of his head for just long enough to give Mackey a target.

He fired once. The gunman fell back and dropped dead in the hallway. Mackey could see half of his head was gone.

Another shot rang out from the study, striking the wood frame high above his head. Mackey darted to the right side of the hall and crept along the wall toward the study where Grant must be hiding. He had been in the room several times before and knew the layout. There was a side door where he could duck out into the hallway and into the kitchen.

He pointed to the one officer who had followed him inside, pointed to his eyes, then at the hallway. The man seemed to understand and aimed his Winchester in that direction.

Mackey flinched when the sound of rifle fire echoed from outside, shattering the windows of the study and smacking into the plaster ceiling.

Mackey yelled back to the guard still in the doorway. "Cease firing, damn it!"

The guard yelled to the men and the shooting stopped.

Grant laughed from somewhere within the oak-paneled room. "What's the matter, Mackey? Afraid one of them will get me before—"

Mackey realized the voice wasn't coming from behind the heavy oak desk, but from the couch just inside the room. He switched the rifle to his left hand and brought it up to his shoulder as he rounded the corner of the doorway.

Grant was crouched between the heavy sofa and the wall. Mackey fired before the mayor could raise his pistol. The bullet punched through the upholstery and through Grant's left shoulder.

The impact with the wall caused him to drop the pistol as he slumped to the ground. Mackey inched into the room, switching his rifle back to his right hand and sweeping the area behind the desk, but there was no one there.

He yelled out into the hallway. "Check the rest of the house."

He switched his aim to James Grant, who was crumpled awkwardly between the heavy sofa and the wall. The Colt he'd been holding was inches from his outstretched hand.

Mackey kicked the pistol away from his grasp. "It's over."

"How'd you shoot me?" the mayor gasped. "You didn't even clear the doorway to shoot."

"Shifted to my left hand," Mackey said. "Pappy taught me how to shoot with both hands as soon as I could hold a rifle."

"Pappy," Grant sputtered. "That old bastard is more trouble than he's worth." He looked up into the barrel of Mackey's rifle. "Finish it, then."

"Already did."

He set the Winchester on the couch and pulled one of the heavy cords holding back the curtains from the window.

"Is that it?" Grant panted. "You're going to strangle me now?"

Mackey grabbed him by the collar and pulled him out from behind the couch. He put his knee across the screaming man's right arm, pinning it to the ground while he tied the heavy cord around his left shoulder, forming a tourniquet to stop the bleeding. He could tell by the loose way the shoulder moved that Grant would probably lose the arm if he lived. He tied the knot hard enough to make Grant cry out in pain. "That should stop the bleeding until Doc Ridley gets here."

The house filled with policemen, and Edison stepped into the study and looked down at Grant bleeding on an expensive carpet. "That's a sight I never thought I'd see."

Mackey knew there wasn't much time. "Send one of your men to fetch Doc Ridley. I want him in Helena alive."

Edison told three of his men to fan out and find the doctor. "Anything else, Marshal?"

"I don't trust the Hancocks to stay out of this," Mackey said. "I want guards around this place until the doc is finished with him and we can get him behind bars. Might be a good idea to get one of your deputies to grab some shackles from the jail and keep him secured to the bed while the doc is operating."

Edison looked at one of his men and told him to do what Mackey commanded. When the officer left, he said, "Sounds like a lot of foolishness to me. Grant's not going anywhere with his arm hanging off like that."

"I don't want anyone taking him if—"

Mackey looked up when he heard more gunfire and screams echoing through the open windows.

Edison rushed to the window and looked outside. "Looks like that noise is coming from the Municipal Building."

"Or the jailhouse," Mackey said.

Grant laughed until he coughed. "Sounds like you boys have got more to worry about than just me."

Mackey knocked him out with a short right-hand punch to the temple.

Chapter 32

Billy pushed Sandborne to the floor when the first bullets hit the jailhouse door.

"Think that's the Hancock boys?" the young deputy asked.

"It ain't pixies." Billy darted over to the desk, grabbed the Greener he had placed against the wall, and tossed it to Sandborne, who caught it one-handed.

"I want you back with the cells and to lock that door. If you hear anyone in here that's not me or Aaron, empty one barrel into Brenner and the other one into whoever comes in."

Both men flinched as more rounds struck the door.

"Think that door will hold?" Sandborne asked.

"It'll hold until it won't," Billy told him. "Now get in there and stay ready."

Sandborne pulled the door closed and locked it from the inside. The front door was the only way into the jailhouse, so at least he didn't have to worry about anyone sneaking in the back.

But while he knew the door and walls should hold, Billy had been a cavalryman long enough to know any building could be breached, and the old jailhouse was no exception. He had no idea how many Hancock boys were in town, but he put the number at more than thirty by now. If they wanted in, they'd get in, especially if no one was shooting back.

He intended to change that right now.

Billy went to the rifle rack and pulled down his Sharps. He didn't have to rack a load into the chamber. He had already done that before he had put it away last time.

He took a position to the left of the doorway as the Hancock boys opened fire once again. Most of the rounds hit the door, which rattled with each impact. He closed his eyes and listened, knowing they must be directly across the street on account of the cluster of shots. They weren't shooting at the lock from an angle. They were shooting straight on and missing.

"Come on, Jerry," he said aloud. "Where the hell are you?"

The barrage stopped, and a solitary rifle shot sang out across Front Street. That had to be Jerry Halstead, who had been watching the jailhouse just like Mackey had told him to do before going to fetch Grant.

They had probably been firing at the jailhouse from the street and the alley without worrying about cover. Now they were exposed to Jerry's rifle, and the boy was cutting into them from the cover of the livery next door.

Time to join the fun.

Billy threw open the door and brought the Sharps to his shoulder. He saw ten gunmen were clustered at the corner of the alley of the Municipal Building, hiding from Jerry Halstead's rifle. One man was facedown on the boardwalk, while another was slumped against the building with a bullet through his head.

Billy aimed into the center of the group and fired. The big buffalo gun boomed, sending the fifty-caliber round into the middle of the men clustered at the mouth of the alley. He saw three of them spin as the bullet tore through them.

He shut the door and set the big gun aside as the group began firing his way once more. The single-shot Sharps took too long to reload in a firefight this close, so he brought the rifle back to the rack, selected his Winchester, and went back to the door.

Fewer rounds struck the jailhouse, and the gunfire from outside died down considerably, probably thanks to Jerry's skills with a rifle.

Billy threw open the door again and brought the Winchester to his shoulder. He counted five men dead at the mouth of the alley and only three remaining. Billy aimed at a man in front and fired. The shot was rushed and struck the brickwork next to him, sending chunks of brick and dust into the man's eyes. He dropped his rifle as he pawed at his face to clear his vision.

The man behind him aimed a pistol at Billy. The blinded man stumbled back and threw off the man's aim. The bullet went high and buried itself in the ceiling of the jailhouse. Billy's next shot put the man down.

Billy levered another round into the chamber as the second Hancock man decided to risk all and charge the jailhouse, screaming and emptying his pistol as he ran.

Billy and Halstead fired at the same target at the same time. Both shots hit him in the chest before he toppled over into the mud.

The blinded man bounced from one side of the alley to the other, feeling wildly for something familiar to hold on to.

Billy normally would have felt some sympathy for the man. But that was a Hancock man. Pity didn't enter into it. That family had been trying to kill him and Aaron for weeks. He didn't know if this was the last Hancock in town, but he was the last one in the fight.

And the fight wasn't over for him until all of them were dead.

Billy stood and brought the Winchester to his shoulder. He drew a bead on the stumbling man and chambered another round into the rifle.

"Uncle!"

He lowered the rifle and saw Jerry Halstead in the middle of Front Street. At that moment, with the sunshine hitting him just right, he was the image of Sim Halstead, his father.

That single word brought Billy back to his senses. That single word reminded him of who he was.

Billy Sunday, Deputy U.S. Marshal of the Montana Territory. He was a lawman, not a murderer.

Billy eased down the hammer of the Winchester. "Best grab him before he stumbles into a ditch or something. We'll lock him up in here."

Young Halstead sprinted after the last surviving Hancock man on foot. He envied the boy's speed.

He envied his wisdom.

Billy shut the door, took a box of cartridges from the rack, and began reloading the Winchester.

He stood just to the side of the door leading to the cells. "Best uncock that coach gun, Joshua. Looks like we're still alive."

Even through the closed door, he could hear the boy lower the hammers. “Is it over?”

Billy thought of Aaron and how he’d gone to arrest Mayor Grant. “I don’t know, but I’m going to find out once Jerry gets back.”

Chapter 33

From his chair in the hallway outside Grant's bedroom, Mackey could hear the commotion his father was causing downstairs.

"I don't care who you are or what you've been told, damn you," Pappy bellowed. "I'm the marshal's father, and I demand to see him."

Mackey went to the top of the stairs and shouted down to the men guarding the house. "It's fine. Let him up."

Pappy bounded up the stairs, his old Army Colt and flap holster on his hip. The fighting was long over, but his father was known as much for his caution as he was for his bluster.

He stopped at the top of the stairs and looked at his son. "You seem no worse for wear."

Mackey suddenly felt very tired. "I'm fine." He nodded toward the closed bedroom door. "Grant's in there. Looks like he's going to lose the arm."

"That's it?" Pappy cried. "I heard the bastard was dead."

"I wouldn't give him the satisfaction," Mackey said.

"He's going to stand trial, Pappy. I'm going to watch him swing for what he's done."

"I'd love to see that," Pappy admitted. "Too bad it's in Helena."

"Maybe you'll see it after all."

Pappy put his hands on his hips. "I hope you're not talking about a lynching, boy. Because if you are, you could've saved us all the bother and just shot him where you found him."

Mackey closed his eyes and breathed in deep. His father's mind worked in such strange ways sometimes. "I'm talking about the hanging. In Helena. You might be there to see it."

"What would I be doing in Helena? I wouldn't go just to see that rat swing."

"No, but you'd go to protect your daughter-in-law, wouldn't you?"

Pappy broke into a wide smile. "Aaron, you mean you've finally proposed?"

Mackey felt himself smiling, too. "And she accepted. This afternoon, in fact. But everyone in town knows about us, especially the Hancock boys. She's in danger every second she's here."

"I'm pretty sure Billy and Jerry cleared out the last of them this afternoon," Pappy said. "You should've seen the pile of them on Front Street."

But Mackey was in no mood for his father's tall tales. He knew there had only been eight of them and one of them was still alive. "All it takes is one to try to hurt her. With Sandborne helping Billy and Jeremiah at the jail, she's only got two lawmen protecting her.

I don't want her protected. I want her out of town quietly and tonight."

Pappy thought it over. "It's been an age since I've been on the trail and Helena's many days' ride from here, but I'll manage it. How much food should I bring for us and the horses?"

He smiled as he touched his father's arm. Yes, his mind certainly worked in strange ways. "You can eat on the train. There's one leaving from the station tonight at ten. All you have to do is get her packed and ride along with her to Helena. There'll be some of Mr. Rice's men there to help you get settled. I telegraphed him earlier and it's all set."

His father was taken by his son's faith in him. "You sure you want me to go and not Billy?"

"I need every man I've got here to watch Brenner and Grant. I need the only other man I trust to watch over her."

Pappy sucked in his stomach and stood a little straighter. "Well then, consider it done. You can tell one of my clerks they're in charge when they open up tomorrow. I won't say a word to anyone before I leave." He fixed his son with a stare. "I mean that, now."

"I know you do." Mackey got up and hugged his father. His father hugged him back. "Just don't let anything happen. To either of you."

Pappy clapped his son on the back and laughed. "Haven't you heard? I'm indestructible."

He reached up and ruffled his boy's hair before heading downstairs to carry out his son's request.

* * *

Mackey had dozed off for a moment, but woke when the bedroom door opened and Billy stepped into the hall, carefully closing the door behind him.

"How's the patient?" Mackey asked his deputy.

"You didn't leave much of that shoulder," Billy said. "Just helped Doc Ridley take his arm." He dropped onto the couch next to him. "Had to work fast to stop the bleeding, but he got it done."

Billy dug out a cigarette he'd already made and offered it to Mackey, but Mackey refused. "Glad to see you're back to your old self, Captain," Billy said as he lit the cigarette. "I was worried you might be slipping back into your old ways."

"I was worried we were both slipping," Mackey said. "But today proves I was wrong."

"Guess it does," Billy agreed. "Glad you got Grant, though. He's been asking for it for a long time."

Mackey looked at the black-varnished door. He thought of the proud man lying in the bed behind it. He thought about the loss of his arm and the trial he would endure. He thought about a town suddenly without a mayor and a company without someone to run it. He wondered if he would incur Mr. Rice's wrath for causing him so much trouble while statehood was pending. He wondered if Judge Forester would give Grant a fair trial and hang him like he should. He wondered if the Hancocks would let this go or dig themselves deeper into the soul of Dover Station. He wondered if they'd try to kill him again. He imagined they would.

He wondered if this all might blow up in his face and if he had just cost himself and Billy their jobs.

He wondered too many things at once and began to give himself a headache.

Aaron Mackey shut his eyes and rubbed his throbbing temples. He surprised himself by saying aloud, "I wonder if we finally got James Grant or if he finally caught us."

He was glad Billy sat and smoked his cigarette in silence. Some questions could not be answered right away.

Keep reading for a special excerpt . . .

THE DARK SUNRISE

A SHERIFF AARON MACKEY WESTERN

Terrence McCauley

The sun has finally set on the violent hellstorm that fell on Dover Station, Montana, like a scourge. But when disaster returns, it falls to a lawman armed with a fistful of vengeance to make things right once more . . .

THE BURDEN OF THE BADGE

At long last, U.S. Marshal Aaron Mackey and Deputy Billy Sunday will see crime baron James Grant and his kill-crazy cronies stand trial for the mayhem and suffering they unleashed on the people of Dover Station. As Montana Territory's statehood is approaching, murdering devils like Grant can no longer be tolerated in positions of political power.

Or can they? Montana's capital of Helena follows its own set of laws—laws that not only set Grant free but give peacekeeping authority to a sadistic murdering gunslinger like Colonel Warren Bell, Mackey's commanding officer during the war. The city's leaders prefer keeping killers like Grant and Bell under their thumbs.

Mackey knows there's no controlling these bloodthirsty madmen. And if they think they're above the law, then Mackey and Billy will just have to appoint themselves judge, jury, and executioners . . .

Look for THE DARK SUNRISE.
Coming soon wherever books are sold.

Chapter 1

Dover Station, Montana Territory, late summer 1889

"Looks like they're coming," Deputy Billy Sunday said from the jailhouse porch. "A whole lot of them, too."

But U.S. Marshal Aaron Mackey had already known that. Adair had begun to paw at the ground a few moments earlier, when the wind along Front Street had shifted and carried the smell of men and torch fires her way. He knew the Arabian was not fussing out of nervousness. The warhorse was fussing because she was anxious to ride into the fray, just like her rider.

Despite the approaching darkness, Mackey counted about forty torches among the men marching down Front Street toward the jailhouse. He pegged the actual size of the crowd to be more than sixty or so.

He and Billy had been expecting something like this since word spread that Dover Station Police Chief Walter Underhill had finally succumbed to the belly wound that had been plaguing him for weeks. Mackey knew the townspeople blamed James Grant and Al Brenner for Underhill's death. Mackey blamed them, too.

But unfortunately, Grant and Brenner were currently his prisoners, awaiting extradition to Helena on the morning train. Underhill's death was only one more charge to be added to the numerous other charges they already faced in Judge Forester's courtroom.

But the big Texan had always been popular in Dover Station, and people did not want to wait for the scales of justice to tip in their favor. They wanted blood for blood, and they wanted it right now.

Aaron Mackey and Billy Sunday had never lost a prisoner to a mob before. They had no intention of starting now.

"I'll head out to meet them," Mackey said. "Turn them if I can."

"And if you can't?" Billy asked.

The marshal glanced down at the big Sharps rifle leaning against the porch post of the jailhouse. "Then you're going to have a busy start to your night."

Billy grinned as he picked up the fifty-caliber rifle. "Ride to your left so I can have my choice of targets. They'll start dropping on your right if it comes to that."

"Let's hope it doesn't." Mackey had barely lifted the reins before Adair began walking up Front Street on her own steam. She was moving at a quick pace, and Mackey saw no reason to make the mare move any faster.

Mackey could not swear to it, but the mob looked

like it slowed down just a bit as the lone rider on the black horse moved toward them.

He reined Adair to a stop about thirty yards in front of where the mob had stopped. He angled her to the left, so the butt of the Peacemaker on his belly pointed right. He could draw, aim, and fire quicker that way if it came to that.

He looked over the crowd and saw few familiar faces among the torchlight. So many strangers had moved into his boyhood town so quickly that he hardly knew anyone anymore.

"Evening," he said to none of them in particular. "What are you boys up to tonight?"

"Justice," a tall thin man in a slouch hat and long face said. "Justice for our friend and yours, Walter Underhill."

"Me, too," Mackey said loud enough for the crowd to hear him. "That's why we were scheduled to take Grant and Brenner to Helena tomorrow. To stand before Judge Forester for what they've done and answer for it. That was before Underhill died, and I promise his death will be added to the charges read out to them."

"Charges," one man in the middle of the crowd said. "Courts. Judges. Juries. A lot of folderol and fuss over a couple of cold-blooded killers. We're here to string 'em up, Marshal. String 'em up right here and now and save you the trouble of a trip to Helena."

A murmur of assent went through the mob.

"On behalf of Billy Sunday and myself, I appreciate the sentiment, boys. But the judge would look poorly on us and this town if we were to hand them over to you like this. I think he's looking forward to hanging them himself. It's never a good idea to disappoint a federal judge, believe me."

"Judge Forester is way down in Helena," came another voice in the crowd. "And we're right here right now ready to dispense justice. We aim to do that this very night, Marshal."

Adair raised her head, sensing a change in the air.

A change that Mackey sensed, too. "No."

The gaunt man who had spoken first said, "We've got a lot of respect for you, marshal, and we hate to go against you like this, but we're taking Grant and Brenner with us and there ain't a whole lot you and your deputies can do to stop us."

"And don't go countin' on Chief Edison to back your play, either," said another voice from the crowd. "They was all mighty partial to Walter and are as anxious to see Grant swing as the rest of us."

He had not seen any of Edison's men coming to break up the mob, even though this was technically a town matter. He had not counted on their support, either. Grant and Brenner were his prisoners. His responsibility. His and Billy's. And they would defend them, just like they had defended all of the other prisoners they had held over the years.

"Doesn't matter what Edison and his men do," Mackey said. "Only matters what Billy and I do. And we say you can't have them. You boys best put out those torches and go home before someone gets hurt. We're burying Underhill at first light. No sense in having more men to bury tomorrow."

"Only one around here who'll get hurt is you, Marshal," said yet another voice from the crowd. "If you know what's good for you, you'll move out of the way."

Adair blew through her nose and raised her head higher. The men on the left side of the mob flinched.

Mackey felt her muscles tense as she was getting ready to respond to his command.

Mackey's hand inched closer to the butt of the Peacemaker. "I'm not going anywhere, boys, and neither are my prisoners. I told you to go home. I won't tell you again."

Then Mackey heard the unmistakable sound of a hammer being cocked on his right side.

In one practiced motion, he drew, aimed and fired, striking a man who had raised a pistol at him. Mackey's bullet struck him in the chest and put him down against the boardwalk.

Mackey shifted his aim to a man behind the fallen man, but Billy's big Sharps boomed as a fifty-caliber slug punched through the rifle stock and obliterated the neck of the man holding it. He was dead before he hit the boardwalk.

And despite the gunfire, Adair had not moved an inch.

Mackey brought the Peacemaker back and aimed it down at the gaunt man who had spoken for the mob. "Anyone else want to die?"

The gaunt man glowered up at Mackey. "Damn it, man. Underhill was your friend, too."

"He was," Mackey told him. "And he wouldn't want this. He'd want Grant and Brenner to stand trial, which they will. I promise you that. But if any of you take another step, you'll die. I promise you that, too."

The gaunt man and the rest of the mob did not

move, though he could sense their resolve beginning to fade. Watching two of their men die had that effect.

Their resolve may have been fading, but Mackey wanted to wreck it altogether.

He kept the Colt aimed at the gaunt man and thumbed back the hammer. "I gave you an order. Move."

Another murmur went through the mob. Their torches sagged a bit. They were having second thoughts.

The gaunt man took a step back, but no farther.

Mackey fired into the air, making the men jump. "I said move!"

He picked up the reins and Adair shot to the left side of the mob. The men scrambled out of the way and moved backward. Mackey brought the black horse around and rode along the front of the crowd, pushing them back even farther. A few on the right side held their ground until he turned Adair sharply and her flank knocked them back.

She snorted again as Mackey began riding back the other way, pushing them some more. The gaunt man broke first and the rest of the men followed. None of them wanted any part of the dark mare or the man who rode her.

The mob broke slowly and began to slip backward, back up Front Street.

Mackey brought Adair back to the center of the thoroughfare and stood in the spot where he had turned them, watching them go.

The gaunt man picked himself up off the ground and glowered at Mackey. His mob may have been broken, but his resolve had not. "You've made a whole lot of enemies for yourself here today, Marshal."

Mackey kept the Colt aimed at him. "They're in good company. Now get going while you still can."

The gaunt man looked at the two dead men on the boardwalk. "You just gonna let them stay like that in the street?"

"I'll stay with them while you fetch Cy Wallach to fetch them. The quicker you move, the quicker they'll be tended to."

The gaunt man pushed the mud of the thoroughfare off his clothes as he backed away. "You're a hard man, Aaron Mackey. And that ain't a compliment, neither."

Mackey had not taken it as one.

He holstered his Peacemaker when the man moved out of sight and stood watch over the men he and Billy had killed while he waited for the mortician to come.

He may have won the battle but knew he had lost the town. But he did not bother about that. He had lost it long ago.

As soon as Cy Wallach brought his wagon to pick up the dead bodies, Mackey turned Adair and rode back to the jailhouse. He climbed down from the saddle and wrapped Adair's reins around the hitching post. He patted the horse on the neck. "Good girl."

The Arabian nudged him before lowering her head to drink water from the trough in front of the jailhouse.

Mackey climbed the front steps and found Billy waiting for him. "That went about as expected."

Mackey walked into the jailhouse. "Didn't count

on having to kill anyone. There was a time when we wouldn't have had to."

Billy followed him into the jailhouse. "Time was they wouldn't have formed a mob. The town's changing, Aaron. We're smart for changing along with it."

Inside, young Joshua Sandborne locked the heavy jailhouse door behind them and was eager to talk about what had just transpired. "You turned them, Aaron. Turned them all the way."

He knew the young deputy looked up to him and Billy. He did not want the young man to get the idea that gunplay was the first order of being a lawman. "Turned them after two of them got killed. That's nothing to be proud of, Josh. Things could've just as easily gone the other way. Let's just be glad it didn't."

He broke the cylinder on his Colt, pulled out the spent round and replaced it with a fresh bullet from the rifle rack. He snapped the cylinder shut and placed the pistol on his desk. "Come on, Billy. Time to get the prisoners ready for tomorrow."

The young deputy looked like he had more questions, but he always had questions. Mackey was not in the mood to answer them. He and Billy still had work to do.

Chapter 2

James Grant sat up in his cot when he heard the rattle of keys at the door to the cells. He had heard the shouts and the gunfire outside. He hoped the mob had won, even thought it would mean death for him and Brenner. The trip to hell would be worth it if he knew Mackey was already there waiting for him.

But he was not surprised when the door opened and Billy trailed Mackey into the cells. Evil was tough to kill if it ever died at all.

These two men had dragged James Grant through all seven circles of hell in the year since he had come to Dover Station. And despite his current predicament as their prisoner, Grant had every intention on paying them back for it.

He hid his disappointment in their survival by applauding them. "Bravo, Aaron. You pushed back the horde and saved our lives in the bargain. I should have known better than to think a mob of shopkeepers and laborers could best the Savior of Dover Station. Al and I are in your debt."

"Speak for yourself," spat Al Brenner, the former police chief of Dover Station. Brenner was as mean as he was big, which said quite a bit, because Brenner was quite a large man. "I ain't in his debt nor anyone else's. I'd rather get lynched than let him have the satisfaction of watching me hang."

"You'll hang," Mackey assured him. "Both of you, but at the end of Judge Forester's rope, not theirs."

Grant forced a laugh. "I take it the temper of the townspeople is still a bit raw after news of Underhill's demise?"

"They'd be in here beating both of you to death right now if it wasn't for us," Billy told them. "But you'll have your day in court in Helena."

Grant admired the friendship between the marshal and his deputy. Other than Mackey being white and Sunday being black, there was little difference between them. Both were just north of thirty, a shade over six feet tall, and lean. They still had the military bearing they had acquired while serving in the cavalry together, where Mackey had been a captain while Sunday had been his sergeant. Their partnership had continued after Mackey had been drummed out of the army. When Mackey became sheriff of Dover Station, he named Billy Sunday his deputy. And when Mackey later became the United States Marshal for the Montana Territory, Sunday had become his deputy.

Grant had underestimated them when he had first come to Dover Station. He had tried to buy them out and when that failed, he had tried to push them out. When they had outsmarted him at every turn, he had no choice but to hire men to kill them.

Now he was their prisoner.

Under other circumstances, James Grant might have admired their loyalty to each other. But as that loyalty had led to his arrest, wounding, and incarceration, he loathed the arrangement.

He decided there was no point in goading the lawmen any further. He might say too much and tip his hand. That would only spoil his plans. Plans that were already in motion. Plans that would ultimately win Grant his freedom.

But for now, he had no choice but to endure the indignity of incarceration at the hands of his enemies Mackey and Sunday.

Mackey nodded to his deputy. "Best tell them what we came here to say, Billy. No sense in being around these two any longer than necessary."

The black man cleared his throat. "Tomorrow's the day we run you two down to Helena for your trial. Whether it turns out to be a good day or a bad day depends entirely on the both of you."

Mackey added, "The four of us will be taking the nine o'clock train to Helena. I'll expect both of you to be dressed and ready to leave by half-past eight. If you're not, it won't matter to us. We'll drag you onto the train naked if we have to."

"Oh, we'll be ready, Marshal." Grant grinned. "The only question is, will you?"

"Which brings us to the reason why we're talking to you two right now," Mackey said. "There's two of you and two of us. Those are even odds, and given Al's size here, we wouldn't blame you for thinking you could overpower us. Maybe make a run for it, even though you'll be chained together the entire time."

Mackey looked each prisoner in the eye. "Bet you've already got some kind of plan worked out between you."

Grant saw no point in denying it and was glad Brenner kept his peace for once.

But Brenner moved to the edge of his cot when Billy slipped the key into his cell door.

"Whatever you're planning won't work," Mackey went on, "and we're about to show you why."

As soon as Billy unlocked the cell door and pull it open, Brenner charged toward his possible freedom, propelled by weeks of rage that had built up in his tiny cell.

Billy Sunday fired a straight right hand that struck Brenner flush in the jaw. The force of the blow, combined with the bigger man's momentum, caused the prisoner to drop like a sack of wet flour to the floor of his cell.

Sunday brought his boot down on Brenner's neck as he grabbed the big man's left foot and raised his leg. Grant watched Sunday pull a bowie knife from the back of his belt and hold it behind Brenner's knee.

Mackey leaned against Grant's cell door. "See how easy Billy did that? Brenner's a big man, way bigger than you, but he's still a Hancock. That means he's as stupid as he is tough. That's no match for our training and determination. Billy knocked your boy cold with one punch. He'll do it again if he has reason to. What's more, he's got his knife to the back of his leg. One flick of the wrist will cut Brenner's hamstring in two. He'll be a cripple for the rest of his life."

"Even though he won't be alive much longer," Billy added.

Mackey rattled Grant's cage door. "If either of you tries to escape, we'll cut both your hamstrings just to be fair. Prison's tough enough for a man with two good legs, Grant. It's even worse for a cripple."

Billy dropped Brenner's leg and tucked the bowie knife away as he stepped out and relocked the cell door.

Grant was disgusted by Brenner's stupidity. The big fool had played directly into Mackey's trap, but Grant hid his disgust as he said, "Consider us both sufficiently warned, Aaron. You've already crippled me once." He rubbed the shoulder that still ached from Mackey's bullet that had cost him his arm. "I have no intention of giving you a second chance."

Mackey grinned. "I don't expect you to live long enough for it to matter one way or the other. Judge Forester will have you dancing at the end of a rope inside of a month at most. Guess you might as well try to keep as much dignity as you can in the few days you've got left."

"That's sound advice, Grant," Sunday added. "Why limp into hell when you can walk in on two good legs?"

"Why indeed?" Grant sat back on his cot his one arm lying across his belly. It was time to begin planting seeds of doubt in their minds. "In fact, who knows how much time any of us has left? Don't forget it's more than a day's train ride to Helena. A lot can happen between here and there. Weather problems. Trees across tracks. Bandits attacking trains. Mechanical problems. Engine boilers are fickle machines.

Almost anything could happen to upset your plans. Anything at all."

Mackey leaned against Grant's cell door. "I know that brain of yours always has something cooking up, so I'll lay it out as plain as I can. If either of you try to run, you both get crippled. If anyone attacks the train, you both get shot in the belly. If the train makes any unexpected stops, for any reason, you both get shot in the belly."

Grant did not like the sound of that.

Mackey went on. "I know you ran the railroad in this part of the territory, Grant, and I know you probably still have some people loyal to you. I also know you've paid men to rob your trains and split the profits with you in the past, so Billy and I have decided not to take any chances. If the train stops, you die. Shooting you will be an abundance of precaution on our part."

"What if the train breaks down?" Grant asked.

"Better hope it doesn't," Billy said, "because like the marshal just said, you'll get shot in the belly if it does."

Mackey added, "We're bringing both of you to Helena for trial one way or the other. Straight up or over the saddle makes no difference to us."

Grant enjoyed the bravado of the lawmen. He would have enjoyed it more if they were not every bit as tough as they thought they were.

That was why bringing them down when they got to Helena would be so satisfying. He only hoped he saw the look on Mackey's face when it happened.

But that would come later. For now, as he sat in that cell, words were his only weapon. "I envy you your confidence, Aaron. Yours, too, Billy. I always have. The confidence to believe that your way of seeing things is the only way there is. You think there is only one way to convict me and one way to free me. Perhaps you're right. Perhaps I'm wrong. I guess we'll find out for sure when we get to Helena, won't we?"

Billy opened the door to the jail and walked into the office.

Mackey stayed behind. "Talk in circles all you want, Grant, but remember all the words in the world lead right back to you being a prisoner and me being a free man. By this time next month, I'll still be alive and you'll be rotting in the ground."

"Just like your friend Underhill." Grant smiled again, sucking his teeth. "It's a shame that such a good man should be cut down in the prime of life like that. And by a lowly drunkard, no less."

Mackey gripped the bar of the cell door a little tighter. "A drunkard you sent to kill him."

Grant shrugged. "So you've said many times, but still can't prove. I suppose it'll depend on Judge Forester's mood when we get to his courtroom, won't it?" He cocked his head to the side. "Or will it depend on more than that? I wonder. Territorial capitals can be such complicated places. I guess it's something for all of us to think about in the miles ahead."

Mackey pointed at the pile of clothing on the stool next to Grant's cot. "Be ready in the morning or you ride all the way to Helena in your drawers."

"But fly to my eternal reward on angel's wings," Grant called after Mackey as the marshal walked into the jailhouse. "Enjoy the funeral. Give my condolences to—"

But Mackey had slammed and locked the door before he could finish his sentence.

It didn't matter much to Grant. The marshal had always been an easy man to read and even easier to rile. Grant had always had an uncanny ability to get under his skin, though he had never been able to figure out why. Perhaps it was because he—a stranger—had amassed so much power so soon in Mackey's beloved hometown?

Grant did not bother wasting time wondering about the reasons for Mackey's hatred. As the lawman had said, all the words in the world ended with Grant still being in jail and Mackey taking him before Judge Forester.

At least for now.

He looked through the bars of his cell at Brenner as the big man began to moan. The left side of his jaw was already beginning to swell and was possibly broken. It served him right. The big fool had run directly into Mackey's trap.

Just as Mackey was about to run into Grant's.